TWO KIDS: WILLIE AND BILLY
BILLY THE KID'S EARLY YEARS

TWO KIDS: WILLIE AND BILLY
BILLY THE KID'S EARLY YEARS

A Novel

GREGORY J. LALIRE

SUNSTONE
PRESS

SANTA FE

Sunstone books may be purchased for educational, business, or sales promotional use.
For information please write: Special Markets Department, Sunstone Press,
P.O. Box 2321, Santa Fe, New Mexico 87504-2321.
Printed on acid-free paper
∞

Library of Congress Cataloging-in-Publication Data

Names: Lalire, Gregory, author.
Title: Two kids: Willie and Billy : Billy the Kid's early years / Gregory
    J. Lalire.
Description: Santa Fe : Sunstone Press, [2023] | Summary: "Little is known
    about the boyhood of the real Billy the Kid, but this is the way it
    could have gone for him during his growing-up years, shared here with
    his fictional best pal, Willie the Kid"-- Provided by publisher.
Identifiers: LCCN 2024003505 | ISBN 9781632936356 (paperback) | ISBN
    9781611397376 (epub)
Subjects: LCSH: Billy, the Kid--Fiction. | LCGFT: Novels.
Classification: LCC PS3612.A54323 T86 2023 | DDC 813/.6--dc23/eng/20240205
LC record available at https://lccn.loc.gov/2024003505

WWW.SUNSTONEPRESS.COM
SUNSTONE PRESS / POST OFFICE BOX 2321 / SANTA FE, NM 87504-2321 /USA
(505) 988-4418

Dedication

For all the historians and novelists who have been inspired by Billy the Kid and to my younger brother, Rex the Kid, who ages ago played cowboys with me.

INTRODUCTION
Brushy Bill, Billy, and Me

All right, I admit it. Several years ago, in 1939 to be exact, I heard about this crazy fellow in the next state, Texas, who called himself Brushy Bill Roberts and claimed to be Billy the Kid even though Billy had died fifty-eight years earlier. I was curious, retired, and liked to travel some, so I drove over from my home in Silver City, New Mexico, and said point blank to this odd old fellow (I was the same age as him, by the way), "How the hell can you be the Kid, when I'm the Kid?"

I meant that as a sort of joke because I was once upon a time known as Willie the Kid and my best pal growing up was none other than William Henry McCarty, who was always Billy to me and became Henry Antrim when his mother married in Santa Fe, then took on several aliases (most notably, Kid Antrim and William H. Bonney) along the way before becoming Billy the Kid once the entire nation had taken notice of his exploits in New Mexico Territory. In other words, when I said that "Kid stuff" to Brushy Bill, I was only kidding. Trouble was, I never was much of a kidder (unlike the real Billy the Kid) and this Brushy Bill wasn't kidding one bit. He looked me straight in the eye without a wink or a blink and said, "I haven't revealed this fact to the world yet, friend, and I ain't sure how you found out about it and found me, but I am the legendary Billy the Kid, sure as shooting." I was not amused, but if he was going to make that outrageous claim, I figured I might as well give him a taste of his own medicine. After our unreliable introductions, our conversation that day went something like this:

Me: I learned about you from Delbert Jones, an *El Paso Times* correspondent I had worked with many years ago when I was a reporter. Delbert stopped to see me while passing through Silver City on his way back to Texas. He said that while in Las Vegas, New Mexico, digging up information for a retrospective column on whether Jesse James had ever met Billy the Kid, an old-timer told him, "Why not ask Billy." That naturally puzzled me. Delbert Jones laughed impishly but eventually clarified, saying the man he was going to see next was Brushy Bill Roberts of Hico, Texas.

Brushy Bill: That would be me all right. I have known many Joneses in my lifetime, including Barbara Ma'am Jones who was like a mother to me in the fall of 1877, but no Delberts that I can recollect.

Me: Are you sure? Delbert Jones writes his weekly column under the pen name "Red Harden." You don't remember a burly red-haired fellow with a squeaky voice asking you about Billy the Kid and Jesse James? It couldn't have been more than three years ago.

Brushy Bill: Yeah, Red Harden. I wanted to forget the son of a bitch. I told him how one Sunday in July 1879 I had enjoyed a dinner at the Old Adobe Hotel in Hot Springs with Jesse, who was calling himself Mr. Howard at the time. After my friend Dr. Henry Hoyt told me Mr. Howard's true identity, Jesse and I talked some more. He wanted me to join his gang but I politely declined his offer, telling Jess I wasn't interested in robbing banks, trains, and stagecoaches. That extremely rude Red Harden laughed right in my face. He didn't believe one word I said. If Red Harden ever wrote anything up in some damn newspaper, I wasn't about to read it.

Me: I don't recall any such dinner with Jesse James. I never went to the Old Adobe Hotel.

Brushy Bill: Which proves you ain't Billy the Kid.

Me: It only proves Dr. Hoyt's outlaw dinner is a tall tale.

Brushy Bill: Outlaw? I was "wanted" but I never considered myself an outlaw. Governor Wallace ought to have pardoned me like he did everyone else involved in the Lincoln County War. I didn't rob banks, trains, or stagecoaches, and heaven knows you hack writers never should have portrayed me as a cold-blooded, murdering gunslinger. I never killed twenty-one men, not by a long shot.

Me: I never wrote about myself.

Brushy Bill: Whoever you are. I haven't written my autobiography either since I'm technically still wanted and have been condemned to hang for Sheriff Brady's murder, even though I didn't do it.

Me: Neither did I.

Brushy Bill: One of these days, though, I'll tell all the world the whole truth—that I am Billy the Kid and that, all things considered, I'm not such a bad man. I'm getting up there in age, and I need to straighten out this matter before I die. First, though, I want to see about getting that long overdue pardon I was promised.

Me: If you're Billy the Kid like you say you are, you'd know the name of your best teacher when you lived in Silver City.

Brushy Bill: Miss Mary Phillips Richards, beautiful and intelligent. She left teaching to marry a fellow named Casey.

Me: All right, smarty. Tell me this then: Who was your very best pal in Silver City?

Brushy Bill: Hard to say. I was a popular kid. I had many pals.

Me: Bad answer. I know the correct answer: Willie the Kid Bonnifield is his name.

Brushy Bill: Says you. I say you weren't even there.

Me: I was there. I'm Willie the Kid.

Brushy Bill: Says you. Never heard of you. Anyway, you lied when you told me you were Billy the Kid.

Me: I never said I was him exactly. I admit I was sort of leading you on. But I was right there at his elbow most of his boyhood. Besides, you aren't Billy the Kid, either, and I suggest you admit that unless you want people to think you're insane. Sheriff Pat Garrett shot Billy dead in Fort Sumner, New Mexico Territory, on the night of July 14, 1881.

Brushy Bill: Wrong. I was there, you weren't. Don't believe everything you read. The sheriff shot an older man with a darker complexion, black hair instead of light brown, and a thick black beard. Fact is, in those days I wasn't even able to grow a beard. Garrett knew he shot the wrong man but said nothing. He wanted the reward. I was in Fort Sumner at the time, but my friends helped me slip out of town. I couldn't show my face in the territory anymore so I hightailed it to Mexico and later came to Texas to live in peace.

Me: That's ridiculous. Besides, even allowing for aging, you don't look like your picture.

Brushy Bill: Unfortunately, that's the only photograph that survives from my early days and it does me no justice, just as that dear girl Paulita Maxwell said. My teeth didn't really protrude all that much, and they certainly never bothered Paulita. She said I had a pleasant, boyish face but the damned tintype made me look downright rough and uncouth. Never should have posed for it.

Me: As far as I'm concerned, Mr. Brushy Bill Roberts, you never did. Doesn't seem likely we will settle this matter here. I best be going home to New Mexico. But from now on, if I were you, I wouldn't go telling people you are Billy the Kid. It doesn't make you look good and who is going to believe you anyway?

Brushy Bill: Not the likes of you or that cynical Red Harden that's for dead sure. You can't handle the truth. And just who do you think you are coming into my house and acting so bloody rude to a genuine survivor of the Lincoln County War and all those other trials and tribulations I went through in the New Mexico Territory?

Me: Like I told you, I'm Willie the Kid, the boyhood pal of Billy the Kid, and I'm still alive and kicking at age eighty. But then nobody shot me down when I was young. So long.

Enough about Brushy Bill Roberts, that not-so-great pretender. I turned eighty-six today and I am of sound mind and astounding body, if I do say so myself. Now you know who I am, dear reader. And you already know who the real Billy the Kid was. What follows is our story.

—William Tweed Bonnifield,
Alias Willie the Kid,
Silver City, New Mexico
May 1, 1945

1

MY FIRST TWO WOMEN

The story goes that in the womb I kicked like a confined mule and somehow orchestrated many false labors until Mum's sexual activity triggered true labor and brought forth Freya O'Neill from the basement. Mum was eighteen and uncertain who the father was when on May 1, 1859, the Irish midwife with insistent hands tugged me out of darkness into the flickering light and stagnant air of our "rear-house" tenement on New York's Lower East Side. According to Mum, when Mrs. O'Neill slapped me on the bottom, I laughed instead of cried because I didn't know any better. Red-haired Charlotte Bonnifield was not ashamed of herself or her unwed motherhood. She named me William Tweed after a powerful politician who couldn't possibly have been my father. She wouldn't let her friends and lovers talk her into leaving me on the doorstep of the St. Brigid's Famine Church, and, once she got the hang of it, raised me as right as rain. It's not her fault that like a cottonwood slab I became warped from all that rain and it took me seemingly forever to emerge as my own man. But can you blame me? Billy the Kid was so much more captivating.

Like Billy, I had a great, if peculiar and often unappreciated, sense of humor. It came to me naturally even though I was the son of a solemn but sensuous woman and some unknown man of low character who possibly was already in the grave by the time I was born. Ancient Freya O'Neill, who had assisted in four-dozen previous births including a dozen of her own, was shocked by a newborn's laughter and accompanying drooling, attributing these things to a demonic spirit. Despite her years of experience in such matters, she dropped me on Mum's belly and fainted dead away. Mum had to cut the umbilical cord herself. I then thrust my tongue out and didn't put it back until I had latched on to a nipple.

Mum, always tougher than she looked, was not spooked by my premature and, according to Mrs. O'Neill, devilish merriment. Mum, in all seriousness, was just thankful after all the kicking, jabbing, and elbowing I did in the womb and my rough trip through the birth canal that I came out alive and looking almost normal, except for the inexplicable grin on my puffy face. It was during the seventh month of her difficult pregnancy that she had decided—if I turned out to be a boy, of course—to call me William Tweed Bonnifield, but seeing me in person drooling and sticking out my tongue ahead of my time, she knew I would never be able to live up to such a grandiose appellation and soon gave me the nickname that stuck—Willie the Kid.

Freya O'Neill, after reluctantly agreeing to help Mum care for me, got over the idea I had been possessed in the womb and was now a devil child. After all, I slept through most nights, cried sparingly, quickly outgrew my unnatural grin, stopped drooling for the time being, never fussed when she instead of Mum handled me, was eager to nurse but would settle for mother milk substitutes, and, though not exactly cute, was far from grotesque. One flaw in my babyhood that persisted, and amused neither Mrs. O'Neill nor Mum, was my tendency to stick out my tongue when they waited too long to change my cloth diaper or simply left me too long in my lonely wooden cradle. They both took it personally, though I couldn't possibly have been intentionally sticking my tongue out at the two most important human beings in my life (there really was nobody else in those early days).

Freya, who was disapproving of the politics and power of my namesake William Tweed, never called me William or Tweed. She tried "Billy" at first but it upset her too much. She later told me that the nickname of her late first husband was "Billy Goat" since he had "pointed ears, goatee, hoof-like feet, everything but the horns, and a tendency to stagger around like a buck who had gotten into the Irish whisky." For a time, upon seeing me each day, she would greet me with "And how is my bonny Bonnifield baby on this lovely morn?" Eventually, though, she tired of that and began calling me what Mum called me, Willie the Kid. "I like names that are fitting, and Willie fits you like a diaper," Freya said. "You're a far cry from a Billy or a Buck; you're just a kid. And how can you be a William Tweed? Impossible. That old goat lies, cheats, and bosses. I can't imagine him ever having been a kid."

I got the story of my first years in New York City piecemeal from young mother and ancient midwife. They came to see things the same way when it came to my disposition—not high energy, not headstrong, not difficult, not a disciple of the devil, not even irritating except for that tongue thing. Because Mum worked long, enervating hours as a factory seamstress to keep food on the table and also had this other love life that did not involve me, I spent more time with Freya O'Neill every day of the week except Sunday. Mrs. O'Neill had her one day off from babysitting duties on the Sabbath, and Mum would skirt many Manhattan churches on her way to the Emigrant Landing Depot at Castle Garden. There we would sit all day in a brownstone building so she could watch the newly arriving immigrants being received and processed to the United States. Perhaps she was expecting to see somebody she knew from the Old Country (but who, as far as I know, never showed up) or else was excessively attached to the place where she herself had arrived on the three-mast *Dreadnought* in 1857.

The two women in my life never did see eye to eye about my namesake. The son of a third-generation Scottish chairmaker, William Tweed had been one of the corrupt city aldermen known as the Forty Thieves and had served a two-year term in the U.S. House of Representatives. Soon after arriving at the Port of New York, barely seventeen-year-old Charlotte Bonnifield (she did look a few years older) bumped into the rising politician when he was out among the people proudly showing off a snarling red Bengal tiger in a French lithograph. She was taken by the powerful presence of both man and beast and became instantly infatuated with Mr. Tweed. He, in turn, was struck by her loose waves of red hair, full lips, straightforward face, and sublime shape. What ensued was at best a dalliance on his part; Mum, on the other hand, hoped it would lead to a lasting relationship or at least a rise out of poverty even though Mr. Tweed was a married man and as stingy with his ready money as he was with his affection.

When appointed in 1858 to the New York County Board of Supervisors, his first vehicle for the large-scale graft practiced by the Tweed Ring, he told Mum he was in no position to rendezvous with her ever again. Although spurned by the man destined to become Tammany Hall's Grand Sachem, otherwise referred to as Boss, Mum never stopped admiring him from afar. That certainly didn't stop her from *seeing*—and otherwise engaging—lesser men of little means, one of whom became my father. Mrs. O'Neill who had outlasted three husbands and half her children, called Mum's relationship with the cad Mr. Tweed "cupboard love," meaning Charlotte Bonnifield had insincerely professed her love of him for the sake of gain. Maybe so, but even after all hope of gain was gone and she was impregnated by another, Mum still named her first and only child for New York City's most powerful man.

I reckon I got attached to my midwife/nursemaid before I did Mum, who in the beginning wasn't around much during my waking hours and didn't come across as a warm-blooded, milk-providing creature. It took me some time to realize she was capable of more than awkwardly cooing back at me and offering high-pitched baby talk while mostly holding me at arm's length as if afraid I'd break in half. Freya O'Neill was different. She brought me my milk in a glass bottle with a cork nipple, talked to me in full sentences using adult words, and wasn't one to baby me, though she held me close to her enormous bosom whenever she felt danger near —in the form of roustabouts, ruffians, rapscallions, and rats. "Your mother's world was infested by bad men," Freya told me later.

At some point during my third year, Mum decided the past was past and was best forgotten—everything except her time with Mr. Tweed. She never mentioned the names of the other men who had come and gone and were now regulated to the trash heap of history. If they were alive or dead was of no matter to her. Mrs. O'Neill suspected that a few of them either ended up lifeless in the East River or were serving time in Sing Sing Prison, and she admitted she had no idea—no more than Mum anyway—which one was my daddy. "Your Mum, as if obeying the voice of the Lord, has turned over a new leaf," Mrs. O'Neill told me when I was almost old enough to understand. "She got to believing there were never any roustabouts, ruffians, rapscallion or rats in her life and that this revelation put your presence in a new light. In short, Willie the Kid, you were suddenly the product of another virgin birth. Hail Mary!"

Even if Old Freya was engaging in hyperbole and no miracle took place, Charlotte Bonnifield truly did make a dramatic change for the better (of course, I am personally biased on the subject). She became a much more driven mother. When not focused on me—now her sole purpose in life—in the present, she dwelled on my future. "You are my shining star, a unique blessing," she told me each Sunday night at bedtime when she planted a kiss on my forehead and stroked my nut-brown hair. "You shall embrace your fears, laugh away your boyhood mistakes, and grow into a self-confident man, your own man. I'll see to that!" Yes, after seeing the light—or manufacturing it herself—she became not only more loving but also more controlling and overbearing. Freya liked to point that out to her. I never did. Mum meant well and I could adapt to most anything as long as I felt her profound love.

It wasn't until I was five years old that Mum admitted she wasn't born on the streets of New York City but in the "Old Country." I assumed that meant Ireland, since I learned early on that New York had two hundred thousand Irish, making up nearly twenty-five percent of the city's total population. One day while Mum was at work, I was corrected by Mrs. O'Neill, who hailed from the barony Fews Lower in County Armagh, Northern Ireland. We were in my bedroom. She sat on a chair too small for her great bulk, but it was the only chair there. I was across from her on the edge of my bed, thoughtful and attentive as usual whenever she sat me down for a chat.

"I'll have you know your Mum was born and raised in south-central England," the midwife turned nursemaid revealed. "'Twas the county of

Oxfordshire to be specific, home of the famed University of Oxford, but the Bonnifields had nothing at all to do with any kind of education. Since medieval times they have been strictly a sheep family."

"Oh, yes, woollies," I said. "They are so much warmer than people."

"Your Mum told you that?"

"No. I thunk it myself."

"But you know that sheep produce wool. She has told you something."

"I know it from her rhymes. Bah, Bah a black Sheep/Have you any wool?/Yes merry have I,/Three bags full,?/One for my master,/One for my dame,/One for the little boy/That lives down the lane."

"Bah! Her master has it all. Mr. O'Rourke is a skinflint and a slavedriver. He has never paid a decent wage to any of the seamstresses working fourteen hours a day in his sweatshop. He pulls the wool over the eyes of all the poor immigrant Irish women."

"But Mum isn't Irish."

"You are a good listener, gossoon. I know she isn't Irish. You know she isn't Irish. But Mr. O'Rourke don't give a fig as long as she puts in the slave labor, the ignorant bastard."

"Poor sheep. It must hurt them to have their wool pulled over the eyes of ladies."

"Don't fret over sheep, gossoon."

"Okay. Tell me, Freya, am I the little boy who lives down the lane?"

"Certainly not. That makes no sense. How can you be such a boy when you live right here with your mother on the third floor?"

"And you live below?"

"Yes, in the basement."

"I am glad. I never want to be the boy who lives down the lane."

"Don't worry, gossoon. You'll be with your mother a long, long time."

"And with you, too, Freya?"

"I won't be here forever. None of us will be."

"Oh. I don't like that."

"I said not to worry. Where has your laughter gone? You are terribly young. Most everyone will go before you do."

"And I'd be alone?"

"Of course not. There will be people around not even born yet."

"I don't like to think about it."

"Then think of something else."

"Oh, no. Now I'm thinking about the Yankees fighting the Rebels."

"Well, let's hope that our President Lincoln will put an end to this terrible war soon and there can be peace."

"I like peace. I hate war."

"Ah, but it seems we must have both in this world. That's life. But let's not talk of sad things. What would you like to talk about?

"Sometimes when I look out my window, I see boys playing soldiers in the street. The ones who get shot fall down but don't die."

"True. Their guns are made of wood, big and little sticks. That's a good thing. And you won't die either as long as you play."

"I don't play soldiers. Mum doesn't want me to."

"Shall we play a card game instead?"

"Maybe later. But first, let's play the pig game Mum showed me. It makes me laugh. Do you know it?"

Mrs. O'Neill snorted and grunted like a pig. "No, tell me."

I proudly recited the nursery rhyme Mum said those times she pulled and tickled my toes: "This little piggy went to market/This little piggy stayed home/This little piggy had roast beef/This little piggy had none/And this little piggy cried 'wee wee wee' all the way home."

"Oink, oink," said Mrs. O'Neill, holding her nose.

"You're funny," I told her.

But suddenly she wasn't. A dark shadow came over her face the way clouds blow in and hide the sun. I thought she might be thinking about the bluecoats and the graycoats dying in the Civil War, and I didn't want to talk about that anymore. I waited for her to stop worrying herself, hoping she would oink again. It was no use; she had lost her playful mood. She lifted her heavy body from the little chair and shuffled over to the narrow window, peering out as if trying to find the sun. "The piggies," she said, "all went to market not to buy food but to get slaughtered and butchered. Sheep usually have it better. They lose their wool, not their lives."

"I'd rather be a sheep then, but not a black one."

"What do you know about black sheep, gossoon?"

"One of them is my daddy."

"Your Mum told you that?"

"No. I thunk it myself."

2

GOODBYE, NEW YORK

I was too young to remember much about America's Civil War. Like the country as a whole, New York City was a divided place. For mostly economic reasons involving the cotton trade (beyond my comprehension as I was more interested in wool), Mayor Fernando Wood supported the Confederacy and suggested the city should declare itself the "Free City of Tri-Insula" and secede from the Union. Next came the New York Draft Riots in which primarily Irish Catholics violently protested being forced to fight in the Civil War and lashed out at black men, who were not subject to the draft and not required to join the fight against slavery. I didn't understand any of that because half my acquaintances were poor Irish and the other half poor Negroes and in our games of hide-and-seek we played fair—taking turns, working effectively in teams, and overcoming conflicts between participants—while all resenting the insulated upper-class kids of the better neighborhoods. After President Abraham Lincoln's Emancipation Proclamation, many working-class whites in New York City feared that free black people would take their jobs. Not Mum, though.

"The darkies can have my job," she said over and over again right up until the summer day in 1864 that she walked out of Mr. O'Rourke's sweatshop for good. When she got back to our rear-house tenement that fateful day, she made her grand announcement: "Being a seamstress for that son of a bitch is unseemly. I told him as much, and I quit. You hear me, Freya, I quit!"

"It's about time," said Mrs. O'Neill. "Willie the Kid is napping."

"Dreaming the sweet dreams of the innocent. How nice for him."

"Yesterday, he woke from his nap screaming. He said he was playing soldiers in a muddy field when men in gray coats began shooting at him for real and he couldn't run away because his shoes kept getting stuck in the mud."

"If I told him once, I told him a thousand times not to play those war games."

"That's why he has to dream about it, I'm supposing."

"Never mind that. There is something more serious to consider. I am out of work, and you know what that means: No more money coming in!"

"You shall find another, more suitable vocation, Miss Bonnifield... Charlotte."

"In the meantime, how will Willie and I survive? We must eat, I must pay rent, and...there is you of course."

"Me? '

"Yes, you, Freya. You do expect to continue being paid for your services?"

"Only when you're able."

"It's not only that. There's this place—the dim rooms with tiny windows or none at all, the insufficient water-closets, the connecting cesspools outside, the nearby brothels, the surrounding stables, and the absolutely unbearable and perilous stench."

"What else is new? Holy Mother of God! You've always been a bloody complainer, Charlotte Bonnifield."

"I have every right to complain. This is America."

"I live in the dank, sunless basement and you haven't ever heard me grumble or moan. I accept my lot in life. Like our boy. I'm here all day with Willie the Kid and I've never heard him make a fuss. He pretends he's a knight in a medieval castle, a sailor on the seven seas, or a brave New York Yankee soldier shooting the Rebels at Gettysburg."

"And wakes up screaming. I'll have no more of it."

"You plan to control his dreams?"

"I do have plans. I didn't quit without a plan. I'll tell you what's new, old girl, I'm not taking it any longer, not O'Rourke, not this place, not you."

"Not me?"

"That's right. I'm pulling up stakes and I'm taking my boy."

Freya O'Neill did not let me go without a fight, but it was one she couldn't win. She was more than a midwife, more than a nursemaid, but she wasn't kin. She called my mother an ungrateful hussy, among other things I didn't understand at the time, but Mum was within the law to take me wherever she wanted and not bring Mrs. O'Neill along.

The place Mum chose was Binghamton, New York, about 180 miles from the Lower East Side, and, yes, it was because of another man. But this one was an old widower, old enough to remember the War of 1812, who had made the trip to the hated big city to pay his last respects to a veteran of that often-forgotten war. The widower's name was Prosper Davis, and though he was no Boss Tweed when it came to money or power, he did own a prosperous dairy farm in Broome County that he worked with his thirty-year-old son Elroy. Prosper wanted Mum, who told him she was a poor widow, to cook and clean for him and to meet Elroy.

When she heard what was behind the move, Mrs. O'Neill rolled her eyes so vigorously that I lost sight of her eyeballs and believed they had fallen inside her head. It made me laugh and I was determined to learn how to do that trick myself. "It figures," Mrs. O'Neill told Mum. "The leaf you done turned over turned out to be rotten underneath. Once a hussy, always a hussy."

Mrs. O'Neill was like me in believing the expression "turn over a new leaf" referred to the leaf of a tree. Well, this Prosper Davis turned out to be an educated farmer and he told me that the expression dated to the sixteenth century when books were referred to as leaves and turning over a new leaf meant turning to a blank page. I also, from some boyhood misconception, thought hussy meant female cow. Again, it was Prosper Davis, prosperous and educated dairy farmer, who set me straight. "You must be thinking of a heifer, son," he told me while Mum and I were still adjusting to farm life. "But heifers are female cattle that have not given birth to a calf. Cows are female cattle that have had calves at some point in their lives. We have to breed out cows every year so that they keep producing milk. Catch my drift, son?"

"I think so, sir. If we were cattle, I'd be a calf and Mum would be a cow, not a heifer."

"That's right. Not a hussy cow either, I'm sure. You wish you were a calf, son?"

"No. I'd rather be a lamb. How about you, Mr. Davis?"

"I'm happy being an old bull."

The old bull treated Mum and me fine, not like indentured servants, though that's what we technically were, as I later found out. Yes, there was plenty of cooking and cleaning for Mum to do around the farm and, though I was only five, I spent many hours in the barn helping to train heifers to become milk cows by scratching their necks, bellies, and udders; brushing them all over; lifting their hind legs; and telling them what great mama cows they were going to be. On occasion I would bellow like a calf wanting to be fed or roar like a bull wanting to impress the lady cows. It fooled some of the female bovines some of the time, but I'd always be sure to tell them afterward that I was only joking.

Unlike the young big city men who laid their eyes on Mum, Prosper Davis had no designs on her. But he was not so old that he didn't recognize that she was a solid, sober, prepossessing female of breeding age. He wanted his wayward son to have her or she to have him. Trouble was Elroy Davis reminded Mum of those cads she had tried to forget. He was thin-skinned, thick-headed, and prone to combativeness, especially when crooking his elbow (and not to milk cows). Prosper hoped that level-headed, attractive Charlotte Bonnifield could do what he couldn't— keep Elroy down on the farm. Most evenings Elroy galloped the five miles to Binghamton on his piebald gelding, affectionately named Rummy, to frequent the taverns. Usually, he kept drinking till the cows came home or had given up all their milk. Every few months Elroy needed to be bailed out of jail for public intoxication, brawling, or taking liberties with a barmaid.

Mum had no interest in Elroy. But because she was an indentured servant, Mum was a good sport, often putting him to bed (without joining him there) and soothing his nerves when he got out of bed by serving him the "hair of the dog that bit him." Prosper was pleased with how Mum handled his son, but Elroy felt teased, not touched, by her solicitude. On one winter morning, though in his cups as usual and naked as a jaybird, Elroy sprang out of bed on his own and like a young bull rushed into the kitchen and charged Mum, who was brewing coffee for the old man. I was sitting at the table in the corner waiting for my bowl of porridge to cool and thus witnessed the terrible spectacle that followed. In short, Elroy tore off Mum's apron, ripped open the top of her plaid wool dress and—there is no polite way to say this—tried to milk her. Early-rising Prosper was busy out in the barn and I, having not yet turned six, had no idea that Mum was in trouble. I hate to admit it, but I thought it was just a man and a woman having grown-up fun. I laughed nervously while waving my spoon over my head until Mum poured the full pot of hot coffee over Elroy's head, causing him, in full distress, to bellow. At that point, the ingenuous me recognized that the spectacle was indeed terrible, and I stuck my tongue out at Elroy.

Realizing that Charlotte Bonnifield had more than her hands full with Elroy and that there was no point keeping him close if he wasn't going to milk any cows, Prosper Davis sent his son to the newly opened New York State Inebriate Asylum in Binghamton. He justified his decision by singing its praises to Mum. "It's the first public hospital in the United States to treat alcoholism," Prosper told her. "The institution is a work of faith in humanity and hygiene and is the most healthfully and beautifully situated medical facility in the entire Empire State. The progressive doctors at this edifice understand the pathology of oenomania and are dedicated to invigorating and revivifying self-willed minds in what clearly is a well-designed temple of health. Let me tell you, Charlotte, when one stands on its palatial walls, one can't help but drink in the inspiration of the pure bracing atmosphere."

Mum let her employer's words sink in. Finally, she spoke her mind. "That's well and good, Mr. Davis, but can this fabulous asylum cure a mean drunk?"

"They'd better. Those philanthropic physicians charge a pretty penny. But do not call Elroy *mean*. He's a moral young man. It's just that intoxication leads to increased aggressiveness and sexual adventuresomeness."

"My apologies. I didn't mean to call your son mean. Overexcited might be a better word."

"Apology accepted. Now about tonight's meal. I've had a standing rib roast in mind."

"Elroy's favorite. But he'll be dining in the asylum for a while, won't he?"

"Nevertheless."

❖

As it turned out, Elroy Davis lasted in the New York Inebriate Asylum until March 1865, when he smashed a whiskey bottle over the head of the head physician and busted out of the temple of health with another patient, Levi Finch, originally from Indianapolis, Indiana. Elroy, sober on the surface, returned to the dairy farm with Levi, not to work but to extract funds for travel from the old man. Levi felt guilty about sitting out the whole Civil War so far and wanted to make amends by enlisting with an Indiana unit. Elroy didn't feel guilty about anything, but he thought that Levi would make a fine drinking companion and that Indianapolis was far enough away to put him out of the reach of his father, the sobering doctors, and the Binghamton authorities.

"That parasitic place was a joke," Elroy reported to my mother without so much as a how you doing? "Those speculative medical sons of bitches with their crazy ideas for a cure tried to turn us into teetotalers. Ten times a day, they made us recite that damned pledge: 'We agree to abstain from all liquors of an intoxicating quality whether ale, porter, wine, or ardent spirits, except as medicine.' It was enough to drive a fellow to drink."

"Not me," said Levi. "I do aim to take a good deal of medicine."

The two men looked at each other, toasted each other with invisible wine glasses, and challenged each other to see which one could produce the heartiest laugh. Mom, of course, didn't even smile, but that laughter of theirs was pretty contagious and I was a vulnerable little fellow. Mum became annoyed at my display of mirth and lifted a hand to my face. But at the last second, she realized how precious I was to her and instead of slapping me rubbed my cheek with her knuckles.

In the next few days, while Elroy and Prosper Davis were bickering over responsibilities, finances, and whether a grown man should drink milk instead of whiskey, Mum was taking a shine to Levi, who had decided it was warm enough to take off his shirt while he chopped firewood for the farm. He had more muscle, smarts, and gumption than Elroy, and she confessed to him that the sight of all those udders on the farm was making her shudder and that she

❖ **21** ❖

had never in her whole life been west of the Chenango River, a tributary of the Susquehanna. Elroy had no immediate luck trying to gain his father's support, but Mum made out well with Levi.

"I want you to come with me to Indianapolis," Levi told Mum point blank after she had been hinting in that direction for forty-eight hours.

"I'm afraid my time isn't up yet here," she said, dropping her head, and wiping her eyes, though they looked fairly dry to me. "I am obliged for at least three more years. You see, I'm an indentured servant."

"Hmmm. Even with milky skin and red hair?"

"That's right. I signed a contract with Mr. Davis so I could get the hell out of that horrible city, where I had lost my job and as a poor widow was trying to raise a young son single-handedly in a run-down tenement house with poor ventilation."

I didn't mind her lying about being a widow; it elicited far more sympathy than if she'd revealed she was never married and was uncertain which lover was my despicable father. But I did think she should have at least mentioned Freya O'Neill, who had spent so much time with me and was still in my bedtime prayers. But I wasn't one to interrupt adults when they were engaged in serious conversation.

"Won't he let you out of your contract early?" Mr. Finch asked.

"It doesn't work that way. Well, as I understand it, I could stop being Mr. Davis's indentured servant if I became his daughter-in-law. That is to say if I married Elroy and we settled down together on the farm."

"Not interested?"

"You must be kidding."

At that point I laughed, which I realized was inappropriate when Mum glared at me and Mr. Finch, who hadn't previously noticed my presence, said, "Hey, that nosey kid of yours is listening."

"Never mind Willie the Kid. He's a born laugher but he doesn't mean to be rude."

"So, it's safe to say you're interested in me and want to go home to Indianapolis with me."

"Yes. I know it's a city, but I'm sure it's not as monstrous as Manhattan."

"Of course not. It's growing, but probably less than fifty thousand live there right now even if you include the cattle. I understand New York City has well over one million people and seventy-one hundred places licensed to sell alcohol." Levi smacked his lips. "But don't you worry. I never did count how many taverns we have in Indianapolis, and anyway I wouldn't be frequenting such establishments knowing I had you waiting for me at home."

"Yes, Indianapple sounds fine, but ..."

"Indianapolis."

"Right, I want to go there, but there's something you should know. I never plan to get married again. My beloved husband tragically died in the Civil War and ..."

"Look, I'm not planning to ask you to marry me, Mrs. Bonnifield. Anyway, when I get there, I won't be making myself at home again right away. You see, I intend to enlist and fight for the Union against slavery and maybe against indentured servitude, too."

"How noble. All I need is to get there safely. I'm used to taking care of Willie by my lonesome."

"Oh, right. The kid. He's part of the deal?"

"Naturally. My son is everything. He goes wherever I go. He is all I have."

"Right, Charlotte. I can call you Charlotte, can't I?"

"As you wish, Mr. Finch."

"Levi. I can't at this time afford travel by train. We'll need a wagon and another horse or two. We'll have to see if Elroy can win over his daddy, Mr. Dairy. Those asylum money-grabbers have left me a little short. But if all goes well, the four of us will be headed west right soon."

"I suppose Elroy has to be part of the deal, too?"

"No way around that. But no worries, Charlotte. Drunk or sober, I won't let my pal touch a hair on your pretty red head."

3

HELLO, MR. MAYOR

Elroy Davis could not get his father to agree to a loan. So, the son went to Plan B. He used money stolen from his father's home safe (which was located in the parlor behind a framed portrait of stern, bearded Prosper Davis in overalls and holding a pitchfork) to pay for travel by train to Indianapolis for himself, Levi Finch, Mum, and me. There was enough money left over for Elroy to rent a room in the back of the Finch family home. Mum did not wish to share it with him, but she and I were allowed to stay for free in the room Levi Finch grew up in because Levi preferred to "rough it" in a tent he set up in the backyard. "Need to prepare myself for serving the Union Army," he explained.

At 11 p.m. on April 9 word reached Indianapolis that Confederate General Robert E. Lee had surrendered at Appomattox Courthouse in Virginia. Wild public celebrations ensued, and nobody celebrated more than Elroy Davis, even though he had avoided the war thanks to his father's paying three hundred dollars to have a young farmhand enlist as a substitute for Elroy. First Elroy indulged in hard cider before stripping to his undergarments and draping himself in a thirty-three-star flag that he took out of a trunk in the Finch attic. Such a flag had flown at Fort Sumner four long years earlier when Confederates bombarded the South Carolina fort and forced the Union garrison to surrender.

It wasn't clear to anyone if Elroy was trying to make some kind of statement with his chosen attire. He provided no explanations as he danced around the Finch home, first with Mum (who soon broke free and escaped to the bushes behind the house) then with Levi's mother and father (before the wary couple retreated to their bedroom, and finally with me (I was helpless as he swung me clear off my feet). Dizziness at long last put an end to his dancing, and he collapsed on the floor with my small body caught beneath his heft and me screaming for mercy. I was relieved when he left the house to continue his drinking in the Indiana Avenue neighborhood where he toasted every black stranger—man, woman, or child—he stumbled upon. It wasn't until dawn that three Negro businessmen carried him into the Finch house on a carriage door that had somehow separated from a black one-horse carriage. The flag he was wearing had been shredded during the celebration, which the *Indianapolis Journal* described as a "demented display of patriotism."

Levi Finch, by contrast, took no part in any celebrating. He was a Union man all the way but was disappointed the Civil War was over before he could help win it. When Mum felt it safe to come out of the bushes, she went to his tent and found him sober but sobbing. He told her that he was joining the 159th Indiana and that in three days the unit would muster into service for a year. "I got to do it; I finally got to do the right thing," he told Mum. "Some of them unrepentant Rebels are still running loose and who's to say Tricky Bobby Lee won't wave his saber again and raise another traitorous army." Mum couldn't talk him out of his crazy notion. His tears did affect her, though. She had never seen a grown man cry before and it struck a sympathetic nerve.

When I recovered from the squashing Elroy gave me, I went out back to look for Mum and heard her groans coming from inside Levi's tent. I naively rushed in without knocking (or whatever you're supposed to do before entering somebody's tent). Yes, what I saw was my biggest shock since the time in Manhattan I witnessed two beer barrels fall off a runaway horse-drawn wagon and crush to death a man trying to cross Delancey Street. I won't go into detail, but Levi wasn't wearing even his undergarments and Mum was underneath him apparently not getting squashed. Before leaving the Lower East Side she had vowed to have nothing more to do with prurient men, but I suppose those tears of his made Levi seem less prurient. Besides, the poor man was about to go off and fight for his country, even though the war was over.

Less than a week later enough tears were falling in Indianapolis that one would have thought the White River had flooded. President Lincoln had been assassinated in the nation's capital. When his funeral train passed through Indianapolis on the way to Springfield, Illinois, on April 15, Levi's parents and ten thousand other people stood in long lines to pass the president's bier at the Indiana statehouse, where his remains lay in state. Mum didn't attend. Once when she was slaving as a seamstress for the despicable Mr. O'Rourke she had voiced her opinion of President Lincoln: "So he freed the slaves—big deal. When's the Liberator going to rescue poor uneducated immigrant women from low-paying, fourteen-hour-a-day jobs with working conditions that are harsh, dirty, unsafe, and humiliating." Not that she wished the violent death of any man (well, O'Rourke and one or two former lovers were exceptions), and she expressed sympathy for Mrs. Lincoln and her two living sons, Robert and Tad.

Anyway, Mum had a darn good reason for not being there to say bon voyage to the president's remains. She was busy at home dealing with a sick son. I had bloody diarrhea, stomach cramps, vomiting, and fever—dysentery, but then known as "bloody flux" or "camp fever" (lots of Civil War soldiers got it, too, as did Levi Finch). Mum kept encouraging me to drink water against doctor's orders, and I didn't suffer too long before the infection cleared from my system. Within a few months I was even engaging in privy humor about diarrhea with some of the other boys in the neighborhood. But, of course, there was nothing funny about the disease. Despite numerous treatments—such as bloodletting, blistering, ingesting lead salts, and emetics—Levi Finch died from severe dehydration before summer arrived in Indianapolis and before he could prove his worth to the 159th Indiana.

The funeral took place in the Finch home. Levi's mother, Imogene, dressed me in a little black suit that used to belong to Levi, and Levi's father, Edward, loaned me a black armband that had been passed down by the Finch family for generations. Mum decided that under the circumstances (her and me sharing Levi's old bedroom rent free, her having once had amorous congress with Levi, and Levi's parents being so kind) she would go into deep mourning instead of half mourning. She wore a black dress with no trim and a long veil made of crepe at the funeral and for three weeks after that she put on the same dress but without the veil. Levi was embalmed by one of Indianapolis' first businessmen-undertakers, Mortimer Underwood. The severe looking man had been one of the many locals to view Lincoln's remains at the statehouse, and the concept of a non-decomposing body was so appealing to Mr. Underwood that he decided to earn an income by selling his services as what would later be called a mortician.

Elroy Davis complained to Mum that she should stop dwelling on the dead and think more about the living, of course implying himself. He also became jealous of Mortimer Underwood, who, the first Sunday after Levi's funeral, asked Mum to go on a picnic at Indianapolis's new park-like Crown Hill Cemetery. Mum, though, had no interest in either man. She kept turning down excursions with Mr. Underwood and fending off Mr. Davis's incursions into our bedroom. Mortimer was not easily discouraged and only dropped his courting notions after Elroy threatened to embalm him alive and bury him without a casket. Elroy, though, was relentless. Edward and Imogine Finch noticed and told him he must vacate his rented room in thirty days. That wasn't soon enough for Mum.

She had been cooking and cleaning for the Finches, but she went out and found a job as a live-in domestic on the other side of town. Of course, she wouldn't have taken the job if I hadn't been allowed to come along or if the single man who owned the house hadn't been so respectable. John Caven looked as stern as Mr. Underwood, but he was set in his ways and looking only for a housekeeper, not a wife. It didn't matter to him that she had falsely portrayed herself as a "respectable poor widow woman." He never crossed the line with Mum, always behaving like a kindly uncle not only with her but also with me. He served as the ninth mayor of Indianapolis through 1867. We stayed with him through that time and well after it, too.

Mr. Caven was the first man to want to teach me anything or to talk to me as if I mattered. He spoke to me about building street railways, creating a city library, securing education for black children as well as white, and the notorious Reno brothers. Outside of Seymour, Indiana, on October 8, 1866, John and Simeon Reno, along with Frank Sparks, pulled off the first peacetime train robbery in American history, making off with twelve thousand dollars from the express car of an Ohio & Mississippi train. That was only the beginning for the Reno Gang, and I couldn't get enough of his stories about those Indiana outlaws. His tales, usually offered me during his daily constitutionals but sometimes after Mum had already kissed me goodnight, did come with warnings I took to heart: "Don't grow up to be a train robber, Willie; Crime pays for only so long, young man; Living is serious business and can make you cry, but when you want to cry, sometimes it helps to laugh instead; Any man who says he understands criminals or females is telling you a windy."

Mum was also impressed with Mr. Caven because he knew when to act like an employer and when to act like a decent human being. She got so overexcited when she learned he had introduced and seen through an eight-hour ordinance for city workers that she overstepped her bounds and kissed him on the cheek. She apologized but he said to think nothing of it. After that she never had anything as long as an eight-hour day cleaning, washing and cooking for him.

I of course had nothing but free time, until Mum, after consulting with Mr. Caven, enrolled me in primary school in fall 1867. At first, I didn't like going because I believed I learned far more interesting things at home from Mr. Caven. One day during my second week I skipped school and the mayor took me to his woodshed and produced a hickory switch. No, he didn't use it. Instead, he waved it like a magic wand and told me a story about how teachers in his school days struck students for the mildest of offenses, such as looking out a window to watch a murder of crows gather in an American elm or dipping into an inkwell the pigtails of a haughty girl sitting in front of him.

"Thank the good Lord there are still American elm and girls with pigtails," he said. "And thanks to School Superintendent A.C. Shortridge, we now have in Indianapolis nothing but qualified teachers who want to teach and not punish. In other words, the rod has been entirely banished from the classroom and the fear of punishment is no longer the incentive for obedience and order. Our teachers secure desirable results by milder and more lenient methods. So, Willie, you're a lucky boy."

"But nobody hits me at home either, Mr. Caven. And you talk about more interesting subjects than Miss Amanda Crabtree does. She knows nothing about the Reno brothers. School is boring."

"Look, I have a successful law practice and I know enough to be a mayor who gets things done, but I couldn't have gotten this far if I still spelled cat K-A-T, couldn't read the printing of the council proceedings, and didn't know enough about figures to oversee the city's income and expenditure."

He had me scratching my head, but then I said, "C-A-T."

"Fine, but now spell catastrophe. And it would be a catastrophe, young man, if you didn't stay in school long enough to fully grasp reading, writing, and arithmetic. Our teachers go by this theory: 'Nothing is accepted as known until it is fully expressed by a good English sentence or written on a slate.'"

I didn't grasp everything Mr. Caven said that day at the woodshed, but I trusted him to know what was best for me. From then on, I never missed a day of school in Indianapolis. I did put Miss Crabtree to the test several times by staring out the window at a quarrel of sparrows (rather than a murder of crows) and sticking into an inkwell one of the braids of a girl who was demure rather than haughty. Indeed, both times I was spared the rod and the switch. But for half a school day each time I was obliged to wear a dunce cap and sit in a corner where I could see neither birds nor girls.

I was too ashamed to tell either Mr. Caven or Mum about those schoolroom punishments dished out by my teacher, but neither did I totally mend my ways. Now and again I couldn't help myself and went on to earn the dunce cap distinction three other times. One morning I got to the school room twenty minutes early and placed a wormy apple on Miss Crabtree's desk. Once she got over her shock and revulsion, she made me hold the rotten apple in my lap as I sat in the corner for an hour. Another time while the class was reciting the Lord's Prayer before the opening exercises began, I drew a poor caricature of Miss Crabtree (she looked half pig, half sheep) on my slate. She made me draw a self-portrait (I gave myself a mustache) while I sat in the corner through recess. The third time I was eating a cold pancake at lunch when a new boy in school threw a hard-boiled egg at my head and didn't miss. Miss Crabtree didn't see that unprovoked attack, but she witnessed me retaliating by hurling my lard sandwich (I liked cold pancakes better) at him but missing and instead grazing the cheek of that poor demure girl with two braids.

My rude and thoughtless act earned me not only the dunce cap in the corner but also a visit to the principal. No hitting occurred there either, only a lecture about how little girls were full of sugar and spice and everything nice and if I ever maltreated one of them again, my mother would be summoned to the schoolhouse. The new boy got off scot-free because I never did tell on him. At the time I didn't even know his name. Two days later he told me I wasn't a bad egg and he appreciated me for not being a snitch like his younger brother Joe. We had a laugh over our short food fight, and he asked me my name. I told him, "I'm best known as Willie the Kid." He laughed at that, too, then said: "My name is William Henry McCarty. But you are my first pal in Indianapolis. You can call me Billy."

4

BILLY AND A GIRL

Billy in no time at all acquired many other pals, more than half of whom were girls, including the demure girl in pigtails. He didn't have to work at it. He was a natural. Most of the schoolkids, even some of the older ones, flocked to him. I suppose he was charming with his freckles, sandy blond hair, soft blue eyes, crooked-tooth smile, ability to walk on his hands, proficiency at executing cartwheels, prowess at twisting his hands into a snake shape, finger snapping, knuckle-cracking, one-hand clapping, ready wit, and easy laugh. I didn't like to admit it, though. My laugh came just as easily, but it didn't go over half as well. And when I looked at myself in Mum's mirror, I saw more freckles, sandier hair, bigger blue eyes, and straighter teeth. No matter how hard I tried I couldn't stand on my hands let alone walk on them, couldn't land on my feet after attempting a cartwheel, and couldn't do any tricks with my hands or fingers, but I could run faster than him and beat him at arm wrestling, right or left. I could make as many witty comments as him, too, except, not on the spot. Most of them came when I was back home looking at myself in Mum's mirror.

"You're jealous of your best friend," Mr. Caven concluded the time Billy invited himself over so he could see what a genuine mayor looked like in person. (Billy had been a little disappointed, commenting, "I thought a mayor would be fatter.")

"No," I shouted, my agitated tone surprising me as much as it did Mr. Caven. "I mean No, sir."

"The boy doth protest too much, methinks."

I ordinarily would have laughed away such a remark, whether I understood it or not, but I wasn't in the mood. I crossed my arms and pouted. "He's my best friend, I'm not his best friend. He has more pals than you can shake a stick at."

"That's what I mean. You're jealous of his popularity. But why shake a stick at anyone. Simply enjoy his company when you can and accept the fact others like to be with him as much as you do. He's a likeable lad. I never before thought of myself as svelte. He has magnetism."

"Magnet is him?"

"Yes, the ability to attract and charm people. I know something about that. How do you think I was elected and reelected mayor of our fair city."

"How do I get it, this magnet thing?"

"Well, to be honest with you, Willie, it's sort of a gift. Magnetism can't be learned. All you can do is be yourself and hope for the best."

I felt pretty hopeless hearing those words, but I laughed anyway. "Got it, sir. I'm Willie and he's Billy."

Billy never asked me over to his house, but one day after school I stealthily followed him home. The Indianapolis streets were mostly named after the states, and it turned out he lived with his mother and brother in a tiny three-room house on New York Street, which was fitting since he had been born and partially raised in the Empire State just like me. Instead of going inside he walked down to the end of an adjacent alley, whistled once with his fingers, and began a distinctive, plaintive call—*CooOOoo-woo-woo-woo*. I don't know if Billy knew it or not—and I only knew it later—but that is the sound male mourning doves make to attract a mate. Like me he was seven years old, which is mighty young for human beings but mighty old for lovey-dovey doves.

Anyway, his cooing got results. A face appeared at a small second-story window and a few moments later reappeared at a back door. It was a familiar sugar-and-spice face, though I was more familiar with the back of the head. Yes, this was Laura Blakney, the demure girl with two braids who sat at the desk in front of me at school. Previously I had never seen her outdoors except at recess. She wore a white dress and had a blue ribbon in her hair. They didn't see me at first because they were making eyes at each other and I was crouched behind a barrel that reeked of dead fish. Laura finally blushed and lowered her head, which made Billy laugh.

"I swear by Jove that I could stare down a mad dog," he said.

"Fiddlesticks," she replied. "And, Billy McCarty, I am not a dog."

"Not a working dog for sure. But you could be a spitz puppy, all soft and white. They like to sit on laps."

"I don't sit on anyone's lap."

"I saw you sit on Miss Crabtree's lap when that honeybee stung you and you wouldn't stop crying."

"It hurt. Everybody cries."

"Not me."

"How about when your Daddy whips you?"

"Never."

"Doesn't he hit hard enough?"

"Don't know. Never met the man. Mom uses a hairbrush. I try not to laugh."

"Are you sad not to have a daddy?"

"Not so anyone would notice. I'm the man of the house."

"Nobody seven years old is a man. You're a kid like me."

"All right, a kid. But I can dance like a man." He bowed to her like a gentleman, took her by the wrists and began to swing her around the alley so rapidly that she had trouble keeping her feet on the ground. The breeze they created even reached me behind the barrel.

Besides her braids, I had no interest in the rest of Laura Blakney. At least that was what I thought until I saw her dancing with Billy. There was no music, of course, but soon Billy began accompanying his fast-moving feet with a noisy song. "All around the cobbler's bench,/The monkey chased the people/ And after them in double haste,/Pop! Goes the weasel!" Each time he sang out "Pop!" he stopped abruptly and lifted the suddenly enthralling Laura into the air.

Billy kept swinging his partner closer and closer to me. I wanted to dig myself a hole or hide in the foul-smelling barrel. There wasn't time for that. I decided my best bet was to show them my back and run like a Confederate soldier. But on the next *Pop!* Laura Blakney went up and, when Billy lost his grasp on her hips, came down with one foot on the barrel and the other on my back. Though she looked light as a dove feather, the force of her landing dropped me onto my belly. Meanwhile she crumbled to the ground holding her left ankle.

"Dash it, Willie," Billy said. "How'd you get underfoot?"

"I wasn't. I was behind the barrel ..."

"Forget about it. You're as bad as Josie."

"Who's that?

"My little brother."

"I thought he was Joe."

"The big baby acts like a little girl. Josie sounds more like a girl than Joe does."

"Hey," said Laura, still holding her ankle. "I'm a girl."

"Right you are." Billy knelt next to her, pushed aside her hands, and held her ankle himself. "Does it hurt when I do that?"

"Ouch. Don't twist it. I think it's broken."

"Nonsense. It's just wrenched. All the bones are in the right place."

"Stop touching it. It hurts something awful."

"I know, I know. Wrenched ankles can do that, but why don't you try standing?"

"No. You don't know. No kid is a doctor."

"Doc McCarty says stand up, little girl."

Billy rather roughly raised her off the ground. She wasn't much help, but once upright, she grimaced and tried her best to pull herself together. Billy insisted she put weight on her left foot. As soon as she did, she screamed. "I can't stand it!" she said, and she began to cry.

"She can't stand it," I said, daring to step in and let her lean against me for support.

"Thank you, Willie the Kid," said Billy. "You must be a bloody genius."

I didn't know what sarcasm meant yet, but I knew his words weren't complimentary. I shrugged it off, though. A female in distress needed my help. I imagined myself a knight, just like I used to do in the old days back at the rear-house tenement. So, the first time I entered the McCarty house on New York Street it was with Billy but with a wet-eyed Laura Blakney between us, a stringy girl arm around each of our narrow shoulders.

5

WOODWORKERS OF INDIANAPOLIS

As Indianapolis mayor, John Caven, was a leader who initiated things and saw them through during his first two terms. He was clearly well liked and would serve two terms in the Indiana Senate beginning in 1869 before returning as mayor for three more terms starting in 1875. But in 1868 he was back to being just a lawyer and a Mason. That September he was elected by secret ballot as Worship Master of Mystic Tie Lodge, No. 398, Free and Accepted Masons. He told me that made him top dog in his lodge and gave him considerable powers, but he didn't spell out those powers, only adding that he now presided over Mason rituals and ceremonies at the lodge. "Someday you, too, can be a Freemason and help promote the brotherhood of man," Mr. Caven told me.

Billy McCarty acted as if he knew all about them. I have no idea how he found out about Freemasonry, but he met all kinds of people on the street and he was the brightest boy in our class when he felt like showing it. "They like to wear white aprons like our mothers and keep secrets from everyone who ain't a mason and don't know the secret handshake," he told me one day when we were throwing rocks into the White River. "They listen to the cries of widows like our mothers and of orphans, which you and me ain't."

"Why white aprons?" I asked. "They like to cook? Mum does all the cooking for the Worship Master—you know, Mr. Caven."

"Sure, the old mayor. He's getting fatter, I noticed. The Masons don't cook regular meals like your mother, I'm sure. And not like that witch in 'Hansel and Gretel' who fattens up little children to eat them. I suppose they do cook sometimes when they ain't got wives, and when they do you can bet they put in a lot of secret ingredients. But mostly they like the feel of their white aprons. I heard they're made from the skins of lambs. Most Masons like the feel so much they wear them aprons when they get buried."

"They kill little lambs for their skins?"

"Sure. Most everything gets skinned one way or another—cows, hogs, deer, buffalo, beavers, bears, foxes, fish. Hell, kid. If you get caught by an Indian, they'll scalp you and skin you alive!"

"Poor lambs. I like sheep, especially when they're lambs." I picked up another stone to throw but accidentally dropped it on my foot.

"Anyway, I don't want to be a Mason." With a running start, Billy hurled a rock farther than either of us had done before. "Top that, Kid."

"How come?"

"Because it's a contest to see who can throw the farthest. I win. How are you for skipping?"

"You mean school? I don't do that anymore."

"I mean rocks. We'll have a skipping contest next."

"Naw. What I was really asking is why you don't want to be a Mason?"

"They're old and dumb and fat. I've formed my own secretive kids' club, the Free and Accepted Woodworkers of Indianapolis."

"Really, what do you do?"

"Work with wood, muttonhead. You need a knife to join. We carve horses, wolves, swords, muskets, pistols, Abraham Lincoln, even Miss Crabtree's bearded face."

"She doesn't have a beard."

'You're missing the point. It'll cost you a shiny new Seated Liberty dime to join."

"I can't carve wood. I don't have a knife."

"Never mind. I'll lend you mine. You can whittle a stick. You do have a dime, don't you?

I shook my head. "Who else is in your club?"

"Why, practically all my pals."

"Including girls, too?" I still sometimes had Laura Blakney on my mind. She no longer sat in front of me in the schoolroom, but by twisting my head a little to the right I could see the left side of her sweet, innocent face and part of the blue ribbon in her hair.

"No, no. Girls aren't Woodworkers. We carve things for them. And sometimes we carve them if they let us." He laughed and with an exaggerated sidearm motion threw a stone that skipped across the water, ten times by my count. "Top that, Kid. The best by far—a dozen bounces!"

"Can't," I said. "I'm tired of throwing rocks. I'm hungry."

"You can't stand being away from Mummy so long."

"Not so, Billy. It's just my stomach that..."

"All right. All right. When you get home, you can ask Mummy for a dime."

"Did I say I wanted to join your club?"

"You don't have to, Kid. Of course, you will. It's written all over your face."

"I might join, but I might not. I suppose you keep all the dimes you get?"

"Every club needs a treasurer. We have a Christmas party planned. I'll buy cake, candy, lemonade, and hair ribbons for the girl guests we'll invite. Three Woodworkers play harmonicas and one got hold of a fiddle with only one broken string. They'll be plenty of dancing."

"I...I don't dance."

"Let me show you, Kid."

Billy latched onto my wrists and began spinning me around despite my protests. I was not light like Laura Blakney. In fact, I was slightly bigger and stronger than Billy. But he was full of boundless, formidable energy and it took me the longest time to break free. When I finally did, I stumbled, tumbled, and slid down the left bank of the White River. I hit the water with the splash of a boulder rather than a stone. I wasn't a swimmer yet and I flailed around some before Billy came down to water's edge and yanked me out.

"Saved your life," Billy said. "You owe me."

That was something of an exaggeration, but I felt like a half-drowned cat and was grateful not to be fully drowned. "All right. I'll go home and split kindling for Mum to earn myself a dime."

"Spoken like a true Woodworker. You won't regret it. We're more fun than the Masons. And I've come up with a secret handshake that makes theirs look tame. I'll show you when you hand over your dime. There's no better club in town."

"If you say so. Besides being the treasurer, you're probably also the club's Worship Master, right?"

"Right." He patted me on my wet back and flashed his crooked-tooth grin. "For life."

The Free and Accepted Woodworkers of Indianapolis didn't stand the test of time, going out of existence in early December. Various mothers of members were in an uproar after two of Billy's pals nearly cut off their thumbs in separate carving accidents and Billy himself thrashed a disloyal member for showing a non-member the club's secret handshake, which involved four hands twisted together and four middle fingers wiggling amid them. The crowning blow was when Billy tired of Joe tailing after him begging to be a junior Woodworker and pushed his younger brother into the White River. Joe easily got out on his own, but he was soaked to the bone and ran all the way home to tell their mother. Unlike the Indianapolis school system and Mum, Catherine McCarty believed in corporal punishment.

When Billy finally returned from the river, he brought me along because his mother liked me. Catherine McCarty had the notion I was a good boy who could possibly have a good influence on her intractable oldest son. Billy McCarty had the notion I had a calming effect on his mother. Nevertheless, right in front of me in the kitchen, she told Billy to touch his toes, and raised not a hairbrush but a wooden paddle, no doubt carved by a righteous grown person.

"What's with that?" Billy asked, looking back and trying to force a smile.

"It's something new just for you," his mother said, tapping the paddle against the palm of her left hand.

"Oh? What kind of wood is it made of, Mom?"

"I have no idea, but I can tell you it's hard wood."

"You mad about something? Willie the Kid is here. He's a real nice pal."

I waved to her and went back to twiddling my undamaged thumbs (I hadn't seriously tried to carve anything yet).

"I know. And Joe is a real nice little boy."

"I suppose, just not much of a brother."

"You had no right to push him in the water. He's two years younger than you."

"He swims like a fish."

"He's liable to catch pneumonia."

"He'll get over it. If you put him to bed, he'll at least be out of my hair."

"You listen to me good, William Henry McCarty. You better be nice to your little brother. Joseph McCarty is a member of our family and has every right to be a member of his brother's club."

"But we use knives and such. We wouldn't want baby brother to hurt himself."

"Boys have already been hurt. What you need to do is form a different kind of club and to include Joe."

"You mean a girls' club that plays with dolls?"

"I've had enough of your sass, William. Touch your toes!"

"I am. I am. Get on with it, Mom. The blood is rushing to my head."

Mrs. McCarty, now red-faced, brought her right arm back and swung the paddle forward with such force that when it connected with Billy's bottom, he tumbled head over heels across the kitchen floor. He ended up flat on his back under the kitchen table

"As I live and breath1!" said Mrs. McCarty as the paddle fell out of her hand and thumped on the floor. "I don't know my own strength."

She and I were too stunned to move at first but then we both cautiously approached Billy, who wasn't moving a muscle. I knew a blow to the backside couldn't kill a person, but I thought it might have rattled his brains.

"Oh, Billy boy, what have I done?" his mother asked, teary-eyed and looking pale as a sheep. She dropped to her knees by his still head. Billy's eyes were closed. Her hands hovered over his face as if she were afraid to touch him. I froze behind her, knowing I was helpless to do anything myself and having no idea if there was a doctor anywhere close to New York Street. As I stared at them, I was reminded of a frightful drawing that hung over the basement bed of my old nursemaid Freya O'Neill. When in her basement, I hadn't been able to take my eyes off it. She told me it depicted weeping Mary Magdalene kneeling at the nearly naked body of a lifeless Christ, who had recently had his hands and feet nailed to a cross. Getting paddled wasn't nearly such a severe punishment, but at the moment I wasn't so sure.

"Is Billy dead?" Joe McCarty, wearing a nightshirt though the sun hadn't gone down yet, had slipped into the kitchen without me noticing.

"No, no, he's just resting," Mrs. McCarty said.

"Under the table?"

"Never mind, Joey. Nothing for you to concern yourself with here. You go back to bed right now and get under the warm covers or mommy will be very unhappy."

"I want a glass of water."

"Later, later. I'll bring it to you in a little while. Go now. I need to wake up your brother."

"No need," said Billy, his eyes now open. He shot backward very fast, like a crayfish, or Indiana lobster, until he was well clear of the table. He then quickly sat up and sprang off the floor without using his hands. "Need to visit the outhouse," he told his mother. As he brushed past me headed for the front door, he winked. "How'd you like my somersault, Kid?" he asked, but he didn't wait for an answer.

6

COWBOYS AND INDIANS

Only a few weeks after the paddling incident that Billy preferred to refer to as the "Great Somersault Affair" (he contended that the paddle his mother wielded hadn't hurt him any more than her hairbrush), the McCarty clan moved from their small New York Street house to a larger residence on North East Street. From there, the enterprising Catherine McCarty operated a laundry, contending no man could dirty clothes as fast as her son Billy, then began selling baked goods as well. While her loaves of white bread sold like hot cakes, her most popular item with the ladies of Indianapolis was something she first baked especially for her younger son Joe—angel food cake. She whipped up so many egg whites for these cakes that Billy called her "Mother Hen." The new house had two extra rooms, so Mrs. McCartney also took in boarders, mostly soldiers who had mustered out of the service but still didn't have anywhere else to go while reacclimating to civilian life.

"Never seen such a catawamptiously chewed up bunch of Yankees in my whole life," Billy told me one afternoon in mid-December 1869 after he had pilfered two slices of angel food cake without asking his mother.

"Catawhat?" I said with my mouth full.

'Catawamptiously. It means all tuckered out but worse. It's my best word."

"What's wrong with them?"

"The Civil War done them all a hurt—on some you can see the hurt, like a mangled arm or missing leg. But on some you can't see it." Billy made a fist and knocked on his head as if it were a door. "Sure is mighty spongy, ain't it?"

"Your head?"

"Ha. Ha. You're a laugh, Kid. Bet you never tasted sponge cake like this before?"

"Never had it before. Mum makes pound cake for dessert once a month."

"I've had it. Dry as a desert. Like eating sawdust."

I shrugged. I didn't want to admit that his mother's angel food cake was ten times better than Mum's poundcake. "Those men in your house talk about the war and such?" I asked.

"Some. They followed their leaders on the ground like sheep. None rode horses. None liked shooting Rebels much. But getting shot at was worse. Soldiers on both sides used muskets, which you load at the end, you know the muzzles. They had to follow nine steps to load and fire a single bullet from one of them muzzle-loaders."

I couldn't quite follow him, but I nodded and said, "That ain't easy."

"I'll say not. I tell you something, Kid, when I get me a gun it won't be no muzzle-loader. I don't aim to get myself catawamptiously chewed up."

"Who would. Where'd you learn a big word like that?"

"From William Henry Harrison Antrim. He was twenty years old in 1862 when he volunteered and became a private with the Fifty-fourth Regiment of the Indiana Infantry."

"One of the musket shooters, eh?"

"I suppose. But he's not like those sorry-looking men staying with us. He ain't catawamptiously chewed up one morsel. He's more substantial. Mom says he wears his mustache well. He lives a few blocks away from us at *Fifty-eight* Cherry Street and has a good job driving for the Merchants Union Express Company."

"How is it you happen to know this Mr. Antrim?"

"Mom met him some time ago but kept quiet about it. She could no longer keep him a secret when baby Josie got frightened as usual and wanted to know why this strange man kept following them and also watched the house from the lot across the street while licking his lips and rubbing his bushy mustache. You see this William Antrim has an interest in her if you catch my drift."

"Sure. Men are interested in Mum, too, but she isn't interested back. Not anymore."

"I wouldn't count on that if I were you, Willie the Kid. For all you know, your mother could be having a high old time with a secret admirer while you're in the schoolroom learning who the father of our country is."

"I know that. George Washington."

"What a genius"

Billy laughed, and I started to get angry. But I counted ten sheep in my head, which always seemed to calm me down. "If there was another man in Mum's life, Mr. Caven would know about it and he'd tell me."

"Not necessarily. What if the fat man is jealous of the other man and is planning to murder him?"

"That's dumb. Mr. Caven would never kill a man who could possibly vote for him—or kill anyone at all for that matter. Anyway, Mr. Craven isn't interested in Mum. I mean, he isn't interested in getting married."

"I'm not talking about marriage, dunderhead. William Antrim ain't interested in marriage, either. There are other things."

I didn't ask him to explain himself. I took my last bite of angel food cake and left when Billy said there was no more.

❧

On my recommendation, Mum started to buy bread from Mrs. McCarty. No angel food cake, though, since she considered it an extravagant expense and Mr. Caven didn't like spongy things. The two women struck up a friendship of sorts after they found out they were both from New York City (they sympathized with each other about that), both had sons the same age (they said they considered us blessings most of the time), and both liked to pass themselves off as widows (they tittered over that). While Mrs. McCarty was known to pat me on the head, Mum didn't have much to say about the two McCarty boys. When I pressed her, she admitted that my pal Billy seemed too boisterous and Joey was a little too tied to his mother's apron strings.

I usually avoided Mrs. McCarty when possible because it bothered me to be patted on the head in front of Billy, although he couldn't have cared less. Joe, on the other hand, scowled at me whenever his mother showed me the slightest attention. I didn't notice when Mrs. McCarty started to behave differently: wiping her eyes and nose excessively, experiencing shortness of breath, wheezing now and again, sweating when others were cold, not wanting to eat her own baked goods or much of anything else. But Mum did. I overheard her point that out to Mr. Caven, who was a lawyer not a doctor but seemed to know something about everything.

"It's the particles in the air we breathe," he told her. "It's happening more and more here in Indianapolis."

"Particles? My education is limited, Mr. Caven. I don't follow."

"Simply dust, dirt, soot, and smoke, my dear."

"Aren't those always in the air. It seemed that way in New York City."

"Yes, and now more so in our fair city, which is all abuzz with commerce. Steam locomotives keep pouring into town, bringing goods and people. Those locomotives are powered by coal, and more and more citizens are now heating with coal. The coal smoke darkens the sky and can cause the problems your friend Catherine McCarty is facing. She isn't the only one."

"I kind of can see that. But can't something be done about all those particles?"

"No, not unless you want to stop commercial growth. Dirty air is here to stay. Progress is at hand, my dear."

"I have noticed myself coughing more lately, Mr. Caven. Should I be worried?"

"No more than you would worry about one of those coal-burning locomotives running you over when you are crossing the tracks. You are perfectly safe in my kitchen."

Mum took a deep breath and sighed. "That's a relief. What kind of meat would you like served for supper?"

Mum's cough went away after a few days and she stopped worrying about dirty particles in the air. Catherine McCarty, on the other hand, continued to worry. She soon was ready to leave behind her baked goods, laundry, and veteran boarders—along with the gray skies of that cold, wet winter— and take the boys not only out of Indianapolis but clear across the Mississippi River. I later learned from an inquiring Mr. Caven that two physicians he knew in the city had told Mrs. McCarty that she had contracted consumption, also known as tuberculosis, and that while there was no cure, her only hope for a longer life was to go to a drier climate with clear air. Wichita, Kansas, fit that qualification in 1870, and also had something else going for it. The year before the U.S. government had opened the Osage Indian trust lands in Kansas to the general public for homesteading. All she needed to do was file an application for a small fee, move onto a 160-acre quarter section, improve the land over five years, and file for deed of title to the property. At the time, Billy wasn't eleven yet and didn't know any of that or just didn't care.

"Great news, ain't it, Kid," he told me, and it wasn't a question. "Mum and I are plain sick of Indiana. It's a joke to call this a Western state. Now Kansas is the real West—the genuine frontier. Wichita is a brand-new town. Only seven years ago Jesse Chisholm, who was half Indian, blazed a trail north and started a trading post at the site of future Wichita. Another trader name of J.R. Mead founded the town in 1868, naming it for the Wichita Indians. Ain't that exciting."

"I suppose, but Indiana was named for a whole bunch of Indians. Anyway, when did you start caring about history?"

"Ever since Miss Crabtree first told us about the Battle of Gettysburg."

"That happened in Pennsylvania, not the West."

"Look, the West is where the action is now. All the fighting Indians are out there."

"Not in Wichita, I bet."

"Stop trying to spoil this thrilling news. What's the matter with you anyway, Kid?"

I hung my head, unable to look him in the eye. I stared at my shoes, which

Mrs. McCarty had recently given me because they were too small for Billy, too large for Joe, and because Billy insisted on going barefoot in the snow until his mother bought him a pair of Western boots, the kind the cowboys wore in Texas and Kansas. "I guess I don't want you to go," I admitted in a whisper.

"Why not? Don't you want me to have fun with the cowboys and Indians?"

"Sure, but...but..."

"But what? Spit it out, Kid."

"There's nobody else...I mean, we have fun here, right? You're my best pal in the whole world. If you leave..."

"Well, it's a fact. The McCartys are departing Indianapolis any day now. But Wichita is in the world, too, you know."

"Yeah, far away. Look at a map sometime. There'll be two whole other states between us—Illinois and Missouri."

"I'd trade you for Josie if I could. Mom won't let me. But it won't be so bad. You can visit me sometime. I'll even let you ride my horse. "

"What horse?"

"The one I'll be getting. You can't be a cowboy without a horse."

"What's so good about being a cowboy? I didn't think you even liked cows."

"Longhorns. You ever even seen one of them. They come from Texas."

"I guess I saw one in a book. I like plain old white sheep better."

"That's the difference between you and me, Kid. I like wild things. You like civilization."

"We aren't so different. I've never been paddled like you, but Mum has scolded me for misbehaving, and so have some teachers."

"Right. Good old Willie 'Dunce Cap' Bonnifield. You were old Miss Crabtree's favorite you know."

"I know no such thing. She liked you, too. I can be as wild as anyone if I have to be."

"Well, fine. When you feel up to being wild again, you can run away from home and become a Kansas cowboy like me. I figure that will be in about five or ten years."

I wanted to be angry at him, to tell him that was no way for a pal to talk. But I knew he was right. And it might even be worse than that. I saw myself being stuck in Indianapolis for my entire life and never once seeing a cowboy on a horse except on paper. I was too sad to be mad. I didn't even have to count sheep.

7

THE CALL OF WICHITA

The three McCartys didn't venture to Wichita alone. A man went with them to dispense support and protection and whatever else a man can provide a woman with two young boys. It was the man with the mustache from Cherry Street, William Antrim. I saw him a couple times before they departed and didn't think much about him one way or the other. Catherine McCarty mostly called him Mr. Antrim but a couple days before the journey west, I heard her call for 'Billy." At first, I thought she wanted her oldest son because he had misbehaved, but that wasn't the case. She needed someone to lift a heavy trunk that my pal Billy couldn't have moved even with my help. It was Bill Antrim she wanted. Mum had met Mr. Antrim only once, when she was buying bread from Billy's mom, and I was surprised when she immediately passed judgment on the man. She was disapproving. After he had gone off to Wichita with the three McCartys, she didn't change her opinion of him.

"I've seen his kind before," she said the next day at our evening meal while she was slicing the last of Catherine McCarty's delicious loaf. "I like Catherine and believe she has made a big mistake going off with Mr. Antrim. He is twelve years her junior. He doesn't strike me as the marrying kind or the kind that will ever make his fortune. No doubt he wants a good woman cooking for him, doing his laundry, and being at his beck and call."

"I never heard nobody mention marriage," I said with my mouth full of bread.

"Anybody, Willie. Talk right."

"Not anybody makes tasty things like Billy's mom."

"No doubt, Mr. Antrim feels the same way. That's part of the problem."

"But not your problem, Charlotte," said Mr. Caven. "I'm sure things will work out fine for her in Wichita. I've never been there, but I've heard Wichita has incorporated as a city this year. I'm sure there are plenty of opportunities for enterprising young people. Who with a few Indian Head cents in his pocket could resist purchasing Mrs. McCarty's baked goods?"

"Sometimes she gave me food for free," I said. "I'll miss her."

"And sometimes naughty Billy would give you stolen goods," said Mum, even though I had never told her any such thing. "I'm sure you'll miss that even more."

"Aw, Billy isn't so naughty. He has a snitch for a brother. I tell you Josie is no little angel."

"Aren't you the lucky one! You have no little brother to tell on the naughty things you did with Billy."

"Me?"

"Well, that little scamp is gone now. That's one less worry."

I stopped chewing and made sure she saw my frown by pounding a fist on the table.

"Mind your manners," Mum said.

"It hurts something awful when a boy loses a pal," said Mr. Caven, looking far off, as if seeing something that neither Mum nor I could see.

"I suppose that's true, Mr. Caven. But there are other boys, other pals to be made. No more bread, Willie, until you eat the rest of the food on your plate."

"And what a divine meal it is," said Mr. Caven, back to concentrating on his pork loin and mashed potatoes. "I can't imagine that Mrs. McCarty prepares finer feasts day in and day out than you do, Catherine."

I'm not sure Mum heard the compliment. She was stirring instead of eating her small portion of mashed potatoes. "I don't think Mr. Antrim will be much help with Billy," she said. "He doesn't strike me as the kind of man who wants to have much to do with little boys."

"You could be right, Charlotte, but perhaps not. As a lifelong bachelor, I never figured I'd take to lads like your son or to Billy McCarty for that matter. But I did. Boys will be boys. Nothing to be done about it but nothing really to worry about."

"Not until they become men anyway. Present company excepted Mr. Caven."

John Caven nodded to Mum as he rapidly filled his mouth. Being well-mannered, he spoke no more.

❖

I never expected to see Billy McCarty again, but I never stopped thinking about him. I kept up with my schooling because that's what Mum demanded and what John Caven encouraged, but I daydreamed inordinately in class and made no new pals. My attraction to Laura Blakney went nowhere. One time at recess she asked me if I knew how Billy was doing. I hinted that I knew plenty, so she agreed to let me walk her home that afternoon. I made things up as I carried her books, telling her that my pal was riding a half-wild horse named Storm, herding cattle and sheep, shooting coyotes and wild Indians, catching frogs by their legs and rattlesnakes by their tails, swimming buck naked in the Arkansas River, playing clever tricks on brother Joe, and dancing up a storm all over Wichita.

I suppose Laura was skeptical but all she did was ask one question, "Who is Billy dancing with?"

I had to think fast. I first thought of cowgirls, then friendly daughters of Indian chiefs but determined those were the wrong answers. If she thought Billy had forgotten her, she would likely stop talking to me. "With his mother," I said. "Nobody else. I reckon he misses you all to pieces."

"I thought his mother was sick."

"Oh, sure. She was. She's better now, at least up to dancing with Billy. The air is much better in Wichita than Indianapolis, you know."

"No. I don't. And I don't know how you reckon to know he's missing me."

I was in over my head now, but I couldn't back down. "Billy said as much in a letter. Didn't you get a letter, too?"

"Billy never wrote me. Wouldn't a boy who missed me all to pieces write me a letter, you know in between all that herding of cows and sheep and dancing with his mother?"

"Maybe he was waiting for you to write first. How would he know you miss him?"

"How'd Billy know you miss him? Did you write him first, William Bonnifield?" She stuck out her sweet little chin, practically daring me to tell another lie. The way she answered a question with a question—in this case two rapid-fire questions—struck me as a clever tactic meant to unnerve a fellow like myself, especially when the clever person was a comely girl. Laura Blakney was the comeliest.

"Yes, I...All right, no."

"I thought not. And I don't believe he wrote you and told you all those things."

"But my mother and his mother exchanged letters, and..."

"Give me my books back. I hate boys who lie."

She snatched her three books from me, turned her back to me, and walked away shaking her head so vigorously that her two braids danced behind her.

I didn't protest, though the mother thing was no lie. Catherine McCarty had sent Mum a recipe for angel food cake and told her she not only was keeping a profitable city laundry but also had purchased at $1.25 an acre a quarter section adjacent to Mr. Antrim's homestead six miles northeast of Wichita.

Several months later, in January 1871, I truly did receive a letter from Billy. When I tried to show it to Laura Blakney, she turned her nose up at it and went off with a rich boy who took dancing lessons and wrote poetry to her. Mum later admitted she had asked Mrs. McCarty to have Billy write me the letter, having reckoned I was afraid to write him myself despite being lonely and prone to sitting around like a lump on a log. I wasn't about to thank Mum for orchestrating the correspondence, but I kept the letter under my pillow and referred to it by candlelight every night for three weeks. Billy wrote with surprisingly beautiful penmanship and it didn't bother me that he omitted most periods, rarely capitalized words at the beginning of sentences, and capitalized words such as Cowboys, Longhorns, Pistols, Buffaloes, and Bluebottle Flies no matter where they appeared.

> Howdy, Willie the Kid—
>
> heard tell you are above Snakes and still in Indy Crimany! I expect you forgot what you promised Me a year ago, but I have not and I think you had ought to have come and seen me as I requested you to. every week 20,000 Longhorns are passing through Wichita to the railroad towns, bringing with them Cowboys, who Drink, Gamble, Shoot off Pistols and Do Whatever else they Please Buffaloes are all around and their Hides are laid out in the streets, drawing in clouds of Bluebottle Flies smell won't kill you. sod roof of schoolhouse collapsed nobody killed, which is good, and better still no school 'cept what Mom teaches me at Home and what billy antrim learns me by Accident while in the Fields plenty of dancing gals and horses too. write me, better yet get a wiggle on and come on out to Wichita we'll be getting our own train right soon you'll see
>
> —Your Pal,
> Henry McCarty
>
> p.s. on account of bill antrim always being around and Mom calling him Billy, she now calls me by my middle name which is Henry but don't think you got to call me that 'cause I answer to both Billy and Henry

I wrote back right away, and Mum even corrected my spelling and punctuation:

> Dear Billy (I can't think of you as Henry),

Thanks for writing when you're doing so many fun things. We all miss you—me, Mum, Laura (remember her?), everybody. Indianapolis is boring. No buffalo or longhorns around. We do have flies but don't know what kind. I been wishing our school roof would fall down. None such luck. The kids are no fun. None of them make me laugh. I make some of them laugh even when I'm not trying to. Nobody calls me Willie the Kid the way you do. I wish there was a train to Wichita. I run off once to go see you. Mr. Caven caught me walking on the road out of town. It was just as well. I was headed in the wrong direction—east instead of west. I reckon I'm lost without you showing me the way. But Mum doesn't blame me for trying to run away from Indianapolis. She's bored, too, all the time cooking and cleaning for Mr. Caven. She says that's not the same as cooking and cleaning for a man you're married to or getting paid by strangers who wish to have their linen made clean. She says that she wouldn't mind being like your mom and misses talking to her. I heard they write letters, too, but that's not the same. Mum is looking for new opportunity (she told me to put in that word and told me how to spell it). Me, too, Billy. I want to be a cowboy like you.

—Sincere regards from your pal,
Willie the Kid Bonnifield

Billy didn't write a second letter though I wrote him three more times. I didn't blame him. He was having adventures in wild Wichita; I was having daydreams in boring Indianapolis. Our mothers did keep up a regular correspondence. Catherine McCarty and sons had apparently moved into a frame farmhouse built by Bill Antrim but there had not yet been a McCarty-Antrim wedding. Mum told me that because Billy's industrious mom owned her own land as well as the City Laundry and other in-town properties, she could provide for her two boys without the help of Mr. Antrim but that some women needed a man anyway. I didn't know much, but I knew enough not to ask her *What for?*

I got excited when Mrs. McCarty asked Mum to come help her run the laundry business, cultivate the homestead, and make pies since she had fifty-seven fruit trees on her property. Mum wondered what Mr. Antrim would think of that, but Billy's mom assured her that she was still single, very much her own boss, and in full control of her "young man companion." What's more, much to my delight, Mrs. McCarty wrote, "I'm certain your Willie and my Henry would get along just as famously here as they did in Indianapolis." Mum's initial response was disappointing: "It's a long hard journey to the Kansas frontier for a city woman and her young son, but maybe I'll reconsider once the railroad reaches Wichita."

But we didn't have to wait that long. Along came carpenter Frederick Schellschmidt, a resident of Indianapolis who had been raised in Huntsville, Indiana, with William Henry Harrison Antrim and in 1863 had served ninety days in the 54th Indian Volunteer Infantry with his buddy. Mr. Antrim had suggested in a letter that Mr. Schellschmidt come out to Wichita, Kansas, a land of opportunity, and Mr. Schellschmidt had jumped at the idea. He owned a covered wagon full of cabinets, chairs, and other furniture he had made and intended to sell once he took up temporary residence in Wichita's two-story Empire House. Mr. Antrim had also suggested it might be worthwhile if, before leaving Indiana, Mr. Schellschmidt looked up a fine-looking redhaired widow named Charlotte Bonnifield.

"Bill says the settlers are champing at the bit for the comforts of civilization I can provide," he told Mum during a surprise visit to Mr. Caven's home. "My old pal wrote me that you are well acquainted with Catherine and him and have long considered resettling in their neck of the Plains. Well, you're in luck, Charlotte Bonnifield. I happen to have room for one more in my wagon."

"Really? I don't know what to say, Mr. eh...Schmidt."

"Schellschmidt. Frederick Schellschmidt. You'll soon be calling me Fred."

"I'm afraid you have me at a disadvantage, Mr. Schellschmidt. Didn't Mr. Antrim mention that I don't come alone? You see I have an eleven-year-old son who attends school here and..."

"You're still in luck, Charlotte. I in fact have room for one and a half in my wagon."

"Oh, you do. That's well enough, sir. But even if I wanted to accept your kind offer to travel with you to Wichita, I couldn't possibly pay for our passage at this point in time."

"My kind offer makes no mention of money. I'm a highly skilled and successful carpenter if I do say myself, and I fully intend to make a killing on the wild frontier. All you need do at this point in time is conclude your employment arrangement with Mr. John Caven, pack your trunk, and grab the kid. All I ask in return is that you help with the cooking in camp and oblige me by calling me Fred."

While Mum was squirming and struggling to come up with a response, I stepped out of the kitchen where I had been all ears. Now, I walked right up to the friendly stranger and uncharacteristically was all tongue.

"Wow, what an offer," I said. "We've been talking about going to Wichita for ages. This truly is our lucky day, Mr. eh...—may I call you Fred? I'm sure Mum would agree that you have provided the two of us with a truly golden opportunity."

Never in my nearly twelve years had I been so bold.

8

WICHITA DAYS

Wichita wasn't all that it was cracked up to be. Or maybe it was, but it didn't live up to its promise, not for me. Billy (I seemed to be the only one who wasn't calling him Henry) was no cowboy. The only horse he spent time with was an old plow mare owned by Bill Antrim. My pal was slow growing; his younger brother matched his height and more than matched his girth. The two McCarty boys saw their share of stacked buffalo hides but hardly any live buffalo and only longhorns in passing. The brothers spent much of their time toiling away in the fields under the hot Kansas skies and cold grey eyes of Mr. Antrim, who was more overseer than worker. At night, the full-grown Billy always found the time to explore the new haunts of Wichita with his old Indiana pal, Frederick Schellschmidt.

While it was true young Billy and Joe weren't going to school at present, their mother was schooling them at home in reading and writing as if their lives depended on it. I fell under Mrs. McCarty's rule much of the day because Mum was spending most of her time working hard in the City Laundry to support our family herself and not be so obliging to the overly generous Mr. Schellschmidt. His bringing us safely to Wichita by wagon for free had actually come at what I viewed as a high price: his dogged desire to possess Mum. He had wanted Mum—and I suppose me, as well—to stay with him in the Empire House, but Mum wouldn't have it, so he volunteered to build us a cabin of our own on a town lot owned by Catherine McCarty. I have to say the man looked at Mum in such a way that vexed me; nothing like the fatherly looks John Caven used to give Mum back in Indianapolis. I had enough self-control to only stick out my tongue at him when his back was turned.

My pal Billy on occasion told me tales about hard men wearing sombreros and breeches with hair on who went about their loathsome business in town each armed with a large bowie knife and a brace of Navy Colts. I never saw them. He also told me that the previous February he had witnessed a shooting affair just down the street from the City Laundry pitting U.S. Deputy Marshal

Jack Bridges against Jack Ledford, an apparently respectable hotel owner who had formerly led a gang of horse thieves and had once thrashed the lawman in a fistfight.

"Bill Antrim wanted Joe and me out of his hair that day," Billy recalled. "He didn't say why, but I knew he was eager to work his so-called charm on Mom. Anyway, he gave a couple pennies to me and a couple more to Joe and told us to go buy ourselves some peppermint sticks at Danger's store. Mom can take care of herself, so I went, didn't have to ask Joe twice. We were in the store picking out our candy when we heard shots outside and rushed to the window along with three other customers and Danger himself. Joe found himself behind a fat lady, so I boosted him onto a sack of potatoes to see better. What we saw was Jack Ledford running toward the store. He was spilling blood as he ran. You see there was real bad blood between him and Marshal Bridges, and the marshal and two others were emptying their six-guns at the fleeing man as fast as they could. Well, Ledford made it into the store because somebody opened the door for him, but the unfortunate fellow had been shot twice in the right arm and twice in the back. Joe fainted right off the sack of potatoes into the arms of the fat lady, but I followed the men who carried the wounded man into the back room. I stood in a corner watching Ledford for half an hour before he died kicking with his boots on. I'll never forget his last words: 'Damn. I just bought these boots. Can't trust a lawman.'"

Billy grinned when he told me that tale, but I believed him, and later Bill Antrim confirmed most of it. During my time in Wichita, I never personally saw anyone running from the law let alone anyone getting shot. But I may as well admit to something even though I was by no means a bad boy: If I had gotten my hands on a pistol that June, I might have shot Fred Schellschmidt, for that's when I learned he had put Mum in the family way when Mum and I were already family enough.

Billy McCarty was the one who gave me the news about Mum. I'm not sure how he knew, but he must have overheard something since it didn't seem possible you could tell by just looking. "Could be you'll get a baby brother like I got—and that'll be tough luck for you if he turns out to be a cry baby like Josie," Billy told me.

"I don't want any kind of baby brother," I said. "He'd be too young to play with."

"More likely it'll be a baby girl. She won't be much to play with, but I figure she'll grow up to be a good dancer and actress who uses the stage name Winnie the Kid. How'd you like that—Willie the Kid and his kid sister Winnie the Kid?"

I imagined a dance hall somewhere between City Laundry and Danger's store and a much older Billy swirling young Winnie the Kid around the sawdust floor while I sat in a corner getting sick to my stomach.

"I don't want a sister," I said. "She might look like me, which would be tough luck for her."

"I understand, but I would think she'd favor your fetching mother, red hair and all."

"What's that word mean—fetching?"

"It means someone so good looking you'd want to get her to dance with you even if she were your very own sister."

"And I suppose you'd be dancing with her all the time, Billy?"

"Sure. But first she'd have to learn how to walk."

As it turned out I never got a sister or a brother because something went terribly wrong and whatever it was died inside Mum, who had kept working as hard as ever at the laundry. Mum didn't shed any tears that I saw, but she never talked about it. I reckon one child—that is me—was enough for her even though I was growing up pretty darn fast there in Wichita. As for me, I never mentioned it either, but I felt guilty for never giving the unnamed creature my blessing. I'm not sure what Mr. Schellschmidt felt, but he insisted that he wanted to marry Mum anyway. Mum told Fred he should concentrate on making furniture instead of babies. At least that's what Billy said he overheard one day at the laundry. True or not, Mum didn't seem to me insistent enough about staying single. Fred hung around the cabin he built for us like a rooster in a hen house.

"Fred and Charlotte, Bill and Catherine—four peas in a pod," Billy said to me one day when he decided to leave Joe behind in a cornfield and took me buffalo hunting with nothing but two homemade slingshots.

"Huh?"

"You've heard of two peas in a pod, haven't you?"

"Yes. Your mother told my mother that's what we are—two young peas in a pod."

"This, Kid, is a different kind of pod, an adult pod that holds two widows and two bachelors rubbing elbows and such but in no particular rush to visit the preacher."

That had me scratching my head, though I found myself not liking that kind of pod. "Where are the buffalo?"

We wandered amid the long blue grass and sunflowers for a couple of hours but never saw a single buffalo. Two cottontail rabbits showed their white tails and Billy let loose a stone from his slingshot. He missed and gave chase as if he could run one down, but both zig-zagged in circles and rushed past me to safety, one actually hopping over my planted feet.

"Why the hell didn't you fire?" Billy asked me. "I did all the hard work.

Gave you a clear short shot at long ears."

"Buffalo hunters don't bother with bunnies," I said, the slingshot he gave me dangling at my side.

"You got something there, Kid, but I'm thinkin' maybe your mother is right."

"Right? About what?"

"Remember the time Fred the Hammerhead accused you of taking his favorite hammer to smash large-headed grasshoppers and your mother told him you wouldn't hurt a fly?"

I remembered it was actually Billy who had borrowed the hammer to nail shut Joe's treasure box full of ribbons, buttons, rocks, colored chalk, and saved bits of peppermint sticks. Several grasshoppers might have jumped in his path when he made his getaway, and he did hammer two or three.

"I never tattled on you," I said. "Mr. Schellschmidt doesn't mind killing grasshoppers or most other living creatures, but he protects his tools as if they are made of gold."

"Pals don't tattle, Kid. We don't give each other medals either. We stick together because that's the right thing for pals to do."

"I know that."

Later that summer I did wing a bank swallow that was picking insects off the surface of the Arkansas River. I had been aiming the slingshot just to make a splash.

"You're all right, Kid," Billy said. "I didn't believe you'd do it."

"I only wounded it. I saw it fly away."

"Not far. Fish food. Alligator gars need to eat, too."

"I didn't mean it."

"Don't fret. I won't tell Fred the Hammerhead or your mother or anybody. We're pals."

"I know, I know. But take this slingshot. You can have two. I don't like slingshots."

"Me neither, but Mom won't let me have my own rifle yet."

Catherine McCarty had bigger worries than how to keep Billy from getting hold of a gun or how to keep tongues from wagging about her living with Bill Antrim out of wedlock. Her condition was deteriorating. She had moved from Indianapolis to Wichita in part for health reasons, but the new climate hadn't quieted her coughing. Working in the constant heat and dampness of the City Laundry was largely to blame, Mrs. McCarty said, though Mum spent even longer hours there without any adverse effect on her health, not counting what laboring in such a place might have done to her unborn child.

"Mom has the white plague," Billy told me, though it is doubtful he heard a doctor use that term. "Your Mum was fortunate not to catch the disease, but the baby did. It coughed itself to death inside her big belly."

I reckon I believed Billy's explanation because I preferred to think the white plaque and not my selfish wishing to remain a single child had doomed Mum's pregnancy. I must have worried some about catching the disease myself because each time I saw the Widow McCarty, as she liked to be called, I covered my mouth with a hand and waited for her to begin a coughing spell. But all Billy's mom ever did in my presence was clear her throat—such as when she corrected our pronunciation while we read aloud or when I stood by while she told Henry to mind Bill Antrim or else. The or else never amounted to much even though Billy was minding Mr. Antrim and his mother less and less as summer raced along. Maybe the white plague had left Catherine McCarty too tired to lift a hairbrush or paddle anymore or else she realized that fun-loving Billy wasn't really so naughty and that tattling Joe was getting too big for his britches.

I welcomed Billy's disobedience because he requested my company whenever he took to the streets of Wichita and I always wanted to be alongside my pal. Where else could I find fun? I told him I wouldn't go, though, if he insisted on bringing along those slingshots. After a brief discussion, he admitted we could still enjoy ourselves without them. "I'm no killer, Kid," he said. "I like birds and cats and dogs and girls and most everyone else. And I'm sorry about hammering those grasshoppers and letting you take the blame." I was so taken by his rare apology that I would have done most anything he asked during our in-town sprees.

He found plenty of things for us to do, nothing really so bad. We said howdy to cowboys, dodged longhorns, befriended stray dogs, barked at cats, begged for candy money outside Danger's store, directed strangers to the City Laundry if they wanted to clean up, bumped into ladies on purpose, apologized to them with great sincerity, and to elicit sympathy faked limps as if we were a couple of Civil War veterans. No authority figure had cause to haul us off to the local lockup. No doubt we annoyed some old people, but we amused others. "There go two of the oddest street gamins you're liable to see this side of St. Louis," Mr. Danger told a new customer. It was hard to say whether Billy preferred to annoy or amuse; all of it made him flash a grin. I was always one step behind him, a little wary of strangers and nervous about offending those who recognized me, but in the end not wishing to be anywhere else in the world.

In August 1872, it all ended. Little did I know that Bill Antrim and Catherine McCarty had been selling off their holdings in and around Wichita. Billy claimed to have also been in the dark about it, while Mum had known something was up but had kept it a secret from me in case it amounted to nothing. It did amount to something and I had great cause to bemoan Mrs. McCarty's white plague, which her latest doctor confirmed was the same thing as consumption, which was the same thing as tuberculosis. By any name it was bad. His recommendation was that her infected lungs would get a respite if she relocated as soon as possible to a higher, drier climate—the kind found in the territories of Colorado and New Mexico. The four peas in the adult pod—Catherine, Bill, Charlotte and Fred—were about to break up, which wouldn't have bothered me too much except that it also meant the two peas in the young pod—Billy and me—faced another dire separation.

9

FRED THE HAMMERHEAD

Life went on in Wichita after I lost Billy McCarty, Mum lost Catherine McCarty, and Frederick Schellschmidt lost Bill Antrim, but it was hardly the same for any of us. Mum worked for the new owner of City Laundry until she was denied time off for Thanksgiving. When she threatened to quit, she was sacked. Mr. Schellschmidt threatened the owner with not only a hammer but also a tenon saw. That showed Mum how much Fred was committed to her (his asking her to marry him was apparently not enough) and for that reason and because the laundry had been her only source of income, she allowed the furniture maker to finally move in with us. He had built the house for us on Water Street and been making himself at home there from the beginning, but Mum had previously not allowed him to spend the night. That made little sense since even I knew where the baby unborn came from, but I admit that all those mornings I woke up and didn't see Fred at the breakfast table made it easier to pretend he wasn't part of our small family. But now, as I saw it, he was working with wood all day and playing with Mum all night.

"It's high time you consented to be my wife," he told Mum one late fall morning at the breakfast table when he thought I had gone out to play but was actually in my room planning the best time to run away from home. I wasn't always the best listener in the world but I sure was listening now.

"Would you like two eggs or three eggs, Fred?"

"You must stop avoiding the subject. You know darn well people are talking, Charlotte. It's bad for my business because most of my sales come from church-going settlers wanting to make decent homes here in Kansas."

"People have always talked, whether it be in New York City, Binghamton, Indianapolis, or Wichita. Nothing to be done about it."

"Certainly, there is: Marriage. I already have the ring ready, and I assure you it's not made of wood."

"Oh, I know how generous you are, Fred, really I do. It's just that things feel unsettled right now."

"Unsettled? We've all settled in nicely here. My business is what makes all this possible. I put my good name on the line every day of the week. Homesteaders buy furniture, cowboys don't."

"I know you've sold a good deal of furniture to the two bordellos that opened down the street. Sinners need furniture just like the saints do."

"All right, enough about furniture. I can't expect you to understand my business. I'm talking about families now, one family in particular—ours!"

"I wish you and Willie could get along better."

"There you go again. Every time I try to have a serious talk with you, his name rises to the surface like a hungry mudfish."

"Willie is my family."

"Fine. I want to marry you in any case. I mean I'm willing to support him the way I do you, at least until he's old enough to seek his own fortune."

"You never spend any time with him. You could help him with his home studies or read him a book."

"Those things are out of my line."

"You could take him fishing."

"I don't have time."

"You have time to hunt rabbits and prairie chickens."

"He says he would never shoot a living thing again."

"You could teach him something."

"What? He has no interest in the woodworking trade. He doesn't know one end of a chisel from the other. I wouldn't know what to do with him. He's too young for hard drink or soft women."

Fred's rippling laughter rattled my half-open bedroom, causing me to brace a foot against the bottom of the door and squeeze the doorknob. Mum laughed unconvincingly, as if it were her obligation even if she wasn't his wife. I was more determined than ever to flee our house on Water Street. I wasn't sure where I'd be going, though I knew which way was west now and I favored that direction.

"I admit it's hard to say where Willie's interest lies," said Mum even as Fred's laughter lingered in the air like one of his morning farts. "Teaching him at home isn't as easy as it might seem. He listens with only one ear when I give him his lessons in reading, writing and arithmetic. Perhaps geography."

"What does that mean—perhaps geography?"

"Willie will look for places on maps. I should like to get him a globe."

"You spoil the kid, you know. An only child will take advantage of his mother whenever he can get away with it. If I was his father, I'd..."

"I know, you'd kick his behind, beat some sense in to him. That's part of the problem."

"Once we're married, he'll have to listen to me. He needs a man's firm hand more than anything."

"He needs a good friend. Willie hasn't been the same since the McCartys moved away. For quite a while he and Henry were inseparable."

"Also, inconsiderate and irresponsible."

"Willie is a good boy at heart. He needs to go to school to learn with others and to make new friends. I don't see why they don't fix up the old schoolhouse. It just needs a new roof and some decent desks and...Couldn't you do it, Fred? You are a carpenter."

"Nobody has made me an offer. I built this house for you at my own expense and with little thanks, I might add. That's the end of my volunteer work."

"But I have thanked you, Fred, over and over. I fried three eggs, easy over as you like them."

"Marriage is the proper thanks. That's the respectable thing to do."

"Are we back to that again? Can we discuss this later?"

"No. You always want to discuss him. I want to discuss us. In fact, I demand it. Sometimes it's not only boys who need a firm hand?"

"Don't you dare hit me, Fred. If you do it's over, and you can have your house back."

"Now, Charlotte, you know I don't mean it that way. I would never strike a woman."

"Unless the woman was your wife?"

"By Jove! I don't want to argue, not on an empty stomach."

"Eat up then. Be my guest."

"Is it so wrong to want you to be my wife for life? Just because your friend Catherine McCarty never got around to marrying my friend Billy Antrim doesn't mean that we should follow in their footsteps." Fred was now speaking with his mouth full.

Mum didn't respond right away. The only sound I heard for a minute was Fred's jaw cracking as he chewed and an occasional smack of his lips.

"Perhaps I'd like to follow in their footsteps," Mum finally said. "I received a letter from. Catherine. She and her boys are now in Denver."

I was instantly offended. That was news to me, and I didn't like her sharing it with Fred first. I had wanted to write Billy a letter but hadn't known where to send it. Why hadn't Mum told me Billy was in Denver! I had a map handy that showed both Kansas and Colorado Territory and I spread it out on my bedroom floor. I found the big dot that was Denver. I knew Denver was a bustling place in a territory that was carved out of Kansas because of mining. It didn't look so far away. I figured there were less miles between Wichita and Denver than between Indianapolis and Wichita. I wasn't as much of a dunce as Fred believed. I hurried back to the door to hear more.

Fred was still busy chewing as if it were hard work. Finally, he paused and tapped his fork on the table as if trying to get Mum's undivided attention.

"I know they are in Denver, and Billy Antrim is with them," he said. "You aren't the only one who gets letters, you know."

"You never told me."

"Didn't I? Or weren't you listening? My old pal had little to say about Catherine and her two sons. He wrote mostly about the mining opportunities in Colorado. It seems the gold mining has about played out, but silver discoveries are happening every day. I do believe my old pal may be making the transition from farming to prospecting. He's had a hankering to be a rich man as long as I've known him."

"Catherine didn't mention any mines, gold or silver. She says she is going to leave the laundry business to the Chinese who are flocking into Denver. She's making a living making pies and selling them to the miners and shopkeepers while Henry and Joe are back to attending a real school. Oh, and Catherine is breathing better. The smell of freshly baked pies must help."

"I just remembered something. Bill did mention Catherine in a P.S. He said prospecting was occupying all his time now but once the snows arrived, he'd find the time to marry Catherine."

"Really? He said that? Funny. No word from Catherine about marriage, either."

"You'll both eventually come to your senses. Bill's a handsome, strong man a dozen years Catherine's junior—an excellent catch for an older woman saddled with two sons. And I am...well, you know what I am—a master carpenter and good provider with a chiseled chin and a fine Roman nose."

I imagined Fred the Hammerhead, as young Billy had dubbed him, pushing away his empty plate, winking at Mum, and tweaking his own large nose. Listening in like that didn't make me think any more highly of him or of the idea that one day, after he finally wore Mum down, he would place a ring on her finger and I would be expected to call him father, if not master. It did make me think that Denver, Colorado Territory, was the logical place for me to run away to when I got around to leaving. Fact was, though, I was still only thirteen years old and, despite all my planning, was afraid of rambling by myself on the streets of Wichita, let alone venturing all the way to a wild place that wasn't even a state yet. I was wondering more than ever what the young Billy was up to besides going to some school. He hadn't written me a letter. I assumed he was having more than his share of fun and adventures with an assortment of new pals and had forgotten all about me sitting around in my room in the house on Water Street. Nevertheless, I decided to write him first.

I had high expectations after I sent off my letter. I wrote:

Dear Billy (are you still Henry, too?)

How you doing? You never told me, but your mother told my mother you are in Denver. Now I know where to go when I escape Wichita and the unbearable Mr. Schellschmidt. He is all the time either badgering me or taking no notice of me. Twice he called me a "slug" for not moving fast enough to suit him and twice a "snail" for going into my shell. Do snails go into their shells like turtles do? Anyway, it's a fact I've been sluggish lately (in truth, ever since you left here). And I do often hide from him, but any kid would except you. You'd laugh at him and tell him to mind his own business. I wish I dared to be like you. Mum says she understands how I feel about Fred and takes my side sometimes, but she also says she is beholden to him. I can see that for myself. She be holdin' him all the time. I don't know how long she can hold out, but he keeps telling her she should marry him—doesn't ask, tells! (remember how you used to call him Fred the Hammerhead—well he is that and if I'm a slug, he's a snake). You know I love Mum, but you can see now why I aim to skedaddle. Hope you got room for me in Denver. I'm still Willie the Kid."

—Your best true-blue pal

P.S. Don't mind any bad spellings and such in the above. I of course couldn't show this letter to Mum to correct anything on account of I don't want her to know I'm running off to Denver.

I believed I was serious about slipping out of the house and heading west to Denver, but first I would wait until Billy gave me the okay in a letter. When a letter finally arrived two long weeks later it wasn't from Billy. It was from Catherine McCarty and addressed to Charlotte Bonnifield. Billy's mom had read my letter to her oldest son and had informed Mum of my intentions to leave home, and in turn Mum told me I had better do no such thing or she would send the police and the bloodhounds after me and lock me in a closet if necessary. I couldn't be too angry with Mum because it showed she cared and at least she didn't tell Fred Schellschmidt, who would have told me I was an ungrateful slug who didn't have the gumption to move my lazy bones anywhere. I was angry at Mrs. McCarty, though, and even more so at Billy. Even if he hadn't been mean enough or stupid enough to show my letter to his mother, he shouldn't have left it lying around the Denver house for other eyes to see.

Why should I go way out west and show myself to be a big needy nothing when my former best pal was so mean and stupid and too busy to write me even one measly ungrammatical letter? That's what I kept repeating in my room, having resigned myself to the disappointing life in Wichita. I began calling myself a slug. In December, Mum took me to Emporia Avenue and placed me in a new school that had the first bell to ever ring in the city (counting churches, too). She thought I had totally stopped listening to her and that in any case she had taught me everything she could teach a boy. Besides that, she wanted me out of the house so she could make and sell pies like Catherine McCarty. My teacher, Mrs. West, was too polite to call me a slug, but that's what I was in the classroom, too. I loved that bell but not much else. In the schoolyard I was more of a snail, retreating into my shell to daydream about another life, one spent as a sea captain in the South Pacific (Okay, I still liked geography), a trail boss (Okay, I loved another map I had that showed cattle trails from Texas) or a miner who'd hit a mother lode of silver ore (Okay, I hadn't totally forgotten about Colorado Territory). Mrs. West told Mum she was worried about me, Mum told Fred Schellschmidt she was worried about me, and Fred told me he wasn't worried but I'd better stop worrying the women if I knew what was good for me. I knew even then that deep down I was about joviality not melancholia. By the end of the year, I had stopped being mad at Billy, realizing my old pal was the only one who could bring me out of it and get me back to acting like myself.

Still, I took no action. There's no telling how long I would have continued my sluggish, melancholic ways if not for several developments in January that didn't specifically deal with my problem but that would change everything for me. First there were two letters; no, neither was from Billy McCarty. Bill Antrim wrote Fred Schellschmidt he must come to Colorado to invest in a sure-thing silver mine with him because mining led to a man's fortune and easy living while carpentry meant work and more work right up until the carpenter was laid to rest in a wooden coffin, not necessarily of his own design. That hit home with Fred or at least interested him enough to mention Mr. Antrim's invitation at dinner. The demand for his finely crafted furniture had tailed off, he explained. The cowboys who poured into Wichita only spent money on drink, cards, soiled doves (I had to ask him to explain the term) and an occasional bath, while others who did need furniture settled on cheaper options, such as making inferior tables, stools, and benches themselves.

I was so excited by his news that I interrupted him even with my mouth full of sourdough bread. "Land's sake! A genuine silver mine! Would you be going alone?"

"You'd like that, wouldn't you? But you can't get rid of me that easily, boy."

"No, no. You misunderstand. I want to go to Denver, very much, sir."

"I do not," said Mum, pointing her fork at the man of the house. "Wanting to get rich is not the same as finding riches. Catherine never mentioned any mine. Can Mr. Antrim really be trusted when he claims to have struck gold?"

"Silver, dear," said Fred. "Let's give my old friend the benefit of the doubt, shall we? And even if the mine doesn't pan out, I'll have my tools for woodworking with me. For certain Denver has an affluent crowd that can appreciate my talent and will pay a fair price."

"You'd give up your house here, just like that?"

"Our house. I can build another, a better one. I will not be going alone. You can marry me before or after we leave—your choice, Charlotte."

Mum told me not to speak with my mouth full, though I hadn't said another word. She stood up from the table and began collecting plates. "Denver is something you and I and Willie, too, will have to discuss later. I...we don't want to make any rash decision."

Fred started to grumble but stopped when Mum announced she had made a cider vinegar pie for dessert. He leaned back in his homemade chair and threw his work-hardened hands in the air. "Of course not, dear" he said. "But I want to go, and your Willie wants to go. That's two out of three in favor."

"I need some time. I'll let you know—both of you."

Mum said nothing about it the next couple days, and neither I nor my surprising ally Mr. Schellschmidt pressed her on the issue since she stayed busy cleaning and cooking (and presumably thinking) while displaying a steady and unusually fierce frown. Then she got her next letter from Catherine McCarty. Billy's mom still didn't mention mining, but she invited Mum to help her run a pie business and assured her that the air was clear and dry and that I would be able to attend the recently completed Arapahoe School with Billy and Joe. Mum shared the news with Fred and me while we were taking a rare buggy ride on the bleak Kansas prairie in late January.

"I can't wait for the black-eyed Susans to bloom," she said.

Fred and I exchanged a look of mutual disappointment. It looked as if we'd still be in Wichita come spring. But Mum hadn't meant it that way. "We should go soon. I don't want to travel by covered wagon. Wild Indians are out there and wolves and bears and outlaws. We'll take the train. I don't need to see those yellow flowers one last time. I'm not sure what else I'll miss about Kansas."

Fred and I climbed out of the buggy at the same time. I, being so much younger and spryer, got to Mum first, embracing her fully for the first time in months. I hardly minded at all, though, when Fred stepped in and broke us up so he could wrap his burly arms around her. As he squeezed her tight, he stared beyond all that empty prairie. "Finally, we all agree about something," he said. "We all want to get the hell out of Wichita."

A few days later we all paid a visit to the Douglas Street depot to see about tickets. On the way there we were nearly run over by a herd of cattle, but Mum complained only about the smell of the unwashed cowboys walking past us as if they owned the place. In a way they did. Farmers had worked to stop the Texas cattle drives to Ellsworth, and Wichita had replaced it as the top cow town in Kansas.

"Wichita has busted wide open," Fred said as we neared the ticket booth. "This year the railroad is expected to ship east some 70,000 head of Texas beef. Business is booming. At least some of the people coming here will need nice new furniture or replacements for tables and chairs busted in the saloons. Do you see that sign over there? It proclaims, 'Everything goes in Wichita.'"

"But we're still going, right?" I asked.

"You bet. Aren't we, Charlotte?"

"Absolutely," Mum said. "No second thoughts."

10

THE DENVER CITY JAIL

We were hardly alone in our wish to relocate to Colorado Territory. The Denver Extension of the Kansas Pacific Railroad was bringing one hundred new residents to Denver every day. I was amazed when I stepped off the train in mid-January and saw a familiar face. I thought it was Billy at first glance, but his eyes were brown not blue, his hair too dark, his cheeks too plump, his chin too square, and his teeth too straight.

"Is that you Josie?" I asked, but I was peering past him at the dense station crowd.

"Not even my mother calls me that anymore. I am Joseph. My friends call me Joe."

"You sure have grown, Joe. Have you overtaken Billy as far as height?"

"You mean Henry. Yes. I am taller and bigger all around. Stronger, too. Things aren't the same. Henry now thinks twice before he starts anything with me."

"Good for you. So where is your little older brother?"

"Not here. Couldn't make it."

I of course wanted to know why not, but Fred Schellschmidt and Mum stepped off the train arm in arm just as Bill Antrim and Catherine McCarty reached the platform. The two men greeted each other boisterously and the two women acted like twin sisters who had been separated at birth. I couldn't get in a word edgewise. The four adults were too busy jabbering to pay me any mind, and Joe, knowing I wanted to see Billy not him and having become a wiseacre, enjoyed keeping me in suspense about the whereabouts of his brother.

As we proceeded on foot down Ferry Street toward the wood-frame house near Cherry Creek that Mr. Antrim had managed to buy, I yelled at the top of my lungs, "Where's Billy?"

"No call to shout, little fellow," Mr. Antrim said. "I'm right here. You must be tuckered out from your trip. But don't be discouraged. We'll be home soon."

"He don't mean you, Billy," Joe said, tugging on his stepfathers' coattail. "He has no idea where Henry is at. You think we should tell him?"

"Not me. Go ahead if you like, Joe. Talking about what your brother did will only put a damper on this grand occasion, our jolly reunion with our old friends from Wichita."

"Never mind, Joseph," said Mrs. McCarty. She shook a finger at her youngest son and turned to me. "Henry has been detained. That's all you need to know."

Billy was not in the house when we arrived. Nobody wanted to talk about him. I wasn't sure what it meant for a boy of thirteen to be detained. I thought it might mean that he was kept after school, but not even the strictest teacher could keep him this long. Joe was as evasive as the adults but meaner about it. I was made to lie in a back room on Billy's bed as if I required rest from the train trip, and from his bed across the room Joe kept repeating: "Wouldn't you like to know? Wouldn't you like to know?" I finally went over to the imp, pinned him with my full weight (he had grown all right but I still had a few pounds on him) and told him I wouldn't let him up until he gave me a straight answer about his brother.

"You're a guest in our home," he said after his initial squirming got him nowhere. "You have no right to beat up on me."

"I'm standing in for your brother. Now you going to tell me where he is or not?"

"I'll scream. Mom! Mom!'"

I covered his oversized mouth with my hand. "Billy used to call you a baby. You haven't changed much. Now you're a big baby."

"All right. Take your hand away. I can't breathe. Yes, I'll tell you. I promise, but I can't speak with your hand..."

I slowly removed my hand but let it hover over a chipmunk cheek to let him know I was ready to slap should he break his promise. I had never overpowered anyone in my life. It felt good.

"My brother did something very bad. Crime does not pay."

"What are you talking about? Give me a straight answer."

"All right, you big bully. Henry is in jail."

"That supposed to be a straight answer?"

"As straight as a die, as Billy Antrim always says."

"You don't mean a real jail."

"Sure do. It's the fat brick building at Two Thirty-one Thirteenth Street with large wooden doors and bars on the windows. The words "City Jail" are painted in huge black letters across the front. You can't miss it."

"But Billy is just a kid."

"Henry is bad. He never learned nothing from getting paddled. Maybe now he..."

"What did he do? Nobody gets arrested for fighting with his brother."

"Not that at all. Henry was doing stuff to Sally and Rachel, twin daughters of Mr. Silver."

"Stuff?"

"Bad stuff—the kind of stuff I'm not supposed to know about."

I imagined Billy pulling their braids and taking the ribbons out of their hair, but nobody got arrested for such things, certainly not a thirteen-year-old. When I began imagining more unpleasant things that I really didn't know much about myself, I slid off the top of Joe, turned my back on him, and stood on wobbly knees while staring blankly at the empty bed across the room.

Joe took the opportunity to escape. I heard him jump off his bed and dash for the door. "Mom! Mom!" he screamed. "Willie is bad like Henry."

I can't imagine what the old folks imagined I had been doing to Joseph McCarty. Whatever it was, it wasn't nearly as bad as what Billy McCarty had done, or was accused of doing. Not that anyone wished to talk about it that night. Catherine McCarty merely separated Joe from me, bringing him into the big bedroom to sleep with her in the adult bed while Bill Antrim eventually collapsed on Joe's bed to sleep off a drunk. I heard him come in because I was having a fitful sleep on a strange bed with my thoughts on assorted crimes and punishments. Mr. Antrim had gone out to a saloon with Fred Schellschmidt to celebrate their reunion. Mum had stayed in the kitchen looking at Catherine's hand-written recipes for pies and other baked goods even though she and Fred had been provided the guest room, which doubled as a storage room for Mr. Antrim's shovels, pickaxes, hammers, chisels, and pans. I suppose that Mum and Fred eventually went to bed, though I never liked to think about that.

In the morning no straight answers were forthcoming from the old folks. Nobody confirmed that Billy had lodged overnight in the city jail but the way they all deflected my inquiries told me he must be there. Joe went to school carrying a note that attributed Billy's absence to a head cold. Mum joined Mrs. McCarty in her pie enterprise, headquartered in a two-stove shack on Blake Street, which Mrs. McCarty referred to as "Bake Street." Mr. Antrim took Mr. Schellschmidt on a city tour of places they hadn't seen the previous night or couldn't remember having seen. They made me tag along because they didn't know what else to do with me. Even in daytime Denver looked like a rough-and-tumble place with rows of shacks and log cabins and shady characters, called "bummers" by Mr. Antrim. They stayed out of the saloons but visited a livery, a "tobacco and segar" shop, a gun dealer, a real estate broker, a furniture store and a building housing two carpenters and a builder (for Fred's benefit). When we arrived at an attorney's office on Larimer Street, Mr. Antrim went in alone, leaving Fred and I to explore on our own.

"Why look at this, something that should interest you," Fred said, pointing to a sign on a two-story wooden building. He read the words, "Views of Colorado Mountain Scenery," as if I didn't know how. "We might even see some of those beautiful silver mines I've been hearing so much about. We aren't in Kansas anymore, boy."

He grabbed my arm and pulled me inside. We were greeted by wall-to-wall photographs of landscapes like neither of us had ever seen before. I never saw so many mountain peaks in my life. Fred let go of my arm, proceeded into the room as if it contained all the wonders of the world, and, wide-eyed like a kid, promptly forgot about me. I raced out of the building and addressed the first woman I saw, "Excuse me, madame, but which way to Thirteenth Street?"

Upon my arrival at the city jail, the jailer didn't let me in to see Billy at first. I pled my case, saying that I was his younger brother Joe and that not only did we have no father but our mother was home in bed having coughing spells. That made the jailer talkative.

"A couple of misfortunates, eh," he said, rubbing his chin so hard it sounded like Fred when he was sanding furniture. "Destitute of proper parental care and growing up in depravation, ignorance, idleness, and vice, I assume."

"Yes, sir, it ain't been easy for me and my brother," I said so smoothly I surprised myself. I was finding out that once you put a lie out there it was easy to keep it going, even when talking to an officer of the law.

"If you can believe it, laddie, I myself was once a street urchin in the Bowery of New York City."

"You don't say, sir. My brother and I were also raised on the Lower East Side. We were as poor as church mice."

"I pulled myself up by my bootstraps. Do you understand? You got to do what it takes to rise above being dealt a bad hand in life. That's what you must do, laddie."

"I understand, and I am trying, my brother, too. But it's hard to do when you are locked up like he is and..."

"Look, I'll tell it to you straight because you might listen better than your brother."

"I'm all ears, sir."

"In Denver we don't lock up a boy who hasn't committed a crime but is merely one of the misfortunates. But Henry McCarty has forced our hand. We had no choice when Walter Rittenhouse, silver mine owner and highly respected member of our community, pressed charges."

"Oh. Did my brother steal something from this Mr. Rittenhouse?"

"Steal? Worse than that, laddie."

"He...he didn't have a gun, did he? He didn't hurt Mr. Rittenhouse, did he?"

"No weapon. Your brother didn't touch Mr. Rittenhouse."

"I don't understand. What did Billy...I mean Henry...do that was so bad?"

"I am not at liberty to share the nature of his crime. I will only say that your brother committed several acts of gross misconduct against two members of the Rittenhouse family."

I couldn't speak. I tried to imagine what Billy had done, and it was an unpleasant exercise. I must have turned pale because the jailer suggested I had better go home and take care of my sick mother.

"But first I must see my brother," I finally said. "Won't you please allow that, sir. I have a...a message from mother. No matter what he has done I must give him the message."

"Is that so? What's her message?"

"Eh...That he is breaking her heart. That crime doesn't pay. That she is praying for him. That if he swears on the family Bible to stop conducting himself grossly, she will bake him an apple pie...when he gets out of jail that is."

"It could be a while. I'll give you ten minutes with him. You don't have a pistol concealed on your person, do you?"

"No, sir, not even a slingshot. Mum...that is my mother...She always tells people that I am the good son."

Billy was being detained in a cold jail cell he shared with two grown men whose dark features, unruly mustaches, chin stubble, and fixed stares made them look as if they were posing for prison photographs. But the assistant jailer led the young prisoner and me to a small room with only two inhospitable chairs and one table between them so that people who sat in the chairs could not reach out and touch each other either violently or I suppose lovingly. Billy and I sat in the chairs. The assistant jailer stood against the back wall jingling keys. He wore no gun but carried on his belt a thick wooden stick that Billy later told me was a billy club even when used on Henrys, Johns, Georges, Franks, and Clydes.

Billy didn't act surprised to see me. Nor did he act delighted or ashamed.

He winked and curled a lip as if his detention was merely punishment for one of his mischievous tricks, such as putting fire ants in Joe's knickers. "Welcome to Denver, Kid," he said when I couldn't manage to say a word, not even hi. "I'd love to show you around. But that'll have to wait until I have some free time. I take it the others have caught you up on all the family news."

"I...I can't believe you are here...I mean in the Denver City Jail."

"A temporary inconvenience."

"How long?"

"All depends. I don't mind the break from school."

"But..."

"But what, Kid? I look at it this way: I'm just visiting, I'm not going to live here."

"But you committed a crime. The man at the desk called it several acts of gross misconduct against two members of the Rittenhouse family."

"To be accurate I was accused of a crime."

"Who is this Mr. Rittenhouse?"

"A silver king. William Antrim serves him, hoping to one day get a small share of the Rittenhouse riches. He's a fool."

"Mr. Rittenhouse?"

"No. He's lucky and clever and cruel. That has made him a wealthy man. It is the man who shared a house with us who is the fool. Silly Billy won't marry Mom until he can afford to buy her a pure silver wedding ring. I say it won't ever happen. Not that I mind, but Mom does. She's getting the notion that a marriage might be the best for all of us in the long run. She doesn't need him but likes to think she does."

I couldn't quite follow what Billy was saying. In any case, I wasn't there to talk about Catherine McCarty and William Antrim. "But what about you? Who are those two members of the Rittenhouse family, the ones you showed gross misconduct against?"

"Rachel and Sally. I don't care what they say. There is nothing gross about dancing with girls!"

I remembered Billy dancing on an Indianapolis Street with that girl in braids, Laura Blakney. He was having his fun then, of course, but she hadn't seemed to mind it in the slightest until he swung her too hard. I must have looked as confused as I felt, because Billy grinned, smacked his lips, and announced he would explain. "Maybe you'll believe me, Kid. Nobody else does."

No explanation was forthcoming that day, however. The assistant jailer silenced his keys, took out his billy club, took four long steps, and rapped the big stick so hard against the tabletop that the table trembled and I jumped half out of my chair. "Time's up."

"Already?" I said. "I was just about to..."

"Get up. Both of you brothers. Two men are waiting for you up front. One of them must be your daddy."

"I don't have a daddy," Billy said.

"Neither do I." I said.

The assistant jailer shrugged and pointed the way with his billy club. "You aren't the only ones."

11

BILLY'S GIRL TROUBLE

Before we were even out of the jailhouse, William Antrim began lecturing me on the dangers of Denver, beginning with a brief history lesson. A handful of railroad connections over the last three years had turned Denver into Colorado's marketplace, reaping the riches of the mountain mining districts and of the surrounding farm and ranch production. While the railroads had brought to the "Queen City of the Plains" honest men in search of employment, he cautioned that some of the newcomers would cut your throat and rob you if given half the chance while others would cheat you in all ways available to devious hard men and deceitful loose women. By the time we hopped onto one of Denver's new streetcars, he was through orating, but Fred Schellschmidt picked right up with a lecture on disobedience. It was as if me breaking away without permission to visit my pal in the city jail was as bad as whatever Billy had done to get arrested and land behind bars. Not that either man had anything to say to me about Billy's crime. The conspiracy to keep me in the dark continued at the house, where Catherine McCarty and Mum were still talking pies and Joe McCarty was standing silent in the corner for stealing a cherry pie and consuming the entire thing. He had been caught red-handed and red-faced holding his aching belly.

"How much longer?" he cried while I watched him squirm as if he had fire ants in his pants.

"Not yet," shouted Mrs. McCarty. "I'll tell you when."

"I need to go."

"Well, you can't."

"I mean really go."

"The outhouse will have to wait. A mother must learn things, too. Henry used to steal pies and I did nothing about it and now...Still, how can I believe what they are saying. He couldn't have done it."

Her voice faded, and she leaned against the stove to find support. Mum put a sympathetic hand on her shoulder. Despite all the pie talk, the arrested

Billy was on their minds. I could easily have corrected Mrs. McCarty. Billy no doubt had stolen pies and other baked goods in the past but he would never finish them off by himself; he'd share them with his pals, hungry strangers, and friendly dogs. And it wasn't true that his mother had done nothing about it. She had paddled him.

Mr. Schellschmidt suggested that a paddling would be appropriate for my disobedience today, and Mr. Antrim, though no more a paddler than Mum was, concurred. Mrs. McCarty, apparently a reformed paddler, suggested I stand in a corner, but a different corner from Joe. Mum instead directed me to Billy's bed, where she had me lie down and sat beside me. Instead of scolding me, she asked what was bothering me.

"Billy," I said. "Not him, but what they are doing to him. Jails are for bad men who rob and cheat people out of money and cut throats. Billy is my age. And he didn't do things like that...did he?"

"It's Henry now. And it's no laughing matter, no matter what Henry might think. What did he tell you?"

"Only that he danced with two girls. What's wrong with that?"

"It's far, far more serious than that. Believe me."

"Okay. I believe that you and everyone else think it is serious. But what is it? Joe knows what his brother did, so why won't anyone tell me? What's the big secret, Mum?"

She ended up telling me in a roundabout way. First, she brought up Walter Rittenhouse, who had made a fortune in the silver mining districts but was spending his wealth in Denver, where he owned a fine two-story brick home that he shared with a wife who wore pearls and diamonds and with two daughters, thirteen-year-old Sally and twelve-year-old Rachel, who were the shing red apples of their father's eye. William Antrim worked for Mr. Rittenhouse, not as a miner but as a trusted personal assistant who did everything for his boss from running errands in town to making exploratory treks into the mountains. Mr. Antrim didn't actually own any part of Mr. Rittenhouse's silver mines, but he acted as if he did and promised Fred a position with the Rittenhouse Silver Mining Company that would dwarf anything he could earn working with wood.

"But what about Sally and Rachel?" I asked, sitting up in Billy's bed and nudging Mum in the ribs.

"Three nights ago, Mr. Rittenhouse invited Bill Antrim and the McCartys to dinner for the first time. Catherine told me she never saw such quality help. A chef from Chicago did the cooking and two efficient domestics served them. It was a grand feast with two main entrees—leg of lamb with parsnips in cream and wiener schnitzel with noodles—an assortment of vegetables, including French peas, new beets in butter, potatoes hashed in cream, watercress salad; for dessert, stewed prunes, rum cake, and one of Catherine's angel food cakes."

"Mum! My mouth is watering but my ears want only to hear the dry facts."

"Very well. Clearly the feast at the Rittenhouses made quite the impression on Catherine."

"And on you, Mum. But please go on"

"After dessert, the children were sent to the porch that has the only swings in Denver, Mr. Rittenhouse retired to his den with Mr. Antrim to smoke cigars and talk business, and Mrs. Rittenhouse gave Catherine a tour of the upstairs. Billy swung with Sally, then Rachel. He apparently charmed both sisters. When they heard fiddle music down by Cherry Creek, the trio joined hands and proceeded gaily as one down Ferry Street, leaving Joe on the porch to swing alone. Joe debated what to do next. In the past he might have gone inside and told his mother how Henry had left the porch without permission. But after much deliberation and fast swinging, Joe followed the disobedient ones to the sound of music."

Mum paused but certainly not for dramatic effect. She took several deep breaths and collapsed in a heap on Billy's bed. I sat there hovering over her shoulder, waiting. But she didn't stir. It was as if I were watching a Shakespearean tragedy (something I had never done but had heard about from John Caven in Indianapolis) and the protagonist decided he couldn't face the final act and walked off the stage.

"What's the matter, Mum?" I asked. "It can't be that bad."

She didn't answer. Her eyes were shut and her breathing was noisier than I ever remembered. I wondered how she could drop off so quickly, but then I watched her sleep as if she were the child and I were the parent.

"You mustn't be like Henry Antrim," she blurted out with eyes still shut.

I thought she was talking in her sleep, but she took out a handkerchief, wiped her eyes, blew her nose, and continued. "The fiddler was playing for some emigrant families camped by the creek. Henry and the two girls joined in the merriment. Henry danced with both girls, like he was spinning tops—that's how Joe described it. Joe then saw something that disturbed him even more. Henry carried them off into a dense thicket of chokecherries, the fruit that gave rise to the creek's name. Catherine said the Arapaho Indians named it long before the white men came to..." Mum's eyes sprang open and the words stopped. She seemed surprised to see me sitting there.

"How could little Billy carry off both girls? He isn't that strong."

"One after the other, I suppose. Joe didn't say exactly."

"I suppose Joe then followed them into the chokecherries."

"No. He didn't dare. He heard screams coming from the bushes. He froze."

"So, he didn't actually see anything."

"He heard. Henry...he...he assaulted those two girls, the daughters

❖ 77 ❖

of Walter Rittenhouse, the silver king, Bill Antrim's employer, one of the wealthiest men in Denver. I can hardly say the words, not to my own son, so young, so innocent, so...so removed.

"I know what assaulted means, Mum. Did Joe say that's what occurred? Billy said they were only dancing."

"In the chokecherries? The emigrants on Cherry Creek heard, too. The fiddler stopped playing. The girls reported what happened to their father and to the authorities. Rachel spoke of molestation, Sally of violations. Mr. Rittenhouse called it despoilment. I've said too much. But now you know why Henry is confined at the city jail. No more questions about it. That's all I know. It's an unfit subject for discussion. Mr. Rittenhouse is up in arms and Mrs. Rittenhouse is...well, beside herself. Bill Antrim is worried sick about what happens next. Catherine is in a state of disbelief. Henry was always a mischievous boy of course but never really so terribly bad...now a hardened criminal!'

"Billy's mother doesn't believe it and neither do I. You shouldn't either, Mum."

"Oh, Willie. I'm sorry, I'm sorry. Facing the truth isn't easy for a grown person let alone for a...I didn't mean for you to grow up so fast. You're only thirteen."

"Same age as Billy."

"My God, don't I know that! I wish we had never come to Denver."

What happened next happened quickly. Walter Rittenhouse made a deal with Bill Antrim but only after his two daughters spoiled the open-and-shut case against Billy by recanting their testimony. Mr. Rittenhouse hadn't wanted either victimized daughter to be subjected to questioning but not even a man of his wealth and influence could prevent that forever.

Rachel, broke first, relatively early in the interrogation since she couldn't imagine sweet Henry rotting in prison. She admitted she wasn't sure what molesting meant and that during the "very close dancing" in the bushes, her hands had been more active than Henry's hands. When asked if only bare hands were involved, she said, "Some lips, hips and limbs, too, but everything was dressed except for our lips." She volunteered that the dancing kid had not forcefully kissed her and hadn't even known what to do with his tongue. Why had she then lied to her father and everyone else about being assaulted? "I never said that," Rachel insisted. "I said molestation because Sally told me to say that. Sally knew that Daddy would be angry we left the porch with a boy and that Daddy would turn red as a tomato when he found out we went into the bushes with that boy. Sally can't stand it when Daddy sees we aren't perfectly behaved young ladies."

Sally, who was questioned separately, was harder to crack. She kept using the word "violations" without saying in what way "that horrible boy Henry" had violated her and her younger sister. "He dishonored us," she shouted. 'I can't speak for Rachel, but I only wanted to dance. That depraved dancer is shameless. I mean Henry, not Rachel. He debauched me." Her impressive vocabulary must have made her seem less innocent than the authorities suspected. Under further questioning, she at last confessed that she had willingly gone into the bushes, though mostly to keep an eye on her sister, and that Henry had only violated her freedom by taking an aggressive lead in the dancing as if he were a fully grown man.

In the agreement reached after the girls' retraction, charges against Billy were dropped but he was never to come within twenty yards of either one of them; Bill Antrim lost his job as Walter Rittenhouse's personal assistant and could never again work for the Rittenhouse Silver Mining Company, but, through the Silver King's influence, landed a job as a teamster for Wells Fargo. Fred Schellschmidt had lost any chance, however slim, of realizing a share in a silver mine and went back to carpentry, though it seemed most everything big in Denver was now being built of brick instead of wood. Catherine McCarty was relieved that her oldest son escaped having a criminal record, but she regretted that she would never again be invited to a feast at the Rittenhouse home and that no matter how many pies she made or how much money Bill made as a teamster, she could never afford to enter one of the regional luxurious resorts that offered hot baths and other restorative treatments for consumptives.

Despite the so-far sunny and dry winter and two buggy rides west of town to inhale fresh, invigorating mountain air, Mrs. McCarty believed her consumption was getting worse. She became so discouraged— about her health, Bill's spending all that time on the road, Henry's playing hooky from school, Joe's acting more and more like his older brother—that she didn't feel up to making a single pie let alone a family meal. Mum took care of most of the baking for profit and most of the cooking for the two families since we continued to live together in the Ferry Road house (Fred was planning an addition but couldn't afford to take the time to build it just yet). I went to school every day unlike Billy and Joe, and after school I helped Mum in the kitchen or chopped wood since Mr. Antrim and Mr. Schellschmidt never seemed to be around to do that or other home chores. I suppose I felt Billy drifting away from me (he had plenty of Denver pals who easily replaced whatever I had to offer him) and no doubt I did some drifting away from him, too, because I had seen what the Denver City Jail looked like.

Mr. Antrim quickly tired of his teamster job ("Taking orders and overworking so the bigwigs can make more money is fool's work") while Mrs. McCarty grew even more tired of being single, sick, and alone even with Mum and the three boys around. Mum wasn't married to Fred, either, but I believe that Mrs. McCarty was envious of her. For one thing, Mum enjoyed good health. For another, no matter how hard Fred worked at his carpentry by day, he was there to share a bed with Mum every night. Also, Mum, through hard work and endless trial and error, had surpassed her as both a cook and a pie maker. There was the matter of the children, too. Mum never had to worry about what her one son—me—was up to while she, Mrs. McCarty, was constantly fretting about Henry and now Joe.

"I need to get the heck out of Denver," Mrs. McCarty announced on a rare day in late January when Mr. Antrim was home for supper (made by Mum as usual).

"I'm constantly getting the heck out of Denver and always coming back," said Mr. Antrim. "That's a teamster's life. I wouldn't mind just going. I got a deep-down urge to be my own boss."

"So, let's go." Catherine put down her fork to clap her hands.

"Where to?"

"Somewhere even sunnier and drier than Denver. Somewhere we can settle down in a nice little quiet house. Somewhere you can make an honest woman out of me."

"You seem honester than most, Mom," said Billy.

"More honest," I said without thinking. Maybe it was the old John Caven influence or the fact I never played hooky.

"Did anybody bother to ask me if I wanted to go anywhere?" said Joe.

"Maybe they don't want you to come with us," his brother said.

"They'd want me more than you."

"Boys!" shouted Mrs. McCarty.

"Are you really serious about moving, Catherine?" Mum asked as she served her friend mashed potatoes from a bowl.

"Dead serious," said Mrs. McCarty, coughing twice.

"But it seems like we just got here," said Mum, as she stopped serving the potatoes and plopped into her chair between Bill Antrim and Fred Schellschmidt.

"She said they were going," said Fred. "She didn't mean us, Charlotte. Isn't that right, Catherine?"

"I was talking about Bill and the two boys. But you all can suit yourself."

"I'm with you, Mom," said Billy. "Denver is getting old, and the police here don't like me. We were in New York and then Indianapolis and then Wichita and then Denver. We got to keep moving West. It's the only way to go."

"You'll go wherever your mother and I decide to take you," Bill Antrim said. "You're too young to have a say in the matter."

"That's right," said Joe. "If I can't have a say, you can't have a say."

"What about you, Willie?" Mum asked. "Have you anything to say on the matter? You are happy in school in Denver, aren't you?"

"Pretty happy, sure. But..."

"But what?" said Mum. "Utah and Nevada are to the west of us. California would be as far west as we could go. Interested?"

It was nice of Mum to ask my opinion, but I hadn't even thought about leaving Denver. I had no idea where else I would want to go if we did decide to leave.

"Hold your horses everyone," said Billy. "I thought of something. West is good, but there is another direction we could go."

"Three other directions," said Bill Antrim. "But I'm done with the East and the North is too cold."

"Right. So, we go South. New Mexico just might be the ticket."

"What do you even know about the state of New Mexico, Henry?"

"For one thing it's a territory, not a state. For another, the people there are fun loving. They have siestas and fiestas. The señoritas all love to dance."

"For God's sake, Henry!" Bill Antrim pounded a fist on the table, which caused Mum to jump, Fred Schellschmidt to shake his head, Joe to roll his eyes, and Mrs. McCarty to cough three times in quick secession before covering her mouth with her napkin. "Haven't you learned your lesson yet, boy? Forget about doing anymore damned dancing. It leads to no good."

12

THE SANTA FE PLAZA

Dancing aside, the old folks decided Santa Fe was indeed the place to go next. I'm not sure everything that was behind the move south, but none of them acknowledged it was Billy's idea. There would be no waiting for the Atchison, Topeka & Santa Fe Railroad to lay down tracks. There was no delay at all. We packed up two wagons with all our belongings, including furniture that Fred hoped to sell or trade in Santa Fe since he figured "those people dwelling in adobes must need chairs and tables like the rest of us." We traveled fast and it was smooth going to the Colorado-New Mexico border, where we encountered a twenty-seven-mile toll road built by enterprising trapper Richard "Uncle Dick" Wootton. He charged a dollar and fifty cents for one wagon but let the other pass for free because when we spent a night in his roadside hotel Mum baked three dried apple pies to serve his stagecoach passengers

It so happened that some young folks made the thirteen-mile trip from Trinidad that afternoon for the weekly dance Mr. Wootton held at his house next to the tollgate. He charged a quarter per couple for admission, but nobody would give Billy one cent so he snuck in by a back window after I boosted him off the ground. I then covered for Billy by saying we would be hanging out with the stagecoach horses. In truth, he danced with Trinidad girls all much older than him and got into a minor scrap with a Trinidad boy who accused Billy of being a Mexican troublemaker even though Billy hadn't learned Spanish yet. I saw none of that as I spent the evening in the corral talking to the horses, most of whom had rasping coughs, drooping ears, and fever from equine influenza. Feeling sorry for them, I tried to feed them some of Uncle Dick's sugar supply with mixed results. One of the ill animals bit me, but I hid my wound from Mum and the others. Billy couldn't hide his broken nose, but I backed his story that one of the stagecoach horses had kicked him in the face, and we got away with it. I suppose I wanted to show Billy that I was still his pal Willie the Kid and would be siding with him through thick and thin down in New Mexico Territory.

We covered the 180 miles from Raton Pass to Santa Fe in five days and set up a camp in a cornfield east of town for several days. Corn also grew north and south of the capital city, along with beans, melons, and cotton. To the west was an endless stretch of prairie. At first, we didn't see many Anglos, which worried the four adults but pleased Billy. Most of the farmers were called Mexicans by the Anglos even if they were U.S. citizens, but they referred to themselves as *la gente* (the people). Pueblo Indians also farmed but regularly wrapped themselves in colorful blankets and left their nearby villages to trade in the bustling Santa Fe Plaza, which marked the end of the Santa Fe Trail. None of us had seen anything like the plaza, from the flat-roofed adobe buildings to the variety of people (Mexicans, Indians, and gringos like us), to the number of goods available for trade. Mum and Catherine McCarty were amazed to see silver watches, gold necklaces, fine China, glassware, furs, and bright clothing. Bill Antrim and Fred Schellschmidt were more interested in the fine-cut tobacco and a barrel of exotic alcohol brought all the way from the small town of Tequila in Old Mexico. I was pleased to see horses and mules that hadn't been ravished by equine influenza. Joe thought the burros that transported firewood and hay were cute. Billy pointed out that every grown man was armed with a gun or a knife or both.

I learned that Spanish conquerors known as conquistadors had founded the city in 1610 and dubbed it La Villa Real de la Santa Fe de San Francisco de Asís (The Royal Town of the Holy Faith of Saint Francis of Assisi). Since that was a mouthful for Mexicans and gringos alike, the six thousand residents had reduced it to Santa Fe. Mr. Schellschmidt immediately fit in with the Anglo merchants and lawyers who treated Mexicans as second-class citizens and wanted to Americanize the region. Even Territorial Governor Marsh Giddings, who resided in the Palace of the Governor on the north side of the plaza, commented that Santa Fe was a Mexican city "of the lowest class on God's earth." The Anglos were the ones who could afford to buy Fred's furniture. The town didn't need any more bakers, so Mum decided to run a boarding house. The large adobe we rented filled up fast as Mum wasn't particular about who her boarders were as long as they paid for their rooms in back and their occasional meals at our table. Mrs. McCarty, now forty-four, felt well enough to help out a little in the kitchen, but she had her mind on something else and Mr. Antrim, thirty-one, was of like mind. They decided it was high time to marry.

On March 1, 1873, the Rev. David F. McFarland married them at the First Presbyterian Church. Among the witnesses were the pastor's wife, their daughter, Billy, Joe, and an unsmiling Fred Schellschmidt, who had lost a bet with the groom about which one would tie the knot first. Mum begged off attending, telling Catherine she must placate an unruly but influential American boarder who didn't want to live under the same roof as even a fairly well-off

Mexican. Mum's putting business ahead of the matrimonial ceremony further strained her friendship with Billy's mother, who had begrudged Mum's health and good fortune (Fred was a much better provider than Bill Antrim) and may have agreed to marry Mr. Antrim to surpass Mum in the critical eyes of Santa Fe society. For Mum's part, she was continuing to hold out against marrying Mr. Schellschmidt, who made a fuss about living in a home with boarders. I believe he had begun to annoy Mum as much as he did me. If her boarding business thrived in the next few months, she was considering asking Fred to go register at the Exchange Hotel where he often hobnobbed evenings with the Anglo elite. She never told me that directly but hinted at it so many times that I caught her drift. It couldn't have happened soon enough for me.

Now that she was legally Catherine Antrim, Billy's mother perked up enough to be of more help with family duties if not the boarders, but just as often she would stay in bed coughing and sweating and taking "snake oil" medicines that did nothing to keep her consumption at bay. Since there was no school in Santa Fe, I spent too much time at the boarding house washing sheets and running errands. When I managed to get away, I would join Billy in the plaza, where he watched the trading but was more interested in observing the dark-eyed women who smoked cigarillos or engaging señoritas in conversation ("To learn their language, habits and customs," he said). The aroma of simmering Mexican food inspired us to take on the roles of beggars but only rarely did we obtain enough coins to partake of frijoles, tamales, and tortillas.

A week after his mother's wedding Billy, now known to others as Henry Antrim, surprised me by taking a part-time job doing dishes at the Exchange Hotel, where his stepfather was a part-time bartender. Billy earned some "tamale dinero," as he called it, and enjoyed watching the man he called "Old Bill" tend bar, but what kept him whistling while he worked was the piano music from the lobby. His favorite was a new tune, "Silver Threads Among the Gold," which surprised me because he was thirteen and the song was about growing old and life fading fast away. Often when he saw nobody in the piano seat he'd rush over there, clap his delicate hands together, separate them dramatically, and begin touching the keys as if he were afraid that he'd bruise them. The sound produced was nothing like his favorite song. He would get frustrated and whenever somebody told him to leave the piano alone, he would pound the keys like a sullen child and run back to the kitchen as if retreating from cannon fire. He must have washed the hotel dishes well because the management kept him on.

Billy came to prefer the sounds coming from the plaza outside the hotel. This lively music, provided by violins, guitarróns, vihuelas, and sometimes harps, was part of bailes and fandangos the Mexicans held practically every night. Instead of quitting his job Billy enlisted me to fill in for him whenever he had dancing feet, and I must have washed silverware as well as he did because nobody objected if they even noticed the change. Billy's "dancing" trouble with the two Rittenhouse girls in Denver seemed all but forgotten. Maybe Mr. and Mrs. Antrim noticed that the señoritas were more respectful of their parents and, while they could outdance their partners, were well behaved before and after each number. The usually exhausted Catherine even came out from her sickbed some nights to at least sway to the music while her husband and Fred Schellschmidt amused themselves in the gambling houses or at the cockfights. Mum didn't mind so much me going out, whether to the Exchange kitchen or the plaza, but she preferred to stick to the boarding house because newcomers arrived in town at all hours in search of lodging, however temporary.

❦

Billy didn't spend all his free time listening to music, dancing, and picking up as many Spanish words as he could from the prettiest Mexican girls and their protective parents. With the weather warming in April, he and I spent long hours sitting in front of the Palace of the Governors, which Billy always referred to as El Palacio de los Gobernadores, listening to an elderly one-legged Mexican man. He went by only one name, Maximiliano, which meant "greatest." He never asked for money but each day he placed his sombrero on the ground in front of his stump and passers-by filled his enormous hat with coins of all denominations.

Billy was impressed. "You must be the greatest *mendigo* in all of Santa Fe," he told the old man, who merely shrugged. "I mean you keep talking to us without begging anyone for anything and the coins keep clinking in your hat."

"*El mendigo* means the beggar," Maximiliano said to me, having accurately determined I was far behind Billy in learning the new language. "The conquistador cavalryman who sliced off my leg with a fine Spanish steel sword made in Toledo left me for dead. I died but came back and have been sitting in this spot rambling on in Spanish for three hundred years. I am happy to speak now like an American. In fact, little ones, it's harder for anyone to hobble my lip when I get to palavering in English."

I wondered about his age. His gray beard was speckled with what looked like snowflakes and his extended forehead was yellow and furrowed like a cornfield. He certainly seemed to know everything that had happened in this part of the country for the last three hundred years. Perhaps he was touched in the head but that was no matter to me since nobody else talked like him in the plaza let alone back at the boarding house. "We don't want you to stop talking, sir," I said. "You must be the greatest story teller in New Mexico."

The old man shrugged so hard that his red blanket fell off his shoulders.

I helped him put it back on. "Gracias," he said. "I shall continue in English. Where did I leave off? Oh, yes, at San Miguel Chapel, the Spanish colonial mission church originally built in sixteen ten by Franciscan friars. It was partially destroyed during the Pueblo Revolt of sixteen eighty that I have already told you about. But in seventeen ten, following the Spanish reconquest, it got a new roof and served as a chapel for the Spanish soldiers."

"The Spanish are all gone," said Billy. "I'd rather hear about the Mexicans and Indians. They've done lots of fighting, right?"

"The Pueblos have been at peace with us for nearly two centuries."

"What about the wild Indians—the Apaches, the Comanches, the Navajos?"

"Bands of Indians still run wild in the territory but we have had of late little trouble from them here in Santa Fe. Our government no longer sends out armed parties to slay savages and collect bounties on their heads. Not so long ago, however, the severed ears of slain Indians adorned the walls of El Palacio for public viewing."

"You don't say,' said Billy, flicking his own ears, which stuck out a little. "The Mexicans did this?"

"Grisly tales involve all of mankind."

"Americans, too, right?"

"Taking ears and scalps or whole heads is not limited to any one people."

"I imagine not. And everyone robs and steals, I bet."

"American stagecoach robbers, Mexican bandidos, and young Indian bucks are all known to waylay travelers to and from Santa Fe. You are a thief perhaps?"

"I would never rob a stagecoach or steal from a beggar."

"Glad to hear it, little one."

"With all the guns citizens are carrying, I'm surprised I haven't seen any gunfights."

"We have had our share of duels and shootings and outright murders on our streets, all of which get duly reported in the newspapers. Most gunshots are fired by drunken carousers when little ones like you are tucked into their beds."

"Nobody tucks me in. I'll be fourteen this year."

"Ah, practically a man but still distressed by a boy's bad dreams."

"I never said that. I don't dream. I'm a doer."

"Violence comes to Santa Fe as it does to any place on Earth. But don't be too alarmed, little one. While I don't get out of town you understand, in my humble opinion we are not any more violent than Albuquerque, El Paso, Denver, Wichita, or any other Western town you can name."

"I'm not alarmed and I'm not so little," Billy said. "The West is as wild as the wolves and the coyotes. It don't mean I need be afraid. 'Course I better not mention any grisly stories to my mother as she's sickly and worries like a mother hen, mostly about my younger brother Josie. He's such a baby!"

"And what about you, Willie Bonnifield?" Maximiliano asked. "You a worrier?"

"Sure he is," said Billy. "He worries that his mother worries about him. Why, my pal even worries about the roosters in a cockfight."

"Sometimes," I admitted, "but I am by no means the greatest worrier in the world!"

❖

Less than a week later, Maximiliano, whose tongue never tired, told us of a gunfight at the Exchange Hotel that involved two prominent Americans. Drinking apparently wasn't even a factor. The fatal fight was over political differences, pitting William Rynerson of the Territorial Legislature against John Slough, the chief justice of the New Mexico Supreme Court. In the hotel lobby, near the bar, the two men (both abrasive and quick-tempered, according to the one-legged beggar) met face to face, or as close to that as possible since Rynerson stood nearly seven-feet tall. They had words over taking back things they had said and done earlier. Neither would apologize. Rynerson wanted Slough removed from the Supreme Court. The chief justice had called the tall legislator a thief, a coward, and a son of a bitch. Slough was ready to pull a derringer from his pocket, but Rynerson fired his six-shooter first, hitting the chief justice in the stomach. Slough and his derringer both fell to the floor. It took him only a few minutes to die.

"They had each walked past me numerous times," Maximiliano said in conclusion. "Neither had ever dropped a single coin into my sombrero."

Billy listened intently, mouth agape with incredulity. He made a guttural sound but couldn't speak. I accidentally bit my tongue.

"It's all true," the greatest story teller in New Mexico assured us. "It was in all the newspapers."

Billy kept shaking his head, looking to me like a young boy refusing to eat his turnips. "But I do dishes there. My stepfather tends bar there. How could we have missed the gunfight? Even if we weren't at the Exchange the day it happened, we would have heard about it. You telling us a tall tale, *el viejo*?"

Maximiliano was usually not one to crack a smile, but now his whole leathery face cracked as he slapped both his good leg and his stump and howled. His laughter lasted a full five minutes by my count. I couldn't help but

❖ 88 ❖

laugh myself, even though I was confused. I had started reading the *Santa Fe Weekly New Mexican* but hadn't seen one word in print about the Exchange Hotel gunfight. Billy's face turned red; he liked jokes but he didn't get this one any more than I did.

"My stories are timeless," Maximiliano finally explained. "It happened more than five years ago, December fifteenth, eighteen sixty-seven, if you want me to be exact. Hardly any time ago at all considering I have been sitting here for three hundred years."

It looked as if Billy was about to get angry at the one-legged beggar, but instead he tossed his only coin into the sombrero. "That's one for you, *el viejo*. But the Exchange couldn't have changed that much. Gunfire might again interrupt the piano music, right?"

"Certainly possible," said Maximiliano, "maybe even probable with Anglo politicians occupying the Palacio and pretty much the whole shebang."

But Billy was not to see any gun play in the Exchange or anywhere else in Santa Fe. The newly minted Antrim family had decided by the late spring to move farther south, this time to the south-central New Mexico Territory burg of Silver City. Catherine believed once again that an ever drier, milder climate could improve her health. She also counted on the move to benefit her two sons. She told Billy it was high time he went to a good school where he could be serious again and learn important things rather than to that brazen plaza where he frittered away his time and picked up bad habits. Billy told me that he would go back to seriously playing hooky down in Silver City and that he anticipated greater adventures in a rough and ready place where unruly men were ready to shoot and fierce Apache Indians were eager to abduct, scalp, and torture. As for what Joe thought, I don't know. He had his wild moments but would never be as adventuresome as his older brother. Still, I heard him tell Billy, "You act like such a b'hoy, but you're as much a homebody as me."

Clearly the biggest reason the Antrims were relocating was because the man of the family insisted on it. Bill Antrim had been denied the riches silver mining offered others in Colorado Territory when Walter Rittenhouse turned on him, but now he was getting a second chance. Santa Fe could not provide him what he needed. In short, he was dragging his family to Silver City in pursuit of silver.

"They are really going, you know," I said to Mum as we hung wet clothes on the rope line behind the boarding house. She was ignoring me as if hanging things out to dry required her full concentration. The Antrims' imminent departure was not something she cared to discuss. Running the boarding house was not making her rich but it kept her constantly busy and largely self-sufficient. She didn't have time to school me at home, to enjoy leisure with or without Catherine Antrim, or to tend to Fred Schellschmidt's pervading needs. In May, of his own volition, Fred had left the boarding house in a huff to register himself into the Exchange Hotel, not that I had any problem with that. I was better off without him treating me like a warped piece of lumber impossible to straighten out and not good for building a damned thing. Trouble was, Mum never smiled now. She said she couldn't afford it.

I intentionally dropped my end of a white bedsheet belonging to a boarder who had never hit pay dirt and was now a stonecutter. His sheets and clothes were always cleaner than himself even before Mum washed them. My apparent clumsiness caught Mum's attention. She yanked the sheet out of the dirt, had me hold it over the clothesline. and began to pound it with her fists as if beating a rug or one of the boarders or perhaps even me.

"I'm sorry," I said. "I'm sorry I distressed you."

"I'm not distressed. I am working."

Lately those two things seemed to go hand in hand, but there wasn't time to avoid distressing her further. My one and only pal was about to be taken away from me again.

"I know that, Mum. You're always working too hard. Don't you want to go with them?"

"No. I do not."

"Why not?"

"I'm not a tumbleweed."

I paused at that peculiar comment. But I had to admit that her round tangle of dry reddish brown hair (where had all the brilliant red gone?) appeared ready to roll off her head with the next west wind. I hung some men's socks and some boarder lady's undergarment I couldn't quite identify before I spoke again. "Catherine Antrim is your friend. Bill Antrim is Fred's friend, and of course Billy—Henry Antrim—is my friend. It's good to have such good friends. We need to stick by them. We need to go with them...like always."

"It's not like always. You do better without Henry."

"I don't do anything without Henry except help you at the boarding house."

"By dropping into the dirt things I have just washed. By breaking dishes when you even remember to do them."

"I do dishes at the Exchange Hotel. I don't break any there."

"You only work there when Henry doesn't want to."

"I earn some money. You said every little bit helps."

"You go to the plaza, squandering the money on Mexican chocolates, losing it playing three-card monte with the confidence men, and giving it away to Henry so he can buy roses and hair ribbons for all those young girls."

I had no argument for I had enjoyed a few chocolates, though I had only played and lost at monte once, unlike Billy who had won twice and lost a dozen times. I had indeed given Billy money when he ran out, but that pleased me. He had better use for it. Roses and ribbons were things I didn't want now and figured I wouldn't have reason to buy until the day I found my true love or the night I gained courage by consuming much Tequila or whiskey.

"I'm sorry that the plaza has come to bother you," I found myself saying. "But if we go, I can leave the plaza behind."

"When Henry goes, you'll be able to work steadier in the hotel kitchen."

"It would still be only part-time, like Mr. Antrim does at the bar."

"And not too hard at that, I imagine."

"I don't know. I often see him talking at the bar to Fred."

Mum almost dropped a men's shirt herself. "I suppose that should be expected now that Fred resides at the Exchange," she said, quickly hanging the shirt. "His carpentry work has fallen off, for whatever reason."

"From what I can tell, he's drinking quite a bit."

"That won't help him sell his furniture. But never mind him. He can take care of himself. And so can I, but I'll need your help and I, of course, must find you a school."

"Billy's mom has heard about a school in Silver City."

"Catherine never asked us to come. Things haven't exactly been going swimmingly between her and me. We stopped seeing eye to eye about pie and work and the boarding house and, well, men in general. Even if she did ask, I wouldn't come. My boarding house is here."

"Mr. Antrim has been telling Fred about the mineral riches down there. He's trying to talk him into coming along so they can look for silver together."

"Foolishness. Bill Antrim strikes me as a man who has no luck."

"You said before he was lucky to find Catherine and to win her in marriage."

"Catherine is lucky, too, to get a man so much younger to marry her when she has those two boys, is so sickly, and possesses little money of her own."

"When she feels well, though, she works hard like you."

"She'll have to because I don't expect her husband to ever find his silver mine."

"He could with Fred's help, that is if Fred decides to go with them."

"If Fred wants to go, what do I care! Men are always free to go. I am a free woman now."

Yes, Mum, you are free to be lonely and sad and to work yourself to the bone. That's what I thought to say. Instead, I said something foolish, but only because I was so desperate. "Maybe we could go, too, and you could put up with Fred a while longer."

"What are you saying, Willie? You never took to Fred."

"He never took to me first. All I'm saying is that I think he can...you know, make things easier for you...moneywise, just long enough for us to get settled in and you to start up a new boarding house in Silver."

"What kind of thinking is that for a boy of thirteen."

"Fourteen. I had a birthday on May first, remember?"

"We can forget Fred. He drinks more than ever and has become lazy about his carpentry all because I won't marry him the way Catherine married Bill. Should I feel sympathy for the man? Well, maybe I do, a little. Is that reason enough to marry him? I think not. The fact is, dear son, I don't wish to marry any man in Santa Fe."

"Mr. Antrim told Fred that Silver City has far more men than women but that not all the women are Mexican. What if Fred goes and finds somebody else down there?"

"Willie the Kid! Enough is enough. Fred can find another American woman if he likes. As for me, I've had my fill of men. The way I feel right now, I wouldn't even marry the powerful and wealthy William 'Boss' Tweed if he asked me tomorrow."

"The man I was named for?"

"That's right. But I didn't name you Boss."

13

HELLO, SILVER CITY

In late May Catherine apologized to Mum for not being a better friend (blaming the consumption) and finally asked her to come along with the Antrim family to Silver City. Catherine also said that Billy told her life wouldn't be the same without his pal Willie the Kid Bonnifield at his side. Billy never said that to me directly, and I always figured I needed him much more than he needed me. Nevertheless, it thrilled me to know that Billy cared. It thrilled Mum to know that Fred Schellschmidt had contracted with Governor Marsh Giddings to build six custom-made chairs for use in the Palace of the Governors and would remain in the capital city. Fred had been pressuring her to become respectable by selling the "seedy" boarding house, marrying him, moving in with him at the Exchange Hotel, and socializing with the cream of Santa Fe society, including the governor and his wife. It was largely to escape Fred's hounding that Mum decided to depart with the Antrim family without so much as a goodbye to her former benefactor. "It became too much," Mum told me. "He believes I should be obliged to him for life and submit to his every wish and command. He desires to deliver me into bondage."

To help fund the wagon trip south Mum sold the boarding house in Santa Fe to a widow twice over who promised to keep on all the boarders, including the Mexican ones. We packed two wagons and rolled along the El Camino Real de Tierra Adentro (The Royal Road of the Interior Land). The route crossed desert with little water and in the late 1600s the Spanish conquistadors began calling a deadly stretch of it the Jornada del Muerto, or "Journey of the Dead Man." Bill Antrim drove the first wagon with his wife and Mum beside him. Since we had left Fred Schellschmidt behind, I drove the second wagon. Billy, looking as proud as Zeus, sat next to me with a seven-shot Spencer across his lap. His stepfather had loaned him the rifle in case we were attacked by dangerous characters—either Apaches or road agents. Mum kept looking back to make sure we were close behind. In the bed of the second wagon Joe also kept looking back. That was his job—to make sure we weren't being followed.

Joe kept biting his nails because Billy had told him stories about how Apaches, if hungry enough, ate raw the tender hearts and livers of little boys, but, when their bellies were full, enjoyed hanging the boys by their feet over a small fire until roasted to death. Mum, though, was more worried about being chased down by Mr. Schellschmidt.

The trip tired everyone out except Billy. When it was time to leave the Rio Grande and head west across the Mimbres Mountains to our destination he told me to keep following the river south and cross the border into Old Mexico to have adventures in a foreign land. "Old Mexicans aren't all old," he said. "I know we'll find thousands more señoritas in Mexico City than in Silver City." I told him our American mothers would be grief-stricken if we strayed off course, then shook the reins to stay close to the first wagon. I expected Billy to start clucking the way he sometimes did when I was reluctant to do something that might offend parents or other authority figures. Instead, he grinned and threw a couple pebbles at the hind quarters of the pulling horse to encourage him. "Let's get to where we're going then," he said. "I can always run off to Old Mexico any old time."

We arrived at Silver City in a summer sweat even though it was still May. Our new home wasn't quite what Mum expected. Hotter for one thing and less civilized. The streets were crowded with miners all right but also with tinhorn gamblers, preening sporting women, and Mexican settlers. In fact, Mexicans outnumbered Anglos two-to-one. Saloons like the Red Onion and Blue Goose stayed open all night, and the rumor that a school existed proved false. The courthouse on Hudson Street was a one-story adobe with only four offices. The six of us moved into a simple, gabled log cabin at Maine and Broadway but many residents still lived in tents.

Even though our cabin was cramped, Mum moved into a room the size of a closet so we could board two bachelors for modest rent in her room. For a small additional fee, she washed their clothes and bedding once a week. Catherine Antrim must have felt better or else she felt guilty that Mum was keeping the household going. One morning she popped out of bed while her husband snored off a long night and as excited as a schoolgirl said to Mum: "We once baked together. We can do so again. Who makes angel food cake and bread better than me? Surely nobody in Silver City. And you without doubt are the best pie maker in town. I am ready to go forward. You and me, Charlotte. We'll call ourselves C&C Bakery. We won't have to say whether the first C stands for your name or mine. Billy used to call me 'Mother Hen.' I want him to do that again. Even Joe is losing respect for me. I don't want to give up. That's not me!"

It was a good thing the two women showed a willingness to work together because Bill Antrim spent much of his time in saloons playing faro. He told Catherine he was only "bucking the tiger" to learn about the mining operations in the area, but he must have been a slow learner as gambling became a nightly habit. He started to see in his dreams the tiger that was painted on the dealer's box. At first, he did moderately well, but when his luck went sour, he asked the ladies to stake him at the gambling tables. They did so only twice, but Mum refused to let it happen a third time. Mr. Antrim was forced to find a regular job. He became a part-time butcher at Richard Knight's meat market. Bill soon became restless and, realizing that beating the tiger was an impossible task, began taking long trips to prospect around existing mines near Arizona Territory. He not only had no luck but also lost his butcher job due to his frequent absences.

With no school to attend, our parents busy as digger bees, and no room in our cabin to swing a cat, Billy and I spent most of our time on the streets or among the cottonwoods and pinyon pines along the streams and upland areas. It was rarely just the two of us. Most of the thirty Anglo boys in town ran together, but Billy, though short for his age and weighing only seventy pounds, seemed to attract a following of Mexican children, who outnumbered us three-to-one. We ran barefoot that summer, splashing in any body of water we came across, chasing any mule deer or desert cottontail we encountered, and throwing any rock that fit in our unwashed hands at human and non-human targets. We never did anything seriously wrong, although one newspaper man labeled us "Village Arabs" and suggested we all needed to have our hides tanned.

Sometimes Joe Antrim tagged after Billy and me, though he was reluctant to stray too far from home because of his fear of roaming Apaches, also known as Geronimo's tribe, and javelinas, wild boar-like animals known elsewhere as collard peccaries. We never did see an Apache, though sometimes Billy and other mischief makers stripped down, added feathers, and painted their faces to supposedly look like warriors on the warpath and create chaos among the more afeared boys, as well as several gullible girls. Once Joe was crawling on all fours in the brush looking for a favorite piece of quartz he'd dropped when he saw a rubbery pig-like snout coming toward him. Javelinas don't see so well, and this sixty-pound adult male must have mistaken Joe for a dog or a coyote. When I saw what was happening, I yelled for Joe to run. The best he could do was stand up on wobbly knees, now pressing to his chest the silvery ore as if it were a shield. The beast halted, pointed its tapered, triangular-shaped head at Joe, grunted, and gnashed its tusks, but then bolted when Billy called out to it, "You scared him enough, Jave. Can't you see he's not what you think; he's no threat to you at all. And you don't want him. You eat prickly pear, roots, dead rodents and lizards not live chickens!"

Billy acted as if he had arranged with the javelina to frighten Joe. "Wearing feathers and whooping didn't do it, but old pal Jave came through," Billy told me the next day. "Josie soiled his trousers. That'll keep the tattler off my tail for a while." Joe didn't seem such a bother to me, but that was because I understood his fear and his desire to please their mother far more than Billy did. Joe was always safe at home when real danger came to Silver City in the form of gunfire.

Early one evening in mid-June Billy and I were out and about with Harry and Wayne Whitehill, sons of coroner Harvey Whitehill. The four of us first entertained ourselves by loitering on Main Street near the Orleans Club, where the high-stakes gamblers risked their stacks of silver and gold. We were counting on men coming out and tossing us a few coins either because they were happy winners or simply wanted us to get out of their hair. When we grew impatient waiting for that to happen, we went to a window of the ten-pin alley at the back of the saloon to enjoy the clamor of balls being dropped and rolled and pins tumbling and spinning at the other end. Billy led us in shouting insults and pounding on the glass since owner Joseph Dyer never allowed Village Arabs to come inside to play

Upon being chased off we kneeled in the nearby arroyo to shoot agate marbles before it got too dark. Billy, with his long fingers and dexterous hands, was Silver City's finest marble shooter, but on this evening, I was having such an unusual run of luck that the Whitehill brothers teased Billy by calling me the Marble King. Billy took it for a while but then stood up, said it wasn't his night, and assured us he would dethrone the king tomorrow. He started to walk away from our circle when a bulky drunk from the Orleans Club ran into him, knocking Billy over and scattering marbles. What's more, the man dropped his Colt revolver and it bounced off the heel of my right shoe, causing the gun to accidentally discharge. Nobody was hit, but the Whitehill brothers both screamed and scrambled out of the arroyo, no doubt having visions of their bodies on a hard, cold table being examined by the critical eye of their father the coroner.

"Out of my way," the drunk shouted at either me or Billy as he struggled to pick up his weapon. "You're interfering with men's business."

"That right, mister?" said Billy, now back on his feet and standing his ground. "It's you who is interfering with boys' play."

A running man who Billy recognized as a Grant County sheriff's deputy (from several past encounters) showed up right when the drunk recovered his Colt. The officer demanded the weapon and, after the drunk refused to surrender it, made a grab for it. For a second time in a matter of minutes, the gun discharged. The slug shattered the heel of my left shoe and barely grazed the bottom of my foot. I felt a slight burning sensation but saw no blood. It was my lucky night all right. The deputy hauled off the drunk and told me to sit tight until he took the offender into custody and sent a doctor to the arroyo. But soon after he was gone, with Billy's support, I limped all the way home. There was no real damage to my foot, and Billy told our mothers I had lost my shoe when I stepped into a gurgling mudhole while we were out looking for gold and silver. I remained quiet, not wanting to contradict my pal. Only Joe questioned Billy's story, wondering where we found a mudhole when it had been such a dry spring. "I bet you can't show it to me because it don't exist, Willie," Joe said. Billy told the lily-livered brat that a colossal javelina liked to roll in that mudhole to cool off. Joe shut up. Later Mum learned the truth from the sheriff himself and she kept me in the house for two weeks. Catherine talked disinterested husband Bill Antrim into taking a switch to Billy for lying and for all the other things he had gotten away with in the past. It wasn't until well into July that Billy had the chance to dethrone Silver City's Marble King.

❖

That summer Silver City saw more than a dozen shootings, but Billy and I only heard about them. We did see one stabbing on August 6 while standing on our toes and looking through one of the windows at the Orleans Club. Bill Antrim had gone there to meet with a miner named Wilson who was about to set out on a prospecting expedition to Chloride Flats west of town. We wanted to see if it was true. The two men were talking friendly-like as if they might find reason for a partnership. Billy rolled his eyes. He wasn't sure why anyone would want to be Bill Antrim's partner in anything. His stepfather had little money to put into any enterprise, and while he owned a pick and a shovel, he had no past mining success under his belt.

"I reckon Old Bill possesses a degree of charm," Billy said to me. "Enough of it to make it work with Mom anyway, and she wasn't even prospecting for a husband. As we both witnessed, he finally won her over to that idea in Santa Fe and it sure wasn't on account of his bankroll or good looks. Still, charming a miner ain't the same as charming a woman."

"You don't like carrying his name?" I asked.

"He took my first name away from me and I had to become a Henry. Henry's only my middle name."

"You'll always be Billy to me."

'Thanks, Kid. I suppose Henry isn't all that bad, but I like to still be Billy, too."

"Sure, Billy. How about the last name Antrim?"

"I don't hate it. Hell, it's just a name. What did the name McCarty mean to me anyway? I never knew any man named McCarty, least wise if I did, I was too young to remember him."

"My last name doesn't belong to any man except Mum's father, who was a Bonnifield way back in England. He's dead."

"How come you came to be called Willie?"

"Mum named me after a New York politician named William Tweed.

He wouldn't let her take his last name. Calling a baby 'William' didn't seem right to Mum. She and Freya O'Neill, who looked after me when Mum was at work and such, took to calling me Willie the Kid. My middle name is Tweed, though. Not that I make a habit of telling people that and you may as well forget it. Mr. Tweed wasn't my daddy."

"Who is?"

"Don't know. Mum tells people he died in the war."

"I know how that goes. Mom fancied herself a widow, and that's what she told people she was until she became a wife. I figure she could have done better than Bill Antrim but she also could have done worse. He has only given me the switch a couple times and only because she told him he'd better do it for my own good. Mostly he leaves me alone, which is fine by me."

"At least you have a father even if he's only a stepfather."

"Maybe you're the lucky one, Willie the Kid. I know you didn't want that Frederick Schellshit to be your pretend daddy."

"Schellschmidt. But you're right. I'm glad he stayed put in Santa Fe."

"God bless our mothers, I say, even if they don't leave us alone. Let's skedaddle. I'm getting bored watching Old Bill and that Wilson doing nothing but talk, no doubt making plans bound to fail."

Before we could stand down from the window, though, saloon keeper Joe Dyer came into the picture and argued with Wilson. When they started scuffling, Bill Antrim stepped between them, only to be rudely shoved to the ground by both combatants. He stayed down and shrugged as if to say *Suit yourself, gentlemen, this ain't my fight.*

"Nobody appears to be armed," I said, my nose pressed to the glass.

"Too bad," said Billy. "We miss all the shootings around here."

"Maybe they'll punch each other."

"Boring. Fisticuffs are for us Village Arabs, not the City Emirs."

"What's an emir?"

"The Arabs who have the authority because of their age and power and love to boss us Village Arabs around. In other words, they're the big bugs who carry guns."

"Oh." I sometimes wondered how Billy knew so much about the world when he hadn't had any more schooling than me, but I never knew enough to question his worldly facts. "Mr. Dyer is much bigger than Mr. Wilson. With fists, it would be a mismatch."

"I know of a badger who beat a mountain lion. I'd bet on Wilson it if amounts to anything. His face is redder and look how narrow his eyes are. "

"Mr. Dyer looks plenty mad. Maybe Mr. Wilson didn't pay for his drinks."

"Looks like a deadlock. Wait. Wilson is reaching into his pocket. Could be a little gun, a derringer."

"I hope not. I don't want to see it." I kept looking anyway.

"Never mind. It's nothing but a penknife."

Next thing I knew Wilson put that penknife into action, slashing at Dyer's face. When Dyer crossed his arms over his face for protection, Wilson began cutting into Dyer's belly. I screamed and punched the window with my fist. To my surprise, the glass shattered into jagged fragments, some no doubt sharper than that little knife blade. I screamed again, much louder. Bill Antrim had retreated across the floor on the seat of his trousers, but other men appeared, some pulling Dyer to safety, others pulling Wilson back so that he was only slashing at thin air. Billy didn't have to pull me away from the window. I took one look at my bloody knuckles and fainted.

Nobody called on Billy or me as witnesses to the stabbing. The authorities arrested Mr. Wilson but he pleaded self-defense and was released. He laid low after that, possibly leaving Silver City but at least never showing his face again in the Orleans Club. As for Joseph Dyer's face it showed scars that would last. But, according to Bill Antrim, the saloon keeper considered them marks of honor and a source of public and personal pride. He did start keeping a pistol in a coat pocket.

A physician picked glass out of my hand and it remained bandaged through September. Mum said I was punished enough so she never did anything but tell me to stay away from the Orleans Club. Catherine Antrim ordered Billy to stay away from there, too. I did, but Billy didn't. The very next week the scarred Joseph Dyer waved his new pistol around and scared Billy and another pal, fifteen-year-old Hyman Abraham, away from the repaired window. "I was hoping lightning would strike in the same place twice," Billy told me. It didn't but not long after that, Hyman's father, David, used a shotgun to fatally blast an intruder at the Abraham home. "Hy admitted he slept right through it, and so did his brother Louis," said Billy. "Poor kids." Bill Antrim also stayed away from the Orleans Club after his wife told him his place wasn't with the high rollers. Old Bill didn't even argue the point. He told her that he deeply regretted Wilson's disappearance and blamed Joseph Dyer for ruining what figured to have been a rewarding expedition to Chloride Flats.

14

THE RETURN OF MR. SCHELLSCHMIDT

I didn't dwell on the bad things going on in Silver City—the shootings, the stabbings, the barroom brawls, the water shortage, the influx of impatient prospectors who'd run you over in a second to get a piece of silver or a shot of whiskey. I had neither school nor work to attend to, though my curiosity about life caused me to read Jules Verne's *Around the World in Eighty Days* and *Journey to the Center of the Earth,* and my desire to help Mum caused me to volunteer to do chores in and around our cabin. That still left ample time for running with Billy and the Village Arabs when I was in the mood, playing checkers with Joe when I wasn't, and as often as possible devouring delicious offerings from the C&C Bakery that Mum and Billy's Mom ran out of our cabin. What's more I was learning how to dance at the festive bailes. My teachers were the two "C" mothers, who found enough time and good health to do the Highland Fling and all the Mexican dances with Billy, me, and even strangers. Joe was reluctant to take a whirl, even with his mother, but he loved to fill up on the sweet sopapillas and biscochitos. Whether Bill Antrim liked to dance, I don't know. He was always off prospecting or, if in town, jawing with more successful miners. Those were the halcyon days of my boyhood. All that was missing was one of those lovely señoritas who on occasion would dance and laugh with Billy as if he were more than a mere freckle-faced, buck-toothed boy of fourteen. I did make eyes at them when they weren't looking. That was enough for me.

I suspect there is a thin line between contentment and complacency, and I suppose I was drifting back and forth between the two. By the time the cold weather touched Silver City I felt neither because a figure from the past appeared, threatening my happy times and Mum's too, or so I believed. Neither Mum nor I learned about it directly. One December evening, Bill Antrim stood up at the supper table and made an early New Year's resolution in front of us, including the wagonmaker who had boarded with us since summer. "It's too bloody cold for prospecting, which hasn't paid off in any case" he said.

"You'll be pleased to hear, especially you dearest Catherine, that I shall refrain from drinking and gambling in the saloons this winter, at least to any regular degree. As you all know I am a frugal man, but there comes a time one must make greater monetary contributions, especially when he is a family man. I, therefore, resolve to go back to work. What kind of work you might ask. No, I won't ask Richard Knight for my old job back at his meat market. No, I won't try to farm this arid land. No, I won't be making cakes and pies with you ladies. No, I won't attempt to become a school teacher. No need to thank me, Henry and Joe. Any guesses? Never mind. We all want to eat. I shall work as a carpenter."

It would have been more accurate for him to say I shall try my hand at carpentry, for he was not known to have ever made anything in wood except two irregular wood boxes we used for storing kindling and firewood. Somebody might have questioned his wisdom in choosing to work in wood, but Catherine must have figured it couldn't be as fruitless as his mining endeavors, Billy and Joe were preoccupied with their chewing, and Mum and I were too polite to say a word. Only two days after Bill Antrim's mealtime speech—the longest one I ever heard him make—he set out after breakfast to go to work, and he kept doing the same for a week. Billy grew suspicious and he and I followed his stepfather to a humble adobe structure on West Market Street. We found no widow suitable for peeping into, so we squatted behind a mesquite thicket, waiting and listening.

Billy nudged me with a sharp elbow. "A carpenter's shop in an adobe," he whispered. "I don't believe it."

"It's possible. More likely than someone making adobe in a wood shack."

"Listen. You hear that other man's voice? I bet Old Bill is in there drinking and playing cards to keep it a secret from Mom."

"You keep secrets from your mother, too, like that time you and the Abraham brothers smoked those cigarillos with that Mexican girl on Chihuahua Hill or when you snuck in to see the cockfighting behind that jacal on South Hudson Street."

"You could have come, but you are chicken...kind of like Josie."

"Hey, you want a punch in the nose?"

"I don't fight pals, and I've never seen you punch anyone."

"I beat you at Indian wrestling."

"You don't need to be brave to do that. Nobody gets killed from Indian wrestling."

"I know that. But no need to tell me I'm like your brother. I just don't like the sight of rooster blood."

"Or chicken blood. Or dog blood. Or javelina blood. Or human blood."

"That's right. And smoking makes me sick. You want to make something of it?"

"All right, Kid. I didn't think you would so easily be offended. If you were really like my brother, you think I'd be your pal?"

"I reckon not, Billy."

"Then let me see that smile of yours."

I smiled, but soon Billy waved me to stop as if I were smiling too loudly.

"You hear that?" he said. "They're talking English in there. Don't hear no hammer going."

"I don't hear any drinking or card playing either."

Billy laughed and asked me how I expected to hear sipping and shuffling coming out of those adobe walls. We made a bet of either five pesos or five silver dollars, although neither of us had that kind of money. I bet that his stepfather was actually doing some form of woodwork in that adobe. Billy bet his stepfather was doing anything but carpentry. We got hungry because we had left home without breakfast, and before long we tired of listening to muffled voices.

"I wonder who he's talking to," I said.

"No doubt some prospector who has never found any silver, either."

"Let's go a little closer." I didn't want to sound chicken.

"Much closer. We're going in."

Billy rushed to the only door, and I figured I had no choice but to follow. He pounded his fist on the door, then gave it a push before bursting through as if he expected his stepfather to try hiding a whiskey bottle and cards. Once inside he froze and I ran into his backside. The obstacle in front of us was a sturdy piece of pine furniture about the size of a bureau; it had two upper drawers and a large base cabinet with holes punched to form stars in the tin panels on the hinged doors. Bill Antrim was running a hand over the top as if patting a dog that he wasn't convinced wouldn't bite. His jaw dropped when he saw who we were, and his mouth stayed open even as he scowled at his stepson. Standing next to Mr. Antrim was another bearded man at least a head taller, and all of him—including his thick eyebrows, his brawny arms, and the toothpick in his mouth—seemed to rise higher all at once. As he looked down on us boys, he yanked out the toothpick and pointed it between my wide-open eyes as if threatening me with a dagger. When he spoke, though, his tone was soft, almost gentle, not as I remembered it.

"Yes, Willie boy, it is really me,' he said, now smiling but with only one side of his mouth raised. "Been laying low here for a couple of weeks making this beauty. I wanted it to be a surprise for your mother—your mother, too, Henry."

I couldn't find any words. My stomach growled, but likely not because it was empty.

"It's a beauty all right," said Billy. "What is it?"

"A pie safe. It stores pies and bread and other baked goods, keeping them safe from dirt, dust, insects, rodents, and pesky boys. The punched tin ventilates what's' inside, keeping the food cool. Simple but clever. Won't your mother be surprised, Willie Boy! It's just what she needs, what Charlotte needs, what C&C Bakery needs!"

I suppose I gave him a slight nod. I was thinking that while Mum surely needed a pie safe, she didn't need the man who made it. Billy didn't say anything either, but he touched the star-shaped holey designs in the tin and opened the creaking wooden doors to study the wide empty shelves inside.

Frederick Schellschmidt made Billy and me swear we wouldn't say a word about his presence in Silver City before he had the chance to spring the pie safe on Mum. He had it all planned out with his accomplice, Bill Antrim. They had been corresponding in secret ever since we left Fred behind in Santa Fe. Mr. Antrim had pointed out that while the capital city was an adobe town, Silver City was trying to look like an American city by building with as much lumber and brick as possible. "There isn't any demand for adobe furniture here either," Mr. Antrim had written, perhaps trying to show off his usually hidden wit. The two men had arranged to have a carpentry shop, even though the only space immediately available was made of adobe bricks. Fred had sent the money for that and for Bill to go with a sawyer to the Pinos Altos Mountains to cut down a ponderosa pine and have the valuable wood ready in the shop.

"Silver City is crying out for a skilled woodworker far more than Santa Fe ever has," Fred told Billy and me. "I'm answering the cry. I see a golden opportunity here."

"I see it, too," said Bill Antrim. "It's great to have my compadre at my side once more."

Clearly Bill's stepfather had only turned to carpentry because he would be in the company of a legitimate carpenter who could teach him the trade and, since they were long-time chums, tolerate his mistakes and not overwork him. No doubt he figured he could help the family finances without giving up his dream of one day finding a fortune in silver. As for Frederick Schellschmidt, woodworking and friendship weren't the main reasons he had relocated to Silver City. Two days after my shock at seeing his self-assured, lean-cheeked, bearded face, Fred brought to the house in his wagon not only his proudly made pie safe but also a trunk filled with his personal belongings. Mum and Catherine Antrim, too, acted surprised and overjoyed at this event even though they had gotten wind of it earlier because Billy could not keep the secret more than twenty-four hours. I had hoped Mum's spirited state was entirely due to the clever gift, but that proved wishful thinking. Not that day or that night, but two nights later, she allowed Fred to bring the trunk inside the house. What's more she asked me to help carry it.

It couldn't have been only the pie safe that convinced Mum to welcome Fred back in the fold. Billy told me a grown woman, widow or not, could go only so long without a man, longer than a man who wasn't a monk could go without a woman but still no more than a year. Just because he danced with señoritas didn't make him an expert on the subject, but I didn't argue the point. All Mum said about it was that Fred had always been a good provider, had showed himself to be a conscientious courter, and had promised to be a good father to me. I overheard Catherine Antrim tell her husband that Mum had finally come to realize the importance of morals and redemption and would marry Mr. Schellschmidt. "It can't be a church wedding because we have no churches here," she said. "But it can still be a good Sunday wedding. Those who break the Sabbath with their gambling, drinking, and dancing won't be welcome. Naturally, unless Charlotte and Fred want to travel a long way for their nuptials, they will have to wait until the right kind of minister comes to town." Apparently, that meant one who wasn't a Catholic like most of the New Mexicans, not that Billy's mom had anything much against the dominant religion and nothing at all against dancing the other six days of the week.

The wait was shorter than anyone anticipated. Even though it was a hard winter, a hard- riding circuit preacher from a northern village near Fort Union showed up in early January 1874. The Rev. Thomas Harwood was a pioneer Methodist missionary who since 1869 had been crisscrossing the territory trying to convert the natives to Protestantism. He had traveled south along the Rio Grande to preach in Las Cruces and on his way back north took a side trip to Silver City. He found plenty of examples of Sabbath-breaking but still managed to preach twice on a Sunday. That night and the following night, too, he encountered a fandango that featured shooting along with the singing and dancing. That jarring activity, along with reports of a snowstorm blowing in from the west, convinced him not to overstay his welcome. At the request of Mr. and Mrs. Antrim, however, he married Mum and Fred in McGary's Hall on Main Street before riding quickly away on a rented horse. It wasn't on a Sunday, but Billy, Joe, and I all wore new Sunday clothes for the occasion. Mum wore a muslin bustle wedding dress that was a perfect fit even though it had been worn once before—by Catherine in Santa Fe ten months ago.

A few days later, Billy, Joe and I started going to McGary's Hall regularly because, while Silver City had no schoolhouse, a rented space in that hall and saloon was turned into a classroom. Mum, Billy's mom, Billy's stepfather, and even my brand-new stepfather insisted upon it. Mum was insisting on many things now—that everyone call her Mrs. Schellschmidt instead of Bonnifield (though she allowed me to keep the last name Bonnifield and to continue calling her Mum), that I never miss a day of school (the price was right as school was free), that I run errands for her and Catherine after school, that I polish furniture for Fred on Saturdays, that I read passages from the Bible on Sundays, that I treat my new father with the respect he deserved every day of the week (she had caught me sticking my tongue out at him a time or two), and that I detach myself from the worst of the Village Arabs whether they be Anglo (Billy was never mentioned by name) or Mexican.

The man behind the school, Dr. Webster, was also the principal and the teacher of children between ages five and fifteen. There were nearly one hundred fifty eligible students but only thirty-two were present when school opened on Monday, January 5, 1874. Billy showed up early that first day and put on a show for the early arrivers with the help of Louis Abraham. What they did was re-create an earlier McGary incident Billy had heard about: Gambler Charlie Bishop, believing he was being cheated in a game of monte, used a bowie knife to pin the hand of a Mexican to the table. Louis wasn't a Mexican and Billy only stuck his penknife between his younger friend's fingers, but their classmates applauded. Webster confiscated the knife. But after Dr. Webster rang his little brass bell, Billy didn't disrupt class once, and in the days that followed he usually sat in the first row and was as well-behaved as me. He listened to the teacher, too, and could recite as well as anyone, though he sometimes mangled lines for laughs. Once he recited Edgar Allan Poe's "Annabel Lee" and twice mispronounced the title character's name as "Animal Flea" before Dr. Webster made him apologize to the class. Billy then was in good form until he changed the second-to-last line from "In her sepulchre there by the sea" to "In her spittoon whereby I pee." That last intentional mistake caused Dr. Webster's pale face to turn pink. He made Billy stay after class and write down the poem's six stanzas (with every word correct, of course) on the blackboard three times. But all was forgotten a week later when Billy surprised the teacher by reciting from memory the first thirty lines from Longfellow's "The Song of Hiawatha," with just one early mistake (saying "the shores of Itchy Gumee" instead of "Gitche Gumee"), and that might have even been an honest mistake.

Dr. Webster instructed in English only, but after school Billy picked up all the Spanish he could (no grammar, though) from his Mexican friends. I didn't make friends of any kind as easy as him, and what Spanish words I picked up came mostly from Billy. Anglo and Mexican boys often swarmed to the Antrim-Schellschmidt house after school to play "racehorse." The older, bigger boys, not wanting to work up a sweat themselves, selected lighter boys as their racehorses and ran them in street races of various lengths. Billy was a lightweight all right but he avoided running and chose not to "own" a human horse. He took on the role of judge, making sure the races were run fair and square. Nobody challenged his authority. I kept Joe, who weighed more than Billy but slightly less than me, as my racehorse. He plodded like a plow horse and nobody else wanted him, but he didn't want to be left out of the game and I didn't care about winning. The winners—horses and owners—were awarded with the unparalleled sweetcakes made by Mum and Billy's mom, and Joe and I got those treats at home anyway.

Billy wasn't by any means the worst of the so-called Village Arabs, but he wasn't above a little thievery. One time his mother refused to give him a piece of pie because he had put a harmless tarantula in Joe's shoe, so Billy decided to steal soda crackers from the store of Louis Abraham's father. Louis went along with the plan, and so did I to a degree. I stood at the counter talking to Mr. Abraham about possibly making a purchase while the other two grabbed the soda crackers. We got away with it. To ease my conscience, I ate only one of the soda crackers that Billy and Louis offered me.

We weren't so fortunate in early February when somebody took thirty-five dollars from the money drawer of Richard Knight's butcher shop. Billy and I were there at the time of the theft. I was picking up ham hocks for Mum, and Billy wanted to take home the blood of a freshly slaughtered animal because he had heard that desperate consumptives were trying to cure themselves by drinking blood. His mother was coughing too much again, and Billy was only trying to help. When Mr. Knight noticed the missing money, he immediately suspected Billy, mostly because Bill Antrim had once worked there and been dismissed but also because the idea of anyone but a vampire drinking blood was outrageous and he didn't believe in vampires. It was Mr. Knight's belief that the disgruntled and revenge-minded stepfather had sent the eldest son to rob him and that I was the son's accomplice. We were falsely accused and locked in a closet with hanging carcasses since Silver City's first real jail was still under construction.

Bill Antrim was out of town on a solo prospecting expedition at the time, so Catherine Antrim came around and told Mr. Knight she might try drinking blood since no doctors knew of a cure for her condition. That proved nothing, he said, since the theft was an entirely different matter. She argued that her husband was away and, in any case, would never ask Billy to do anything, good or bad, without first asking her permission. Still, Mr. Knight refused to release Billy or me into her custody. Mum left a pie in the oven to take up the logical argument that if we were guilty why were we carrying less than a dime between us, rather than thirty-five dollars. Mr. Knight suggested that we had passed the stolen money through an open window to a third boy, possibly Joe Antrim.

Finally, Fred Schellschmidt broke away from his carpentry shop and defended the honor of Bill Antrim. "He's a carpenter now and has no regrets about leaving butchery behind," Fred said. "He is neither revenge minded nor a wrongdoer. You, sir, have leaped to a false assumption and I will not stand for it." Mr. Knight conceded that point and now emphasized that "those obnoxious Village Arabs perpetrated their depredations without any parental guidance." Fred then defended me in the weakest manner, saying that if I did wrong it was only because I was under a spell cast by "prankish Henry Antrim, who fancies himself the Arab Chief." At that point Mr. Knight released me from the closet but wouldn't let Billy go until Fred paid ten dollars in "bail" and promised to investigate the crime (that is to get a confession out of one of the three thieves). Joe had not been anywhere near the butcher shop that day, but he'd been in an alleyway trying to roll his first cigarette at the time, so he felt guilty. He might have even looked guilty but no adult who knew him (and Mr. Knight clearly did not) suspected for an instant that he would have assisted his older brother and been the third boy in the theft.

That night we ate Mum's ham hock and bean stew and finished up with Mum's dried apple pie. Billy joked about how he would never take Mr. Knight's "blood money." Nobody laughed but nobody said anything more about the theft either. The real perpetrators were never caught. When Bill Antrim returned three days later from another unrewarding prospecting venture, he heard about the incident but shrugged it off and told Fred: "I hate that you had to hand over ten dollars to greedy Mr. Knight just to free Henry from his clutches. I don't believe Henry did it, certainly not on my account." Billy wasn't exactly the Arab Chief but he was able to use his wiles to find out who committed the crime. He never did reveal who the guilty parties were, not even to me.

15

REST IN PEACE, CATHERINE

Our close call at the butcher shop and another time when he was falsely accused of stealing a barrel of whiskey didn't teach Billy anything except that kids didn't stand much of a chance in an adult world full of greed, duplicity, spurious accusations, supremacy, arbitrary discipline, and rigid punishment. In early March 1874 he hatched a plot to steal jewelry from Matt Derbyshire's store and go sell it across the border since that would be safer and he had been longing to see Old Mexico. He wanted me to go along but I came up with an excuse—a badly twisted ankle from stepping into a prairie dog hole. I could tell he didn't believe me and he closely watched me for a couple of days, but I managed to maintain a consistent limp. "Suit yourself," he finally told me. "Charlie and Henry Stevens are dying to go and they got four good feet."

Maybe so, but at the last minute, Charlie got a change of heart. He confessed the plot to his father, then told him and Mr. Derbyshire that he only went along with it because "Henry had me hypnotized." The boy then had to explain that he didn't mean Henry his brother but Henry Antrim, the "most atrocious Arab." The two adults went to the Antrim home, but got little satisfaction. Bill Antrim was out of town as usual and Catherine Antrim was in bed, exhausted and spitting up white phlegm—suffering too much to even reprimand her oldest son. Joe and I were playing checkers and we both denied knowing of the planned burglary—Joe was telling the truth and I was telling one of those little white lies to protect my best pal. Mum was in the kitchen, and all she said was that she believed Henry was playing "three-way checkers." Frederick Schellschmidt happened to be downtown putting the trim around the windows and doors at the new jail, where Mr. Stevens and Mr. Derbyshire threatened to take the "perpetrator." At that point I stepped up and asked how there could be a perpetrator when there was no crime committed and how could my pal be put in jail when he couldn't even hypnotize Joe let alone the much less susceptible Stevens brothers. The accusers then left, none too happy.

In fact, before leaving, Mr. Derbyshire displayed a wayward elbow that jarred the checkerboard, dislodging half the pieces.

Billy didn't exactly thank me for speaking up for him, but he let me have a few coins that he said he found (I didn't question him) and suggested that sometime we should go take a peep at the woodwork and iron bars at the new jail.

"Remember when I headed the Free and Accepted Woodworkers of Indianapolis," he said. "I was damn good with wood."

"I remember. Maybe you should join your stepfather and go to work for Mr. Schellschmidt at the carpentry shop," I replied.

"I'll be hanged if I ever do such a thing. Forget I ever mentioned wanting to visit the new jail. I'm not that fond of woodwork, and who needs to see iron bars!"

The latest suggestion by the continuously outraged editor of *Mining Life* was that the Village Arabs of Silver City should "be put to work sweeping the streets by day and locked up in the new jail at night." Mum actually wrote Editor Scott that he didn't know what he was talking about because the boys couldn't be sweeping the streets when they were attending Dr. Webster's classes all day and couldn't be sitting in jail at night when they were home doing chores and improving their reading skills, even if only by reading his newspaper. Catherine Antrim continued to feel poorly but at one point she felt well enough to call Billy into her bedroom and have him sit on the edge of her sick bed. With a firm hand on his shoulder, she said: "There's something I must say to you, Henry. I'll put it to you plain. I don't know if you were planning to rob Mr. Derbyshire's store or not, and I'm not asking you to confess to anything. All I'm saying is if you're starting up a life of crime and continue in that vein, you'll hang before you're twenty-one."

Billy wasn't scared straight by his mom's warning, but he did behave better for a while. The first school term ended March 28, 1874, but not before Dr. Webster offered a quote from a foreign fellow named Chaucer. "Idle hands are the devil's workshop!" our teacher proclaimed, and when those words didn't sink into our overworked heads, he repeated that cautionary message from olden times. To keep us busy and off the streets, he had arranged for us to perform in plays and minstrel shows. Billy stepped up and became the leading light in our staged performances, which also helped raise money for building a schoolhouse. I had minor parts with never more than two lines, but that was fine with me because I was shy in front of an audience. I had a long way to go if I wanted to "act" like my pal. Still, I did better than Joe Antrim, who froze and failed to deliver his only line the one time he dared step on stage.

When we performed *Uncle Tom's Cabin*, Billy put on blackface and portrayed the slave Tom in fine fashion until he saved angelic Eva, played by a tiny Mexican girl, from drowning (as the plot called for), but then planted a full kiss on her lips (uncalled for, everyone agreed). Billy was forgiven and next up he played the town drunk in our performance of *Ten Nights in a Bar-Room and What I Saw There*, whose purpose was to show the Village Arabs as well as the more innocent children the evils and dangers of alcohol consumption. Billy performed a little too well for most in the audience. While carrying on in a barroom scene he was supposed to nurse a whiskey bottle full of water, but somehow half of the content was still whiskey. Billy drank from the bottle liberally and when it was time to tell his dying daughter (played by the same tiny Mexican girl, Maria Guerrero) that he would abandon alcohol forever, he instead said, "How about a nightcap before you go, *mi hija*." At least this time he only kissed Maria on the cheek.

After that, Billy wasn't given another dramatic part, but his voice was heard again in the minstrels, especially loud when he stole the show singing "Silver Threads Among the Gold." Bill Antrim was actually in the audience for that performance, and it was one of the few times I saw him praise Billy and actually run a hand affectionately through his stepson's hair. Catherine Antrim wasn't there that night as she was in bed suffering from cold sweats and extended coughing fits. She also gave up dancing because of her illness, and Mum did the same partly out of sympathy for her friend but also because Mum was usually exhausted from her household chores and work in the C&C kitchen. Billy and I continued to attend the bailes without any parental supervision. I danced some but mostly stood around listening to the guitars, violins, harps, and horns while Billy hardly ever stopped twirling on the dance floor, though never with Maria Guerrero, whose mother kept a sharp eye on her.

Catherine Antrim did not regain the spring in her step when spring came to Silver City. In fact, March and April were bitterly cold in the territory, and she grew worse. "She's wasting away right before my eyes," Billy said more than once. Joe usually kept his eyes closed, unable to watch his mother deteriorate. "It's a sad sight to see," I said, although I admit I was secretly grateful that Mrs. Antrim was stricken and not Mum. I suppose Bill Antrim didn't like what he was seeing either, although it didn't keep him from being out of sight for long stretches. It was Catherine's friend Mary Hudson who escorted the sick lady twenty-six miles to sulfur springs in the high desert as a last resort. Catherine stayed at a hotel at the springs for more than two weeks, taking long sulfur baths every day and receiving kind treatment from Mrs. Hudson. Back home, Joe wept constantly, Mum and I wept on occasion, and Billy told everyone to dry their tears because he was certain his mom would come home as good as new. Fred Schellschmidt, who was busier than ever with his carpentry, took a more realistic view, lecturing all of us: "Hot springs have been around even before the Spanish explorers arrived in this land. Let's face the facts. Whatever relief soakers might have gotten for muscle and joint aches, poor blood circulation, and gout, never was there a single lunger saved by so-called healing waters."

Mrs. Antrim came home in May smelling like rotten eggs and looking like a shell of herself. Mum did some of the nursing, but it was more than she could handle with all her other household duties. Clara Truesdell, the mother of another of Billy's pals, had nursing skills and she came to the cabin nearly every day to lend a hand. Even Billy lost hope that his mother would ever be her dancing, enterprising self again. I caught him crying over his mother a time or two.

"It ain't fair for a good woman like her to be dealt such a hand," he told me one night when he was thinking too much to fall asleep. "I'd give up my left hand or anything at all to have her gain the strength to give me one of her old-fashioned lickings again."

"I reckon she'd rather you give up your mischief making and such and not do anything that would call for a licking."

"Ain't that funny, Willie. You're no older than me but at times like this you act like the father I never had."

"I don't. All I'm doing is putting myself in her shoes. Anyway, you have your stepfather."

"Wherever he may be. He has silver on his mind, not sickness."

Catherine Antrim didn't want her two sons sitting by her sickbed weeping and worrying, so she insisted they attend the second school term, which began May 18 in a building that was not in the best of shape. Billy and Joe even volunteered to whitewash the walls, perhaps to get in good with the new schoolmarm, Mrs. Pratt, who had replaced Dr. Webster. I never missed a class and I can't say Billy ever disrupted the classroom the way he had the stage performances between terms. But other boys, with their outbursts and inattention, had Mrs. Pratt tugging her already tangled hair bun. That month, Mum took me and the two Antrim boys to see a traveling Mexican circus, and we did some laughing for a change. Joe laughed loudest at the circus clown, and I joined in even though to me this clown wore mental agony rather than good humor on his bloodless white-masked face. Billy had more fun cackling at the trapeze artists and tightrope walkers and applauding them when they made slips into the safety nets below.

In August rains came, getting heavier by the day. The dirt on the schoolhouse roof turned to dense mud. One morning we were all seated on our benches except for Joe, who stood at the front of the class trying to recite with knees shaking and tongue tripping over Matthew Arnold's poetic words. Some of us noticed something ugly brown dripping from the ceiling onto Joe's head and laughter naturally broke out. Joe finally looked up and a glob struck him right between the eyes. He dropped to his knees and screamed as if he'd been hit by a stone. Mrs. Pratt shot up from her desk, shaking her fist, and scolded Joe for not appreciating "The Scholar-Gipsy," apparently the name of Arnold's poem. But then the teacher screamed herself when the mud spilled through the roof onto all our heads. She told us to remain calm before she ducked under her desk. Most of us abandoned the building. When the danger seemed passed, we congregated at the doorway and waited for Mrs. Pratt to emerge. "Class dismissed!" she yelled. "Forever. I am done teaching you Village Arabs." It was as if she blamed us, mainly the boys, for the heavy mud that caused the roof to be on the brink of collapse. Anyway, the second term ended more than a week early and the children of Silver City were free once more to take to the streets or, in the case of Billy and Joe, to their dying mother's bedside.

Whenever he grew weary and short of supplies, Bill Antrim came home for a while to work for Frederick Schellschmidt, admitting to his understanding employer that the woodworking was necessary to finance his silver prospecting. Together they began constructing a two-story wood house on Yankie Street that Fred intended to be the new home for him, Mum and maybe me. He was tired of sharing the Antrim family cabin, which was too small and too crowded. Mr. Antrim, nevertheless, spent many of his summer nights sleeping in the still roofless Yankie Street house under construction. "I got used to sleeping under the stars," he told his wife. "It's gotten so I can't sleep a wink unless I see their silvery twinkle along with the golden glow of the moon."

His words sounded almost poetic to Catherine, but that only confirmed in her mind that they had drifted apart, rather that he had distanced himself further from his hopelessly sick wife and the two boys he'd usually kept at arm's length. On the first of September she banished her husband from the place he had never really wanted to be anyway for the past four months— their bedroom. He told everyone with a tear in his eye that he had no choice but to respect her dying wish, and on at least one occasion compared her to a wounded female cat who had no further use for the company of a tomcat. Catherine had Mum and Clara Truesdale to manage things and her two boys and me to keep her company even as she became pale and frail enough to look like a ghost. When she coughed, her entire body shook like a leaf about to fall. She had been bedridden for four months, and she knew she would not live until fall. It was mid-September when she called for her sons, all three of them, to gather at the head of her sickbed. Of course, she had only the two sons, but I had become like an adopted son to her, and I didn't object even though I was more than satisfied with my actual mother.

First, Mrs. Antrim reached out and weakly took hold of the hands of Joe. "Josie, dear Josie," she began, going back to the name she used to call him and that Billy still did. "Do not think of this as the end of anything. I have given you the gift of life and you must live on and on and on as best you can, remembering all that I taught you and holding in your heart a mother's love. Listen to Mrs. Schellschmidt and Mrs. Truesdale as you would me and be true to yourself. If you can't always be good—and who can?—then at least be strong. Persevere!"

"I can't," her teary-eyed youngest replied. "I don't want to be severe." He buried his face in his mother's bosom.

I nudged Joe in the back. "She said persevere," I told him. "That's not at all the same thing."

Joe failed to acknowledge me, but Billy pulled him away from his mother with great difficulty, allowing me to move in closer and receive a pat on the hand from Mrs. Antrim.

"Ah, it's you, dear William, Willie the Kid," she said and her lips upturned in the slightest of smiles. "I have lost most of my body but have not lost my mind. I know you are from the womb of another. Still, you are my good boy, my smart boy, my sensible boy. You make sure Josie stays in school and minds his manners. And, you mustn't let Henry stray. Keep him on the straight and narrow. It won't be easy, I'm afraid. Do your best. Henry needs you. I mean Billy needs you. That's what you call him and what I once called him. He can be Billy again. Billy Antrim. Or Billy McCarty. I named him William Henry McCarty. He can call himself whatever he likes now, but he must not call himself a bad boy or a Village Arab or a son of a bitch! Tell me where is he? Where is my oldest son? Where is Billy?"

Billy let go of Joe and rushed forward, knocking aside my arm to clasp his mother's right hand. He didn't excuse himself, but there was no need. I understood perfectly. No matter how different Billy might have been from me at that stage in our lives, we had something very much in common—an unadulterated love of our mothers and an unquestioned love for each other's mother.

"Don't fear, I am right here," said Billy. "No need to say anything more. I know how you feel, Mom. You want to live your life to the fullest as long as you can, and you wish the same for Joe and me and my best pal Willie the Kid. Well, hell, I can promise you I'll be living to the fullest—through the coldest winters, the hottest summers, through storm and sunshine, through thick and thin, through celebration and calamity, through drought and flood, through the 'slings and arrows of outrageous fortune.' That's Shakespeare, Mom. The long-gone Dr. Webster told us that in class. I haven't forgotten!"

"Yes, I know you are smart, son." she said. "It makes me proud. And you can be good, too. But you are squeezing too tightly. Not so hard, Billy."

"Sorry, Mom." Billy let go of his mother's right hand and allowed that hand the freedom to take hold of his wrist. She gave it a squeeze, no doubt not meant to be an inconsequential one, though there was no strength behind it. "And like you said, when I can't be good, I'll be strong!"

"Not too strong. Remember what I said to you earlier about not giving anyone any reason to hang you before you're twenty-one."

"Don't worry. Nobody is going to hang me. Not if I live forever." He laughed so hard that he drooled and pulled his arm away from her to wipe his mouth with his shirtsleeve.

"Do play and have fun, son. But remember that life is not a Shakesperean comedy, nor does it have to be a Shakesperean tragedy. Most lives are something in between. There's only so much drama any of us can stand. Now I need to rest. So go, but not too far. I don't know how much time I have left to advise you and your brothers."

On September 16, 1874, consumption consumed Catherine Antrim. Billy, Joe, Mum, and I were at her bedside to hear her last gasping breath; her husband Bill Antrim was not. He was still off in the hills looking to make a strike. Fred Schellschmidt, who always considered Mrs. Antrim too lax with her oldest son and not attentive enough to her husband's needs, was busy constructing a faro box for the Blue Goose saloon. Mrs. Antrim's last words were "Be good, Billy, goodbye." She then closed her eyes for the final time. Joe had been weeping for hours, but he stopped abruptly, leaned close to his mother's open mouth and waited a minute before blurting out, "Why did you say goodbye to him and not to me?" He got no answer. She was gone.

Mum put her comforting arms across the shoulders of Billy and Joe and tried to reassure them: "There wasn't time enough for your mother to do everything she wanted to say and do. She was once a highly spirited lady who loved you both very much—remember her that way. I promised to watch over you two, and that's what I aim to do." Clara Truesdell, who had been making tea in the kitchen, rushed into the bedroom, only glanced at the deceased woman, and pulled Billy and Joe to her breast. "Your mother told me she was sorry to be leaving you two boys in a wild country and she asked me to do all I could to help you and keep you tame till you were grow'd." Mrs. Antrim had said in her last days the same thing to both Mum and Mrs. Truesdell, essentially:"When you get right down to it, they are now orphans. I can't count on Bill Antrim; it's a lot to ask, but I'm asking—those boys need a woman's touch and sensibilities."

Mum sent me to fetch Fred from his carpentry shop, and he quickly hammered together a coffin while Mum and Mrs. Truesdell prepared Catherine Antrim's body for burial; they washed the body, dressed her in her favorite dancing gown, and took the tangles out of her hair. There would be no waiting for Bill Antrim to return. The funeral service took place the following afternoon in the family cabin. Silver City had no undertaker or hearse. At least a dozen people volunteered to put the body in the coffin, which Fred then transported to the burial grounds in one of his "furniture-wagons." Billy, Joe, and I dug the grave, but there were only two shovels on hand, and I did most of the digging because Billy and Joe kept arguing over the significance of their mother's last words while having a tug of war over the second shovel.

"She told you to be good because she knows I'm already good," said Joe. Billy laughed as he gave up the shovel to his younger brother and replied, "She said goodbye to me because she liked me best, just the way I am."

16
DIFFERENT HOMES

After the funeral, it was time for learning again instead of mourning. Mum and Mrs. Truesdell insisted on it. They sent us off each day to the new one-room schoolhouse that had opened two days before Catherine Antrim's death. For this third term, we had our third teacher, Miss Mary Richards—a refined, sophisticated English woman with the neck of a swan, the face of Helen of Troy (whom she told us about), the waist of a wasp, and the hands of a princess who had never been required to work a day in her life

Unexpectedly but decidedly her right hand proved firm. Joe, looking to get on her good side, went to the carpentry shop and under the direction of Fred Schellschmidt fashioned a thick paddle for punishing mischief makers like his brother. Miss Richards accepted Joe's gift and wielded it liberally for several weeks to keep the class in line. One of her first "victims" was Joe himself for repeatedly doodling on his slate full-figure pictures of Mary of Silver City. "But...I...I only wanted to show how much I...we all...cherish you, Miss Richards," he said, whimpering in front of his peers. She walloped him anyway, explaining afterward to the entire class, "I wish to be appreciated, not cherished; respected, not fawned over, held in esteem, not deified." Billy did no fawning, but he showed his fondness for her by volunteering to straighten our chairs, clean our tables, sharpen pencils, fetch water, and show her the pictures he drew of cactuses, mountains, and sunsets. Joe claimed that his brother was "mashed" over their teacher and deserved to be paddled. Billy didn't disagree, saying, "My interest in schoolwork has been excited and my desire to help out after class has been advanced."

In my opinion both Antrim boys, having recently lost their mother and having a largely absentee father, felt a need for a caring parental figure, and Mum was too busy with baking and looking after me to fill the bill. "I'll have you know the schoolmarm is awfully fond of me, too," Billy told me in one of our night talks. "She is convinced I possess an artistic nature. She can write with either her left or right hand, like me. We might be related. She's like Mom before Mom got sickly and too weak to keep me in line." Miss Richards only paddled Billy once and that was because Billy kept looking at my slate as if to get the correct answer to a history question she had posed to the class. "Of course, I didn't need to do that," Billy told me afterward. "I had a far better answer than you gave about why Samuel Adams urged the Colonial Patriots to break from the British. I just wanted to feel the sting of the hard wood from our schoolmarm. I felt no pain at all. She reminded me of Mom back in the good old days."

Being around Mary Richards by day and Mum at supper time worked well for Billy, who before I knew it stopped wanting to talk about the good old days. He wanted to live for today, which meant finding enjoyment in all he was doing now—gaining knowledge and doing chores in the classroom, devouring Mum's good cooking, performing in minstrel shows (he was forgiven by Miss Richards for his previous lapses on stage), teasing Joe and me for our circumspect natures (Joe far more than me), promenading with his pals on the street, looking for whatever silver linings he could in Silver City. One of those silver linings, he told me, was his stepfather's indifference toward him and Joe. "It makes me almost a free man," he insisted. "I'm happy as a pig in mud, which is not to suggest anything unfavorable about your mother's ability to keep house." After finally returning to town more than a week after his wife's burial, Bill Antrim had not gone into mourning. He spent some time earning money in Fred Schellschmidt's carpentry shop but soon arranged for the care of the two boys he had inherited and took off once more, certain that his luck would have to change and he'd strike it rich.

Happiness, which I suppose I was striving for as much as Billy (at least I tried to laugh as much as he did), has a way of breaking down like an old horse—not that he or I owned a horse of any kind yet. Our domestic tranquility was shattered in late October by something beyond our control. It had nothing to do with Billy's stepfather. I mostly blame my stepfather, Frederick Schellschmidt. He had finished that well-built two-story house on Yankie Street and now, at last, he and Mum could live the way well-to-do married folks were supposed to live. She reminded him it wasn't a good time to leave the Antrim cabin because motherless Billy and Joe needed looking after. Fred told her she had already done enough. "Clara Truesdell and other motherly types are more than willing to take charge of those Antrim boys," he said. "Old Bill has already made the arrangements. In fact, he sold that miserable little cabin before he left town."

I naturally didn't want to be separated from Billy and I suggested that he be allowed to come along to live with us in the new house. Fred said to Mum, without even caring that I could hear him: "No way in hell will that happen. Taking on one fifteen-year-old rascal is more than enough!" Fred liked better my idea of me staying behind and going wherever Billy landed to help the boy deal with his new status as essentially an orphan. Mum wouldn't go for that. "Then you'd practically be an orphan yourself," she told me. "What have I ever done to you to make you not want to have me as your mother?" I assured her that she was a great mother, that the house on Yankie Street would not be many blocks away from wherever Billy was deposited, and that I could still come over to do chores if Fred didn't want to handle them all himself. What it boiled down to was Fred insisting it was Mum's wifely duty to share with him a house of their own and Mum conceding that point. I suppose she was in love with Fred (but never in a way I could understand). In any case she was getting older and was no longer willing to fend for herself. I must say I appreciated her all the more when she put Fred straight on the matter of her close connection to me: "It'll be Willie's home, too, until he finishes school, has the money to buy himself a pony, and is ready to ride off to find his fortune—and hopefully not by searching endlessly among the silver mines like that damned Bill Antrim. Willie's departure could happen as soon as three years from now when he turns eighteen. But I suspect he'll wait until he's twenty-one." Fred didn't argue, no doubt accepting that Mum had her motherly duties, too, and realizing it was best not to ask her to choose between him and me.

Billy and Joe ended up in different homes so that the burden of caring for them both wouldn't be placed on one family. The bickering brothers didn't mind. Billy went to the Truesdell home, in part because the two boys, Gideon and Chauncey, knew things would be livelier with their fun-loving chum around. Their mother, Clara, was obliging, but she made Billy pay his way. The Truesdells owned the old Star Hotel and they put Billy to work waiting tables and washing dishes. Billy hadn't been big on doing chores for his late mother, but he took to having a paying job and, unlike other workers in the past, refrained from stealing any silverware. Catherine Antrim would have been proud of him. He was behaving like a good boy.

It was different with twelve-year-old Joe, whose host family was the Dyers. The father, Joe Dyer, still bore the scars from the knifing he took from a customer at the Orleans Club, that clamorous place he owned on Main Street. He had no use for Village Arabs but he didn't put Joe, who had never caused him any trouble, in that category. He allowed Joe to earn his keep by sweeping and mopping up in the club and didn't object when Joe learned to serve drinks, take bets, and gamble at cards. That's not all the onetime mama's boy did. I heard rumors he had gotten into the habit of slipping over to Silver City's Chinatown to smoke opium with the grown men. Billy heard the same rumors, but he told me he wasn't concerned because Joe had to learn to look after himself and to discover for himself that one didn't need opium or whiskey to have fun. Billy also quoted from the Bible story of Cain and Abel, the former having murdered the latter. When God asked Cain the whereabouts of Abel, Cain replied, "I know not, am I my brother's keeper?" That quoted statement worried me some, as did Joe's bad habits. But Billy assured me that he would never kill Joe and furthermore that a Mexican fortune teller had used a deck of cards to inform him that the younger brother would outlive the older brother by fifty years. I was not reassured.

The Chinese were not popular in Silver City, even less so than the Village Arabs. In fact, the leading white men, the same ones who complained about the Arabs, now encouraged those unruly boys to hound the Chinamen and ideally drive them out of town. None of us Arabs (yes, I was one of them, but barely) carried guns, but we filled our pockets with rocks, and some in our crowd hurled them at the offending Orientals. Despite his scrawny arms, Billy was one of the best rock throwers; he couldn't throw as far as me anymore but was more accurate when we fired away at trees, the sides of adobe buildings, barn doors, and once a line of clothing that laundryman Charlie Sun hung out to dry. Neither Billy nor I had anything against Sun (the red long johns we were aiming at were too irresistible) or his fellow countrymen. But it's true we were both in the neighborhood when a tragic incident occurred.

A collection of good citizens, upon seeing one of the unwanted foreigners, yelled "Rock him" and a half dozen Arabs obliged. One rock caught the Chinaman in the temple and he dropped fast. He flopped around on the ground, "like a yellow perch out of water," said Joe, who happened to be nearby, fresh out of an Opium den visit. The victim seemed on the verge of death and would have to be carried out of town if the white folks didn't want a Chinaman buried in their cemetery. Arabs, innocent or not, skedaddled from the scene. I rushed back to the new house on Yankie Street, ignored a question from Mum about where the fire was, and hid under the bed that Mum had obliged Fred to build for me. Henry didn't run, and neither did Joe, who apparently knew the victim and blamed his brother for throwing the deadly rock. The older brother denied it, and I know he was telling the truth. No adult questioned him, and Joe said nothing further, not wanting it known about his precocious opium smoking. The body was quickly carted away. I don't believe a lawman or anyone else ever confirmed that the Chinaman had died. Nobody ever said anything about it to us.

Silver City became the county seat of Grant County in 1874, but the sheriff, Charles McIntosh, took three thousand dollars   in county funds and bolted without notice that year, probably across the border into Old Mexico. He had been slightly wounded in the line of duty, from an anonymous bullet not a rock, and had often complained about low pay. Still, his crime surprised most everyone, though not Billy. "The sheriff liked to push people around, especially the Mexicans, Chinese, and Arabs," Billy told me. "He treated me like dirt. When he saw me standing or walking too slowly on the street, he'd tell me to move along and get back home. When he saw me in a store, he'd check my clothes to make sure I hadn't stolen anything, then tell the clerk to keep an eye on me. Twice he saw me reading the *Police Gazette* and both times he asked me if I was getting ideas for committing a crime in *his* town. He had shifty eyes for a bully. I bet he'd been planning his transgression against the town and the whole county ever since he realized he was too cowardly to handle the job. If you can't trust a sheriff, who can you trust?"

Even though Sheriff McIntosh had never said a word to me, I agreed with Billy that to be rid of him was worth the county losing all those "spondulicks," as Billy liked to call money. I knew McIntosh's suspicions about my pal were not made entirely out of whole cloth, but I said nothing, not wanting Billy to think me anything like his brother Joe. But Harvey H. Whitehill, who was voted in as sheriff in April 1875, had suspicions of his own and not without cause. Not long after he put on the badge, Sheriff Whitehill received a complaint from a rancher that Billy had taken three pounds of butter from his buckboard and sold the butter to a merchant. There was no doubt Billy had committed the petty theft; he confessed to me, if not the sheriff, that he needed money fast to buy a birthday present for me. He did promise the sheriff that in the future he would behave as if his mother in heaven were looking down on him. Mr. Whitehill, who had attended Catherine Antrim's funeral and knew how Bill Antrim had all but abandoned the boy, accepted the promise to be good and released Billy. I never did get any birthday present from my friend. That birthday, though, Mum went all out and baked me an angel food cake using one-dozen egg whites, a pound of butter, and a pound of sugar. Billy came over to the house and got more than one piece.

"It's as good as Mom used to make and she made the best," he told Mum. "It's a damn shame I can't be sitting at this table every night of the week instead of..."

A loud, stern voice interrupted him. "Be grateful for what you got, boy." It was the voice of Fred Schellschmidt, who we all knew didn't believe in his heart that boys like Billy, or even me, deserved an extravagant treat with "angel" in its name.

While Billy was no angel, he wasn't as bad as some of the Village Arabs or most of the despicable, dangerous, and desperate men who lived mostly for Silver City's nightlife. As a rule, the latter didn't bother Billy. One exception was Levi Miller, the village blacksmith, who liked to torment Billy by suggesting his late mother had made eyes at rich men while selling pies and his absent stepfather had cast aside his bastard sons to have carnal relations with javelinas. On occasion, the blacksmith would manhandle the slight lad and call him a bitch's runt. Apparently, this crude fellow didn't give Joe Antrim the same treatment, and he paid no more attention to me than he would a June bug. Exactly what he objected to about Billy was never clear, but it got to the point where Billy told me he'd see to it that the tyrant never bullied him again. I immediately thought of Billy's efficiency at throwing rocks or slinging them with a slingshot. Billy, though, had something else in mind—borrowing a rusty muzzleloading shotgun that Joe Dyer kept behind the Orleans Club's bar. I followed Billy to the bar but instead of diverting Mr. Dyer's attention so that my pal could grab the shotgun, I began singing at the top of my lungs "The Drunkard's Child," a song about alcohol abuse that Billy and I had learned from Mr. Antrim. Billy was shocked to hear me (a poor, reluctant singer) at first but, unable to resist exercising his vocal muscles, he joined in and drowned me out. Mr. Dyer didn't appreciate the ear-splitting performance and personally escorted us from the Orleans Club. Outside, Billy shrugged, cackled, and said: "What the hell. The situation isn't so dire. I doubt that old muzzleloader would have fired anyway."

❖

School continued with the capable Miss Richards running the show in fine form. She had a way with the wayward boys who leaned toward rebellion outside the classroom but who under her supervision were well-behaved if not always attentive. Joe was an indifferent student, not having a mother to please anymore and not being inspired by the knowledge his teacher imparted or her polished beauty. He usually sat slumped in a chair letting Miss Richard's words go in one ear and out the other. Billy, who continued to be influenced and invigorated by the teacher, compared his brother to a clump of petrified wood and Miss Richards to a fragrant blooming desert. His skill with words greatly improved all around, and that summer he created four lines of verse about her that he had me write down for him and slip onto her tidy desk:

> Our Incredible Instructor
> How fair you are and beyond compare
> So well-informed and, what's more, oh so pretty
> An Englishwoman who has traveled the world
> Yet landed happily for us in Silver City

Always alert, Miss Richards noticed what I did and asked me if I was the scholar and gentleman who had written the unsigned poem. I found a way to not tell a lie by simply saying, "Yes, ma'am, I put the words on paper." She smiled, thanked me, and sent me on my way, but I'm certain she knew the identity of the actual author. One week later, after Billy brought her a plump red apple that he had stolen from the Schellschmidt orchard, she made mention that his "artistic nature" was only exceeded by his "poetic nature." I reached the conclusion that it was Billy's fondness for his brilliant teacher that kept him, for the time being, from putting those dancing Mexican girls under intense scrutiny.

17

THE CLOTHES CAPER

The largely carefree days of my best pal—known to me as simply Billy, known to most others as Henry Antrim, and once called William Henry McCarty—could not last forever, but they ended far sooner than I expected. I suppose you could say it was his own damn fault, but I put much of the blame on a thirty-five-year-old stonemason. As his friend Harry Whitehill, one of the sheriff's sons, told me later: "Henry was a good amigo, not a bad fellow at all, even if he does have dancing eyes like Daddy says. Daddy also said that it was a shame about Henry's mother dying that way and his father not being around to see that he grows up right but that the boy still didn't need to go wrong. I say it was the fault of George Schaefer."

After Fred Schellschmidt brought Mum and me to the new house, Billy had begun to distance himself from me in other ways, at least to a degree that bothered me. I suppose I still saw him more than his brother Joe did but that wasn't saying much. At the same time, he drifted away from Village Arab activity after school and followed around the hard-drinking, sometime stonemason Mr. Schaefer, known by everybody (including Sheriff Harvey Whitehill) as "Sombrero Jack." Now sixteen, Billy decided it was high time he lived by himself and took a room at Sarah Brown's boarding house, where Schaefer also boarded. Billy began to wear his own enormous straw sombrero, and the pair would pull the two-feet-wide brims over their eyes to shade themselves from the sun when they took afternoon siestas together on Main Street. Passers-by looked on in disdain at the drunkard and his disciple, who weren't even Mexicans.

Earning his keep as a stonemason wasn't enough for Sombrero Jack, not when whiskey consumption and sticky fingers gave him grander ideas. On September 4, 1875, he acted on one of those ideas, breaking into Charley Sun's laundry and hauling two-hundred dollars' worth of clothing and blankets, as well as two Colt revolvers, to Georgetown, twenty miles to the east. Billy knew nothing about the theft until Sombrero Jack offered him some fresh duds if he would smuggle the stolen clothes back to Silver City and keep them until they could be disposed of later on. Billy agreed because now that he had a place of his own and could do as he pleased, he wanted to look sharper for the señoritas he'd soon be meeting, if not for his beloved teacher, Miss Richards.

When Billy gave me a brown wool vest with deep pockets for safely carrying a pocket watch (I didn't have one) or throwing stones (I no longer carried them), I was delighted. He said he wanted to give it to me on my birthday last May but he needed to save up more money as the vest wasn't cheap. I could see that and I thanked him profusely, thinking what a real pal he was and not questioning where he bought it. The vest was a little big for me but I figured Billy wasn't a good judge of size. I filled the pockets with a dozen marbles, strips of jerky, fishing line with hook, two pencil stubs, and a wooden-handled folding knife and wore it every day over whatever shirt I had on. Fred Schellschmidt never paid much attention to me, but he noticed that vest because he recognized it, singling out a slight rip in a small pocket "I haven't seen it since Charlotte decided she had too much baking to do and sent my clothes off to Charley Sun for washing," he said. "How in the devil did you get your hands on it, boy?" I knew to keep Billy's name out of it. "Mr. Sun must have given it to me by mistake," I mumbled. Fred called me a little thief but said he wouldn't tell my mother if I cleaned everything out of the pockets and brought it back to the Chinaman to be washed over again at my expense. I agreed, as much to protect my pal as myself.

I wasn't sure whether to mention this vest problem to Billy or not, but before I could decide, Mrs. Brown discovered the rest of the stolen clothes under Billy's bed at her boarding house. She knew Billy couldn't afford all those clothes; he could barely pay his rent. What's more there were several female garments in the mix. On September 23, she went to Sheriff Whitehill, reporting what she had found while cleaning Billy's room. "I couldn't count on him to straighten his own room," she told the sheriff. "I tried to look after him as a mother would, for he could be quite polite and had a pleasing smile even if I suspected he was one of those Village Arabs I read about in the paper. I of course was outraged to see what he was keeping under the bed. I felt it was my duty as an honest citizen to bring the matter to the attention of the law."

Sheriff Whitehill did his duty, too, arresting Billy and taking him before Justice of the Peace Isaac Givens. The two officials grilled the boy and got him to finger Sombrero Jack Schaefer as the mastermind of the clothing heist. The sheriff first escorted Billy to the boarding house to check on his story. Mrs. Brown said that Mr. Schaefer had fled on a fast horse with his rent for the week unpaid. She had searched his room and not found as much as a sock. The sheriff made his own search to confirm what wasn't in Sombrero Jack's room and what was in Billy's room. "I personally have little doubt that the stonemason was behind the burglary," he told his young prisoner. "I cannot, however, ignore your involvement. You are under arrest Henry Antrim, on the charge of larceny. Justice Givens agrees that you must be tried before a grand jury when the district court convenes in two months."

By locking Billy up, the sheriff created an uproar in certain circles. A number of Village Arabs took to the street in front of the jail to demand the release of one of their own, contending that the contrived larceny charge was a way to punish all of them. At the Whitehill home, his two sons, who were almost as close to Billy as me, and even Mrs. Whitehill protested the arrest. The very next day I went to the jailhouse in an agitated state to see Billy but was turned away. I returned, however, with my Mum, who agreed to put in a good word about the prisoner's character. This time, Harvey Whitehill asked us to sit down so he could explain his position. Mum spoke up first.

"I have known the young Antrim boy for years," she said. "He plays with my Willie; they are best friends. He would never do anything really wrong. Catherine Antrim was a long-time friend of mine. For many months our families lived together in a small house on Main Street."

"I am well aware of that, Mrs. Schellschmidt," the sheriff replied. "My sons have played with Henry, too. One important point must not be overlooked: Since his mother died, he has become wilder. This isn't the first time his misdeeds have been brought to my attention."

"Henry is a thoughtful and intelligent boy, one of the brightest in the classroom. You have only to ask his teacher, Miss Richards."

"No need. My sons have said the same thing."

"In all their time together, Henry has never once led my Willie astray."

"I don't doubt your conviction, Mrs. Schellschmidt, but there is the matter of the vest."

"Vest? What vest?"

"One of the items stolen from the Chinese laundry earlier this month. Charlie Sun says it was in the possession of your Willie. This has been confirmed by none other than your own husband."

Mum raised her eyebrows, then gave me her most severe look, those eyebrows lowering and drawing together causing wrinkles I had never noticed before to form on her forehead. I crossed my arms but had to look away from her and the sheriff.

"Billy didn't steal it," I mumbled. "He gave it to me as a present."

"I won't dwell on that matter. I'm willing to accept the possibility you accepted the gift without knowing that it was stolen property."

"The vest belongs to my stepfather. You could say that Billy was returning it to its proper home."

"This is the first I've heard of any of this," said Mum. "Are you suggesting you might put my Willie in your jail, too?"

"Not at all, Mrs. Schellschmidt. Nobody has ever accused your son of being one of the wild Arabs. Willie Schellschmidt appears to be on the timid side, and I'm sure he has done nothing *really wrong*, My boys say he is not bold and adventurous like Henry Antrim, but rather quite the opposite—white-livered and possessing a pudding heart."

The sheriff smiled at Mum and reached over to give me a quick pat on the head. I squirmed in my chair and bit my lower lip. I wasn't exactly sure what being white-livered with a pudding heart meant but I knew I didn't like it. Harry and Wayne Whitehill were Billy's friends, not mine.

"My son is not named Schellschmidt," Mum said. "I have taken my husband's name but I have allowed Willie to keep the last name Bonnifield."

"I stand corrected, Mrs. Schellschmidt."

"But we are here to talk about Henry Antrim, not Willie Bonnifield."

"That's true. You have more to say?"

"My son and I feel, sheriff, that we are obliged to speak up for your young prisoner since Bill Antrim has long been away and we are the ones who know Henry best. That disreputable stonemason who skipped town is the guilty party in this matter. Henry is not totally innocent, of course, but he does not deserve to be behind your cold, hard bars."

"Never fear, ma'am. This is the first time that young Antrim has been arrested and I sincerely hope it will be the last. I assure you he will not stay locked up for long. I am not unsympathetic toward youth. After all, I am a father of two Silver City boys as well as the sheriff of this young county. I am giving young Antrim time to think about what he has done and to consider what kind of punishment awaits him should he continue to act against the law. I can only hope that this short confinement will do him some good."

Mum and I of course recalled that the precocious Billy had been arrested once before in Denver for molesting the two Rittenhouse girls. Those charges were eventually dropped, and we had no reason to correct the sheriff by bringing up that sore subject.

❖

Two days later, I learned he was still in jail, so after school I went there for a visit to tell him that we were all behind him—Mum, me, Miss Mary Richards, the half of the class not jealous of his good standing with the pretty teacher, the Village Arabs who had never themselves been arrested, the Truesdell family, the Whitehill family except maybe the sheriff, Fred Schellschmidt (at least he told me Billy deserved his date in court), brother Joe (though I'm not sure he even knew) and Bill Antrim (who I assumed would be behind his oldest stepson if he wasn't off somewhere continuing his relentless search for silver). Sheriff Whitehill wasn't there, and I was refused entry by the new jailer, a short man with a pale, padded, and bumpy face that reminded me of a prickly pear cactus.

"Nobody goes in to see him who isn't a relative, sheriff's orders," the jailer said.

"His mother is dead, his father is far away, and his younger brother has no interest in the matter because he is smoking opium with the Chinese," I blurted out. "What I'm telling you, mister, is the truth. There is nobody else but me."

"And who are you?"

"I'm Willie Bonnifield, his best pal in the whole world."

"That's what I thought. Nobody."

"Look, mister, we both have stepfathers. It's like Billy and me are stepbrothers."

"*Almost like* is not relative. And the prisoner's name is Henry. Be off with you, scamp."

"I'll wait for Sheriff Whitehill to return."

"He won't be back today. You can't stay here. It's not permitted. Leave at once or else."

"If I don't, would you then arrest me?"

"If I did, I'd stick you in a separate cell and you still wouldn't see him. This is not some one-horse town with a one-cell jailhouse. So, if you know what's good for you, vamoose."

I shuffled my feet, but they weren't taking me away. I gave him some mouth instead, which was unusual for me in those early days. "I suppose you can't help being an absurd person," I told him, having recently learned from Miss Richards about absurdity when she discussed Shakespeare's *King Lear*. "I'll return tomorrow when there is a real lawman in charge." The jailer's face became bumpier and reddened in places as if it were flowering. He opened his mouth to give me a piece of his mind, but as he took a fierce step toward me, only spit came out. That got my feet going. I ran hard for thirty feet before looking back. I slowed down because he wasn't following me. I suppose he was like a trained soldier who could not under any circumstances desert his post. I continued on to my room and stayed there, thinking about my poor pal and trying to make sense of not only the jailer but also adults in general. After I got over being sad and mad, I regretted giving the prickly pear man my real name because I was sure he'd inform the sheriff and get me in trouble. Should that land me in the same cell as Billy, I told myself at last, I figured it would be worth it.

I returned to the jailhouse the next day, September 25, on my way to school. Sheriff Whitehill was there, but he was now the one with the red face and had no wish to talk to me. I heard the jailer reluctantly confess that it had been his own idea to keep Billy in solitary confinement in his cell without any exercise the last few days. I also learned that Billy was no longer there, because the jailer, as ordered by the sheriff, had allowed Billy to stand in the corridor between the cells for ten minutes that morning and the boy had found a way to miraculously escape. The sheriff wouldn't tell me how this was done, but I overheard the jailer saying there was no way in hell he could believe a human being, even one as inconsequential as the prisoner, was capable of climbing through a chimney hole.

Sheriff Whitehill caught me looking around town for Billy and told me he'd do the looking and for me to get off to school or he'd see to it that my hide got tanned. I told him that Mum had never done such a thing to my backside as far as I could remember and she had no cause to do so now. Furthermore, I saw fit to add that Frederick Schellschmidt had promised her he would not lay a hand on me without her permission. The sheriff was in no mood for backtalk and said if I wasn't headed to school by the time he counted to five he'd tan me himself just as he did his own two boys. I waited till he got to four, then took off on the run. I got to school quite late, which was a most unusual occurrence.

"Nice of you to join us, William Bonnifield," Miss Richards said. "Did you perhaps not hear the rooster crow or did you take too long eating your apple pie for breakfast?"

My classmates laughed because they knew playful teasing by our teacher when they heard it. Mum was the remaining partner in C&C Bakery and more than once I'd come to school on time but with pie on my face. I should have expected to see Billy's front-row chair empty, but still when I saw nobody sitting there my stomach went empty as if I were a starving waif instead of the son of Silver City's best cook. "It's Billy!" I cried. "He's missing."

"You mean Henry," Miss Richards said calmly. "We have been wondering about your friend Henry Antrim, as well, because we all expected Sheriff Whitehill to release him this morning so he could return to school."

She didn't explain. Everyone there, even Joe by that time, knew Billy had spent several days behind bars.

"That's right," said Harry Whitehill, and his brother Tyler nodded his head. "Daddy told us he had scared Henry enough. Daddy wouldn't go back on his word."

"Joe doesn't know where his brother might be," continued Miss Richards. "What about you, William. Where is Henry? Why hasn't he come to school?"

"Missing, like I said. He got away clean."

Miss Richards asked for clarification and various students asked for more details. For one of those rare times, the teacher lost control of her class. I told what little I knew about the escape, and one of the brighter boys suggested that our classmate could not have gotten away clean since his clothes would have been blackened by the soot in the chimney. The Whitehill brothers told what they knew about Billy's arrest, Gideon and Chauncey Truesdell suggested that the escapee might have run back to their house because their mother had always treated him so well, and Joe simply walked out of the classroom and back to town (but not to find his brother). Things settled down some when Sheriff Whitehill himself showed up at the school and confirmed that Billy's motive for escaping wasn't due to his worry about missing too many schooldays or his eagerness to see his revered teacher again. The sheriff explained to Miss Richards that Billy was desperate to get away because the jailer had been treating him badly and the boy thought he wouldn't be let out until the district court session began in several months.

The sheriff left to continue his search for his prisoner, who had made the mistake of escaping on the very day of his planned release. We spent only half a day in school because nobody could concentrate on the classwork, particularly not our teacher. I thought maybe Miss Richards wanted to go looking for her prize pupil herself, but later I learned she had other things on her mind and many errands to run. She was on the verge of ending her teaching career for she had fallen in love at first sight with Daniel Charles Casey, a Canadian-born carpenter who had come to Silver City to seek greater fortune and for the time being was in the same business as Frederick Schellschmidt. The couple wasted no time in getting married, and, in fact, Fred was the best man. That happened on October 5. No doubt that sudden happening would have dismayed Billy more than it did the rest of us, but by then he was long gone from Silver City,

Not that the ingenious Billy had left town immediately after clawing his way up the flue and squeezing his slender body through the chimney hole that Sheriff Whitehill described as appearing not even as large as his arm. As the two Truesdell boys guessed, Billy first hightailed it to their house, where their mother fed him and washed and dried his clothes while he took his first bath in weeks. By the time Sheriff Whitehill got around to checking for the young fugitive there, Billy had thanked Clara Truesdell and fled to the Schellschmidt house on Yankie Street. There Bill climbed up one of the apple trees in the back yard and wriggled along a shaky branch to reach my second-floor bedroom window.

"Nothing like a fruit tree bearing fruit," he said, biting into an apple he'd grabbed on the way up. "I don't blame Adam for eating the rest of the apple Eve had bitten into first. Eve must have had big brown eyes. I don't even blame the garden rattler or whatever it was that handed the apple to Eve and tempted her in the first place. Girls like to dance with snakes, even back then. Hell, I don't believe there's such a thing as forbidden fruit, because why would God create delicious fruit if we weren't meant to eat them? Anyway, Miss Richards says it may have been a fig tree, not an apple tree. You can't believe everything you read."

I only had a vague knowledge of what Billy was talking about. Neither of us was from what you'd call a religious family and our church-going through our first fifteen years had been limited. Not that we were raised to be sinners by any means. I suspected that Billy had been doing some Bible reading behind my back, probably after school with Miss Richards.

"Your hair's wet," was all I could think to say, thinking a person would get dirty hair but not wet hair climbing up a chimney.

"Mrs. Truesdell gave me a bath and dressed me in Chauncey's clothes because mine weren't dry yet and we knew the sheriff was getting close. She's a fine lady, wasn't even going to turn me in, but I figured I'd be better off spending the night here, what with the law sniffing around."

"Sure." Billy had entered my room via the apple tree before, but not once since Mum and I had come to live in Fred Schellschmidt's house had Billy stayed an entire night with me. Fred wouldn't stand for that. He figured if he allowed it one time, Billy would make a habit of it. For a long time, Fred had instructed Mum each night to make sure I wasn't sharing my room with irresponsible Bill Antrim's increasingly wild son. Formerly Mr. Antrim's friend and biggest supporter (telling Mum, "You can't blame a man for seeking his fortune in silver"), Fred turned against him because Mr. Antrim had neglected his obligations as a carpenter's assistant and his responsibilities as a father (telling Mum, "That man goes off roaming the countryside for six hundred miles like a damned boar Grizzly bear, leaving the two sons free to carry on like wicked little transgressors."). I never got the impression Fred really wanted me, but if he had to have me around to keep Mum, he would see to it I didn't transgress or embarrass his good standing in the community.

"Your stepdaddy still laboring at his hardwood shop?" Billy asked.

"No doubt, unless he's building something somewhere. Only on Saturdays does he take time off for the Orleans Club."

"Your Mum still laboring in her C&C kitchen?"

"As always. You're safe here until she comes up to say goodnight."

"At which time, I'll hide under the bed. But for now..." Billy brushed past me and swung up onto my bed as if it were a pony. He bunched up my pillow and stretched out on his back, looking as relaxed as a boy lying on a sunny riverbank next to his fishing pole. "Was I missed at school?"

"Yup, by Miss Richards and everyone."

"She knew I escaped?"

'I told them all. You see, I'd been to the jailhouse earlier. But they were expecting you to show up for class even before I told them."

"Impossible. I didn't even know I'd escape myself until I saw opportunity and climbed into the chimney. I doubt you'd have fit, Willie. Sometimes it pays to be short and skinny, if you're clever enough."

"I don't think it paid this time. Miss Richards must have talked to the sheriff or someone. She knew the sheriff planned to let you go free this morning. It would have happened if you'd found out you couldn't fit in that chimney."

Billy sat up on my bed, grabbed the pillow, and squeezed it against his slight chest. "That...that can't be true," he muttered. "The sheriff never mentioned letting me out. He..."

"He wanted to teach you a lesson. Miss Richards wouldn't make that up. And I would never lie to you. It's true, Billy."

"Darn the luck." He punched the pillow but then flipped it back over his shoulder. "Thanks for the news," he said, smiling as if he could even appreciate a good joke on himself. He again lay back on the bed and began to softly sing "Silver Threads Among the Gold."

I grew impatient for him to stop. "So, what now? I asked. "Maybe you can turn yourself in and they'll go lightly on you."

"I can't take back my escape through the chimney. I made the sheriff and that awful jailer look like fools."

"Never mind the jailer. He's probably a fool anyway. Sheriff Whitehill isn't a bad sort. Who knows? You might only have to spend one more night in that jail."

"One night too many. It's something to think about, though. Tonight, I'll sleep on it."

18

LEAVING SILVER CITY

Billy was not discovered in my bedroom that night. He slept in my bed as if he didn't have a care in the world. It must have been considerably more comfortable than his jailhouse cot. I spent a restless night on the floor, using for a pillow first my right arm, then my shirt, trousers, and socks bunched and held together by the leather strap I usually wrapped around my schoolbooks. I woke up with a stiff neck that hurt worse when I yawned and worse still when I turned my head abruptly to see if Billy was really there on my bed. He was, looking almost innocent the way he was curled up and clinging to my pillow.

I dressed in fresh clothes, my school clothes. I went to the window Billy had climbed through the night before. I had never climbed in or out of that window myself. The closest apple tree seemed to droop before my eyes. The morning wind was blowing in gusts from out of the West. An apple fell off the tree on its own. Lying on the ground it looked like the still-life painting Miss Richards had hanging in the classroom. I felt a tear forming and tried to shake it off because I heard Billy stirring on my bed. Neither of us said good morning.

"You awake?" I asked.

"I'm hungry," he said.

"Lots of apples out there."

"I know your mother makes you and Fred the Hammerhead better breakfasts than that."

"I can smell the eggs. They'll be biscuits, too. Come on."

"You bring me some."

"Oh. You aren't going to turn yourself in?"

"Nope. And I'm not staying. I thought it over."

"In your sleep? I thought you'd think better in the morning. Why go?"

"Might as well start fresh somewhere else. Silver City hasn't been the same since Mom died. I'm old enough to try my luck on my own anyway. Joe doesn't need me or even care if I'm around. I'll miss Miss Richards of course,

◆ 135 ◆

and some of the boys, and a few señoritas will miss me even if they don't realize it yet. But at my age, I don't need anyone. How about you?"

"Me leaving to be on my own?"

"Why not? It'll happen soon enough anyway. Fred Schellschmidt would love to get rid of you."

"I reckon, but Mum wants me...I mean, Mum wants me to get all the schooling I can get and...."

"I didn't exactly mean *totally* on your own. Why not come along with me, Kid. We'll be on *our* own."

"Where would we go?"

"Not certain. I do know the direction. We'd be going the way we've been moving all along since our families left New York City—west."

"We've been going more southward since leaving Denver."

"There's plenty of truth in that. Going south from Silver City should land us in Old Mexico. I'm not opposed to that at all. How about you?"

Crossing the southern border to leave the country seemed far more terrifying than crossing the western border to another territory. The wind was blowing harder now, shaking the apple tree as if it were a misbehaving child. A second apple fell, then a third. I gulped the inside air and backed away from the window. "No, you're right, Billy," I said without conviction. "West is better."

"Then it's settled. But first breakfast."

I didn't consider anything settled, but I went downstairs alone. Mum had indeed scrambled eggs for Fred Schellschmidt and me. I gulped the eggs down, hardly chewing. Instead of eating my biscuit, I pocketed it and asked for another. Fred looked at me suspiciously without a word. I thought I could hear him thinking unpleasant thoughts, so I announced that I'd eat the two biscuits on the way to school. He grunted and drank his coffee. Mum asked me where my schoolbooks were. I said upstairs and left the table without being excused. Fred grunted again and asked Mum to refill his mug. I noticed the December 26 edition of the *Silver City Herald* on a side table. As usual, Mum had gone out early to get the paper so that Fred could be up on the news before he went to his shop and dealt with chatty customers. I took a chance and grabbed the *Herald* on my way upstairs. I might have even stuck my tongue out at Fred; I hadn't totally broken the habit. Nobody called me back.

I handed both biscuits to Billy and spread the newspaper out on the bed. We read the short article about him together. Right there in black and white it said how Henry McCarty (using his original last name instead of "Antrim") had been in jail awaiting the action of the grand jury upon the charge of stealing clothes from Charley Sun's laundry. His escape through the chimney was mentioned, but it was left up to the reader to determine how unusual and clever that was. Using information that Sheriff Whitehill must have provided, the newspaper further stated: "It is believed Henry was simply the stool of 'Sombrero Jack' who done the actual stealing whilst Henry done the hiding. Jack has skinned out."

"They got it right, right?" I said when I was done reading.

"Not bad, but I don't like to be called the stool of anybody. And they make it sound like it was nothing to climb that cramped chimney. It surely was not nothing." Billy tried to stuff an entire biscuit in his mouth all at once. It was impossible so he gnawed at it like a rat as he read the article a second time. "Never made the news before, at least by name. Funny how they call me McCarty instead of Antrim."

"I guess, but if I ever make the news, I'll be glad to be listed as Bonnifield instead of Schellschmidt."

"How do you expect to make the news, Willie the Kid? You aren't liable to do anything bad enough to get written up about."

"You sound proud of what you did, like you expect to make more such news in future editions."

"You never know, but not here."

Billy finished off the first biscuit and took the second biscuit to the window. As he peered out, he started to nibble but thought better of it. "Better save this one for the road. Wind has died down. Does Fred the Hammerhead ride his chestnut to the hardwood shop?"

"Sometimes. Why?"

"Just thinking we could use a horse We'd have to ride double, of course."

"I'm supposed to be getting my books."

"You won't need schoolbooks where we're going. We can pick up a dime novel or two along the way."

"Oh. We're really going?"

"You're not dreaming, Kid. I won't be a jailbird in Silver City. We got to go."

"To Arizona Territory?"

"In Arizona I'll be a free bird. I won't be wanted there by anyone. You ready? We'll have to go out the window."

I said nothing. I wanted him here with me. "To go or not to go" ran through my head, carrying a great weight like Hamlet's "To be or not to be" in a Shakespeare play, one I had only heard about from Miss Richards. While my head felt as if it were about to explode (could death come from thinking too much?), Billy told me there was no more time for thinking or discussing. It was time to act. He didn't climb out the window, though. We both heard footsteps on the stairs. He scrambled under my bed.

By the time Mum entered the room, I was sitting on the bed, the folded newspaper across my lap, trying not to look guilty. "Your father wants his paper," she said, seizing the *Herald* but fortunately not trying to read anything herself. She examined the four corners of the room as if looking for dust or cobweb before settling on the three schoolbooks at my feet. She then lifted the strap that still contained yesterday's clothes and held it up for my consideration as if she were a prosecutor presenting damning evidence in a courtroom.

"Are you going to tell me what's going on?" she asked. She dropped the bundle of clothes onto my lap and bent down to pick up a few biscuit crumbs off the floor. She not only made the best food in the city but also could not stand any of her food going to waste.

"I'm sitting here, that's all."

"You aren't still eating yet you aren't ready for school."

"No, ma'am. I mean yes ma'am. I feel too sick to go to school." I pushed aside yesterday's clothes, gave my best groan, and lay on my side holding my stomach with one hand and my forehead with the other.

"But not too sick to go off somewhere with Henry Antrim," she said.

I could only manage a lesser groan. I glanced up at her with awe as if she had the same mental gift as that card-reading Mexican fortune teller I once saw (but didn't have the money to consult) on the Santa Fe Plaza.

"I know he slept here last night," Mum continued. "I heard snoring I hadn't heard since we left the Antrim house on Main Street. I peeked in after midnight. I saw you on the floor and him on the bed. I didn't wake Fred to tell him, but this morning after you had your breakfast, we both heard Henry's voice. And the newspaper was missing. I told Fred I'd bring down his paper and also see about Henry. He didn't want to go himself because he admitted if he caught Henry up here with you, he was liable to start wailing on you both with a strap. So here I am."

"Yes, you are. I'm glad Fred didn't come up. Thank you."

"I see Henry has already gone. Are you planning to meet him somewhere instead of going to school? How long does he expect to hide out? Tell me the truth, Willie. We know what is going on. I have already read today's *Herald*. Fred has now left for work, but on the way there, he intends to pay a visit to Sheriff Whitehill."

I got off the bed. My head and my neck still ached, and the scrambled eggs weren't sitting easy in my belly. I walked right into Mum's arms, though they weren't exactly outstretched. She seemed to be wringing her hands. Hugs between us were not infrequent, but she had initiated almost all of them. Not this morning. I wrapped my arms around her. There was less of her than I expected. Despite her endless cooking and baking, she hadn't put on many pounds through the years. She wasn't too skinny, though. She was just right—not fragile the way Billy's mother was at the end. It was no wonder Fred wanted her with him and was willing to put up with me to have her stay at his side. Thinking of her as a woman instead of just a mother was embarrassing me. I didn't want her to see my face, which I knew must be as red as the rising sun. I pressed my head to her bosom, tightened my hold, and fought back tears.

As she stroked my hair, I wanted to confess to her that Billy hadn't gone yet, that he was under the bed at that very moment and wanted a supply of food before he left town, probably aboard Fred's chestnut if it was still available. But if I said all that, I would have to admit that Billy wanted me to leave with him, and I couldn't do that to Mum. I finally pulled my left arm away to wipe my eyes with my fingers and my nose with the back of my hand.

"No matter what happens," I said. "I love you, Mum."

"And what will happen? You'll go to him?"

"No need for that," said Billy, crawling out from under the bed and quickly rising to his feet. "A good morning to you, Mrs. Schellschmidt. And what a lovely morning it is. Good traveling weather. Any of your fine food you can spare will be deeply appreciated. And the borrow of a horse would leave me indebted to you. Or did Mr. Schellschmidt go off this morning on horseback instead of on foot?"

Mum gently pushed me to the side so she could get a better look at my house guest. "If your poor mother could see you now, William Henry Antrim, it would surely break her dear heart."

"My stepfather already done that...did that," Billy said.

"Fred took the chestnut. And he has gone to the sheriff."

"Yes, I heard. I'd love to converse with you further, Mrs. Schellschmidt, but under the circumstances I'm sure you can understand why I have no wish to ever see Sheriff Whitehill again and why we must press on."

"We? I don't think so. Willie is going to school, and you'd best go with him. Miss Richards is expecting you both to attend class today."

"Not today, Mrs. Schellschmidt."

"You must. I cannot in good conscience allow my son to leave this house with you. If you insist on going, I can't stop you, but you go alone. For the first time in my life, I will not be willingly providing you with food, Henry, and if you take anybody's horse, Sheriff Whitehill will charge you with another theft. I'm sorry it has to be this way because you know I have always cared for you. But there are limits. Now, my support must end."

"No need to apologize, ma'am. I'll make other arrangements. You are a good woman and I respect your wishes. No need to provide additional biscuits or pie or anything at all. Besides, there isn't time. Come along, Willie, we'll go see Miss Richards. . .on foot." Billy then stunned Mum and me by picking my three schoolbooks off the floor and strapping them together. "Hurry, Willie. I know how much you hate to be late."

Billy carried my books to the window and opened it. I took one step with my left foot toward him, but my right foot refused to move.

"Your teacher will insist you stay at school," Mum said.

"Yes, I know," Billy replied, smiling almost like a shy schoolboy. "She is a good woman, too."

"I'm glad, boys. You are making the right decision. And if you are going to school, no need to go out by the window. You are welcome to use the front door."

I believe I did believe that morning there was no need for a long goodbye with Mum. But as much as Billy said he enjoyed classes run by Miss Mary Richards and as much as he wished to say goodbye to our teacher, we did not go to the schoolhouse. After we walked some one hundred yards, he made a 180-degree turn and headed at a brisk pace in the new direction. He had volunteered to carry my bundle of books on a long stick and he still had it resting on his right shoulder, so I continued to follow. We were headed in the general direction of the jailhouse, and I became hopeful he was giving himself up (for I was convinced his coming back to school would happen soon after he did that). Instead, he veered off again and took a path that followed back roads and crossed several vacant lots to the Truesdell home.

"Why have you come back here?" I asked when I saw Gideon and Chauncy come out the front door in a hurry. No doubt they were running late for school.

"Because Clara Truesdell is a good woman like your mother and Miss Richards but with the added bonus she is not as much a stickler for the law."

Billy intercepted the two Truesdell boys. He instructed them to take my books back to the schoolhouse and made them swear an oath not to breathe a word about seeing him and me. When the brothers dawdled, he yelled for them to run and not look back. They did so without question.

We then went inside—Billy eagerly, me dragging some but nevertheless not protesting. Mrs. Truesdell came through for Billy with flying colors. She accepted Billy's assertion that Mr. Schellschmidt had given me an outrageous beating for harboring a fugitive and that Sheriff Whitehill now intended to arrest both of us runaway boys. Without any fuss she packed a lunch for two and hailed a westbound stagecoach passing by the house. She paid the driver for two one-way tickets to the mining camp of Clifton, where she apparently had a cousin who would help us get settled in and stay safe, and told us to be good as we climbed into the coach and waved goodbye.

I suppose I could have backed out at some point before the driver cracked his whip and got those four pulling horses moving. Instead, I went along, not wanting to let down either Billy or Mrs. Truesdell. By going, I of course was letting down Mum and probably Miss Richards, too, but I didn't think about that until we were on a roll west of town. Even living with an unwanted stepfather, I hadn't seriously thought much about running away from home. It naturally wasn't something I would have done on my own or with anybody else but Billy. The driver was keeping the horses in a steady trot and I was crammed in the coach with Billy and five other male passengers. There was no turning back.

When we reached a relay station after the jolting first stretch of the journey, we jumped at the chance to stretch our legs while the horses were replaced. There was also just time enough to eat a meal. While the other passengers dined on hard-to-digest salt pork and mesquite beans, Billy and I enjoyed the chicken legs and bread Mrs. Truesdell had packed for us. It wasn't the equal of Mum's roast chicken and home-made bread, but I wasn't about to say anything. I kept thoughts about already missing Mum to myself.

"Ain't it grand to be free," Billy said, licking his chops.

"Didn't feel that way when we were packed in the coach like sardines."

"That's a good thing. Must be plenty of gold and silver in Clifton if all these folks want to get there."

"That why we're going?"

"Good a reason as any, plus Mrs. Truesdell's relative is there. It also happens to be where the western stage line ends."

"Oh. How far is it from here?"

"Can't say. Don't know exactly where we are or how far we've come. I don't figure we made it to Arizona Territory yet, but it's hard to tell."

"Oh, so Clifton is in Arizona Territory?"

"That's right. I thought you knew where we were going."

"Sure, Clifton." In my head I saw a place that was mostly underground because of the diggings, in the middle of nowhere, and surrounded by high cliffs, savage Apaches, and merciless bandidos.

"Mrs. Truesdell told me that Clifton is ninety miles from Silver City. We have no reason to complain. We haven't run into any hostile Indians or road agents yet. Beats walking all this way by a country mile or even riding double on your stepfather's horse. That old chestnut probably would have broken down by now or steered us way off course."

We stayed on course in our cramped quarters on a rutted road that

❖ 141 ❖

twisted mostly uphill to finally reach a canyon where we were greeted by a line of adobe huts on a stream bank and an impressive adobe smelter where Chase Creek emptied into the San Francisco River. The driver steered the stage around freight wagons, buckboards, horses, burros, and men to reach Clifton's only store. The owner, Charles Lesinsky, introduced himself, found out we didn't want to buy anything, and began rubbing his double chin while shaking his head.

"Looks to me like you made a long trip for nothing, boys," he said while seeming to measure us with his dark eyes. "You have no gold or paper money to speak of, right? It's a known fact that we don't take charity cases at our frontier post."

"We didn't ask you for nothing," said Billy as we stood tired and hungry just inside the general store's only door.

"True, but how are you going to pay for food and shelter? You're too young and soft to work in my copper mines or at the smelter, and all the small mining claims along Chase Creek have already been taken by Mexicans."

"We aren't necessarily looking for gold, silver or copper."

"Nobody from Silver City comes to Clifton for any other reason. Copper is what makes us grow. You running away from something, boys?"

Figuring the store owner must be reading guilt on my face, I put a hand over my mouth and nose and coughed. Billy handled the question better. "We paid full fare for the stagecoach ride, mister," he said. "We're free men."

"If you say so. What are your names?"

"Billy and Willie will do."

"As you like it. What we have here, Billy and Willie, are lots of hard men doing hard work in dangerous country. Mostly Mexicans work for me and my brother Henry. He had to travel all the way to El Paso and Juarez to hire workers."

"Mexicans are fine by me. But we're not necessarily looking for work. We're looking for someone."

"That right? A white man?"

"Yes. Could be he goes by the name Truesdell."

"I know every white man in town, and none of them goes by Truesdell or any other kind of dell. Of course, not every man gives his right name if he's on the run."

"Actually, it could be a lady. All we know is this person we're looking for is a cousin of Mrs. Clara Truesdell of Silver City, New Mexico Territory."

"You boys want a woman?"

Mr. Lesinsky, who had been mostly scowling since we met him, now laughed so hard that he jiggled from jowls to belly. Billy, who usually enjoyed a good laugh, even on himself, now looked as if he wanted to take a swing at the man's fleshy middle. All I wanted to do was back out the door, climb back into that miserable stagecoach, and wait for a return trip to Silver City.

Billy tipped back his hat, which was no Mexican sombrero but had a broad brim, and wiped dirt and sweat off his brow. "I didn't say this person is for sure a woman," he said. "But whoever it is, he or she is related to Mrs. Truesdell, and if you won't help us find him or her, we'll find someone who will." Billy seized my arm and easily pulled me toward the door.

"Hold it, you two," Mr. Lesinsky said, scowling again. "What you said is funny to me as it would be to any resident of our town. You see, females are in short supply in Clifton. We didn't get our first woman until 1873. Dona Juanita came to do laundry for the miners, and she's still at it. Hasn't had much competition for her services. Only a handful of women have come along since then, and they're all Mexican. Therefore, I can assure you that this white person you're looking for and who is a cousin of Mrs. Truesdell of Silver City, must be a man."

"Maybe this Dona Juanita can help us find our man."

"Could be. Every white man in town who wants his clothes washed goes to her."

'Come on, Willie the Kid. Let's go find the laundry."

"That away, boys." Mr. Lesinsky stepped outside after us and pointed south. "You'll find it on Shannon Hill. Next stage to Silver City doesn't leave for a couple days anyway."

"Thank you," I said, because Billy wasn't going to say it.

Hardly any of the town was on level land, but after the road made a bend to match the one in the San Francisco River, we saw many small buildings terraced into the side of a mountain. Painted on one adobe wall was a sign with a single word on it: *Lavado*, Billy didn't bother translating. He walked up the steep incline and motioned me to follow. I was panting by the time I reached the laundry, where Dona Juanita was bent over a fluted copper washboard. She looked up from her washing and cried, "*Oh Dios mío!*" Billy translated this time. "Means Oh my God!" he said. "I reckon it's hard to keep yourself clean traveling by stagecoach."

The laundress spoke some more in rapid Spanish, and Billy nodded his head while poking at his ears. "She says she can wash our clothes while we wait but it will cost extra," Billy said. "We'll have to strip to our long johns."

"But we can't even pay the regular price," I said.

"Right, I'll tell the señora. Keep your shirt on."

Billy tried to tell her in Spanish but she interrupted him: "Ah, Americanos. No pay, no wash." She kept scrubbing.

It turned out that Dona Juanita spoke English about as well as we did. She knew of no one in town named Truesdell, but she said she had at least a dozen customers who, like us, had arrived by stagecoach from Silver City. "All get dirty here," she added, now laughing as she scrubbed. "I know all the

Americano clothes, the Americano faces, and most of the Americano names. The Lesinsky brothers, Charles and Henry, of course. Joe Yankie. Bill Blood. Señor Pierce. Señor Webb. Señor Pollard..."

Billy cut her off. "Names don't do us any good, Señora Juanita. We'll have to wait for them to bring in their laundry or else try to look them up." He turned to me and socked me on the upper arm. "Why in the hell didn't we think to ask Clara Truesdell the name of her cousin."

"Señor Metcalf. Señor Stevens. Señor Roberts..."

"Never mind, señora. We can do without any clothes washing. But do you have a place we can wash up? And we could really use a bite to eat if you can spare it Any tamales perchance?"

"Señor Brennan. Señor Patton. Señor Solomon. Señor Antrim. Señor Longfellow..."

"Hold on there, señora. I believe one of those names rings a bell. You did say Antrim, didn't you?"

"Yes. Señor Antrim. Sounds like ant and rim. Blue plaid shirt. Tan wool vest. Heavy brown coat. He does not come often; not for a long time does he come. Says he can pay no more. Washes his own clothes in creek. You know this hombre perhaps?"

"Indeed, I do. We both do. I knew he was out here somewhere but had no idea it was this far out. He hasn't stayed in touch with me much since my mother died. You see, señora, this man Antrim is my stepfather. I guess all this copper in Clifton hasn't made him rich."

"I think not. No pay, no wash."

19

THE CLIFTON CONNECTION

B illy was surprised enough to learn his stepfather was so near, but he was in no rush to look him up. Dona Juanita took some pity on us, but she didn't believe in charity cases any more than Charles Lesinsky did. By splitting wood from a pile in back of the laundry we were allowed to wash our faces and hands in a water barrel and sit down at a table for the best tamales I'd ever eaten. Of course, Mum never made them. If I ever got home, I'd ask her to try her hand at preparing that delicious dish.

"Excelente," Billy said when he had finished seconds. He sat back in his chair and patted his belly as if he was the owner of a hacienda. "Tell me, Señora Juanita, do you have no daughters?"

"Nor do I have sons. Not even *el marido*. I am *la madre* de Clifton."

The two of them began to converse in Spanish with a few English words sprinkled in, and I felt left out. I couldn't follow what they were saying though I heard Billy refer to señoritas several times despite our host being a señora. Neither noticed my yawning or how my tired head drooped almost to the tabletop.

"What about him, your stepfather?" I said when I finally saw an opening. "I thought you wanted to find him."

"I never said that. I wanted to find Mrs. Truesdell's cousin."

"But we don't know if he's Pierce, Pollard or one of the others. We know who your stepfather is."

"Right. But that Bill Blood she mentioned sounds more interesting. Who'd want to get on the wrong side of an hombre who calls himself Bill Blood?"

"Be serious, Billy. It's getting late. You don't want to get on the wrong side of your stepfather either."

"It wouldn't be the first time. It's not like he knows we're even here. And when he sees I've come all the way to Clifton, Old Bill Antrim is likely to be none too pleased. I bet he says right off: 'What the hell you doing in Arizona Territory, Henry? You don't belong.'"

"Señor Antrim has camp higher," said Dona Juanita, pointing to the ceiling. "You go up hill to the top, then over for a short way. But darkness comes soon. Comes early on this side of the mountains."

"Old Bill will keep. My pal has sleepy eyes. A good night's rest will do him some good. You happen to have a place we can bunk? Most anywhere will do."

Dona Juanita reached out and lifted my chin with two fingers that were long but had short, broken nails. "*Pobrecito*," she said as she studied my eyes and offered a warm smile. I admitted to myself that the only time lately Mum had smiled at me in that consoling way was when Catherine Antrim's death brought me to tears.

"We can stay, *si*?" Billy said.

Our host patted the top of my head and stood up, turning her attention to the plates and glasses on the table. "You wash dishes, you can sleep."

We set out up the mountain the next morning with our bellies full of tortillas and beans. Billy promised to pay her back for her hospitality if his prospecting stepfather possessed any mineral riches and was willing to share any of it. After we were out of Dona Juarez's hearing range, Billy said to me: "I didn't have the heart to tell the kind lady how big an *if* it is. Me saying to her I'd return with money from Old Bill is like a man in the desert telling his partner dying of thirst he'd bring him a drink if the mirage ahead turned out to be a waterhole."

We found a prospector's camp that Billy said must belong to his stepfather because hanging inside a partly torn tent was a tan vest and blue plaid shirt and in a far corner was a broken shovel that had a rusty blade, a splintered shaft, and no handle. Little else was there—an unrolled bedroll, one blackened pan for cooking, two gold pans made of tin, a pick, a wood spoon, a fork with a broken prong, three tin cans (two were empty, the can of peaches was open and half full), a jug of whiskey, and a weathered copy of Mark Twain's *Roughing It* laying open to a section about 1860s mining on the great Comstock silver lode, which even I knew wasn't anywhere close to Clifton.

While waiting for Bill Antrim we finished off the tinned peaches and each took an unpleasant swallow from the jug. After an hour we figured he must have been hard at work somewhere so we tramped up and down the mountain for a couple more hours before coming upon a man with the longest nose I'd ever seen, an overgrown gray beard, and a curt manner. He kept a long rifle pointed in our direction while telling us that Old Bill had passed by earlier on his way to town for supplies. The miner, keeping a safe distance, pointed out the path to take and shouted after us: "The son of a bitch won't have much luck. Money-grubbing Lesinsky ain't taking no more IOUs." I kept looking back and each time the miner was still eying us as if he suspected we'd turn around and come back to steal whatever gold or silver he had accumulated.

When we got down the mountain, Billy started laughing, a delayed reaction to Gray Beard's parting remark.

"Nothing funny about Mr. Antrim wanting to use IOUs," I said. "If he still isn't doing well, how's he going to help us?"

"Don't expect he will. I'm not laughing at his bad luck. I'm laughing because I never heard anyone call my stepfather a son of a bitch before. A cheap bastard, yes, but not an SOB."

We found Bill Antrim, whose black beard looked rather trim, sitting on the ground in front of Lesinsky's store, his back to the wall. He wore a heavy coat and was puffing on a corn pipe, but the pipe dropped out of his mouth when he saw Billy and me coming up the street.

"Land sakes!" Old Bill said. He picked up his pipe but not himself. He slouched and tapped the pipe bowl against his knee. "Where in thunder did you two come from? There was no stagecoach today."

"Willie and I arrived on yesterday's coach; we spent the night at Dona Juanita's laundry," said Billy. "You were able to buy tobacco, I see."

"Why not. Plenty of tobacco available. Our store has most everything I need."

"But I heard you might be short of funds to pay for anything."

"Don't be a wiseacre, Henry. Somebody in Silver City suggest that you come out here to check on me, Fred Schellschmidt perhaps?"

"No. Nobody there knows exactly where you are as far as I can tell. When you came back for that short time after Mom's funeral, I thought you were having better prospects somewhere but didn't want to reveal the location."

"I've had some ups and downs. That's to be expected. There's not all that much gold or silver in them hills. This is copper country."

"I heard. This one of your down times, sir?"

"Not so down, boy. I'm working for Charles Lesinsky's brother, mining copper at four dollars an hour. It's only temporary. I'm building up another grubstake before I move on. Whoever said I had money problems is dead wrong. Who said it?"

"Heard it from a prospector with a long rifle, long nose and gray beard. We ran into him over in the Shannon Hill area, not far from where you're staying."

"You don't say. That would be Red Longfellow. His beard used to be reddish. He's been sticking his big nose in my business since I got here. Our partnership didn't work out. We both thought we were stealing from each other, and, let me tell you, there was very little worth stealing. Where's your brother Joe?"

"Saw no reason to bring him along. Don't see much of him anymore, except when we go to school."

"Shouldn't you be with him in school right now? That's what Catherine wished for you two scamps. There some kind of trouble back in Silver that caused you to make this long trip to see me?"

"It was a surprise to find you here. We came looking for someone else."

"That right? Who was it? I'm sure it couldn't be that old maid washerwoman. Dona Juanita is as avaricious as the Lesinsky brothers."

That made me finally interject something into their family conversation. "She treated us nice, Mr. Antrim," I said. "We ate well and slept well."

"No fooling? She must have a soft spot in her stony heart for two wayward boys. I have no doubt you paid her well for her trouble. Have much money on you, do you? Does your mother know you're here, Willie? I didn't think so. She would never permit you to go off like that."

"Clara Truesdell knows we are both here," Billy said. "She told us we could look up her cousin in Clifton. Trouble is I didn't catch his name."

"You already met him, boys. Red Longfellow is Clara's second cousin once removed or something like that. If you're looking for him to help you, you're out of luck. I found out the hard way that he's a surly, ungrateful son of a bitch, not to mention a petty thief."

After Mr. Antrim went back inside the store to pick up his meager supplies, Billy and I helped carry them back to Old Bill's tent, where we made a fire outside the front flap and cooked beans that the three of us ate out of the same pan. Finding Red Longfellow again and telling him that his cousin in Silver City sent us didn't seem like such a good idea anymore. It was not Mr. Antrim's opinion, however, that we were better off in his camp. In fact, he said the two of us should take the next stagecoach back to Silver City so we could continue in school and finish growing up into men.

"Fifteen ain't grown up," he said once he had taken two gulps from the whiskey jug.

"I turned sixteen," said Billy. "So did Willie."

"That don't change a damn thing. It's a hard life out here. I carry this for protection." He opened his overcoat and gave us a glimpse of a Colt six-shooter with walnut grips he had tucked into his waistband. "Clifton's no place for a good woman or children of any kind."

"We ain't a couple of kids." Billy stood on his toes to look taller and put his hands on his hips to look wider. "We ain't a-feared."

He's not speaking for me, I felt like shouting. Instead, I silently moved closer to the fire and stayed there even though smoke was getting in my eyes.

Mr. Antrim took another swig. "You're loco to want to stay here, boy." He poked Billy in the chest. "I made arrangements for you and Joe to be looked after in Silver. Now get on back there and get looked after." Mr. Antrim then turned to me and gave me a quick shove away from the flames. "And you, Willie the Kid, were about to get your pants set on fire. Go home. I know Fred can be a pain in the ass at times trying to shape everybody the way he wants them to be as if flesh and bones are no different than blocks of wood. Even I, who was his best friend, can see that. Still, the man is your stepfather and he comes with your mother, a good woman. Hell, you're lucky to have a mother who's still alive! How could you run off on Charlotte this way? No doubt she's already sicker than a dog with worry."

"Her health is fine, thank you," I said, but I stepped back from the fire and crossed my arms on my belly. I wanted to go home.

Billy was more defiant. He used his tongue to free a bean caught on a back tooth and spit the bean into the flames. "You know plenty about running off, stepfather," he said.

"Your mouth ain't getting any smaller, boy. You best mind your tongue. I am your stepfather goddamn it."

"That's what I said. Yet when I come to you in trouble, all you can say is you don't want me here."

"You didn't say anything about being in trouble. What kind of trouble you in, boy?"

"I escaped from Sheriff Whitehill's jail."

"Jail? You were in jail?"

"That's right, for a robbery I didn't commit."

"Falsely accused again, huh? Don't tell me Willie did it."

"Of course not. Willie wasn't even involved."

"Then why is he here with you?"

"He's sticking by me."

"Because you're innocent?"

"Not exactly. He is my pal. That's what pals do."

Billy glanced at me, so I gave a slight nod. Mr. Antrim then tilted his head to look at me, and he looked hard, biting his lower lip and narrowing his eyes as if he couldn't quite make out my face away from the flames. I wondered if he might be thinking about his strained relations with old pal Frederick Schellschmidt. But I wasn't thinking of Fred. I was still thinking of Mum and feeling as if I had committed a worse crime than Billy. I had deserted the one who had given me birth and nurtured me for sixteen years. Billy, on the other hand, couldn't very well have deserted his mother when she was already dead.

"Tell me then, who did this robbery if it wasn't you or Willie?" Mr. Antrim said.

"A lowdown fellow name of Sombrero Jack. He skipped out and left me holding the bag, the clothes actually."

"What clothes?"

"Fred's vest and other stolen garments."

"Garments? All you did was take some clothes, and Whitehill put you in jail for that?"

"I already told you. I didn't do it...I mean the stealing part."

Mr. Antrim threw his hands in the air but then quickly lowered them to lift the jug again. He took his largest mouthful so far and swished the whiskey around in his mouth before finally swallowing vigorously. "I don't usually take to the jug this much," he said. "You can sure enough drive me to drink, boy."

Billy now crouched before the fire. "You aren't going to help us, then?" he asked.

"Help you? I didn't hear you ask for help. I can't give you any money, boy, if that's what you mean. I don't have it. Maybe I'll get it after I leave here and make a strike someplace else on my own. Then I'll bring you some, you and Joe."

"You want me and Willie gone then?"

"In a word, yes. Go back to Silver City, like I already told you. If I don't know where you are how can I bring you money once I have it."

"There's no going back there for me. You're off on your own. Well, I can do the same."

"Suit yourself, but I'm not going to support you here. I have enough trouble feeding myself."

"Fine with me. I don't need your kind of support. It's weak as piss."

"If that's the kind of boy you are, get out...get out of my camp this instant."

"You bet I will." Billy stood up and looked out into the darkness. An owl gave a hoot. "We both will...in the morning."

Mr. Antrim took one final swig and his head kept nodding until he nodded off.

❖

Billy and I slept under one blanket toward the front of the tent. Bill Antrim lay in his bedroll at the back. For the longest time I heard him sucking on the stem of his pipe or blowing over the opening of his jug to create a hollow whistle. I finally fell asleep, long after Billy did but before his stepfather stopped sucking and blowing.

At dawn Billy woke me by whispering into my left ear: "It's time. Listen to the old goat. He sounds like a pick breaking up ore—hard, worthless ore." I listened with only one eye open and didn't disagree though I had never swung a pick and I don't think Billy had either. I shut the one eye, squeezed both eyes tight, and tried to get back to sleep so I could go back to dreaming I was in another place. Billy would have none of that. He either spit in my ear or stuck his tongue in it. "Get out of bed, you sleepy head," he said, pulling the blanket off my shoulder. I had heard that saying before, from both Mum and his late mother. I curled into a ball and cradled myself. But when he punched me in the back of the neck I straightened up. I also must have howled.

"Shhhhhh," he said, none too softly. "You want to wake the dead?"

He meant his stepfather, who of course wasn't dead. The old man was snoring. But he may as well have been dead. Billy was done with him.

"What's up?" I asked.

"We're going. Find that beefy jerky he bought yesterday. We'll need something for the road and there are no biscuits or apples."

What road? I thought, but I kicked off the blanket and crawled around in the dim light trying to find Mr. Antrim's supplies. We had slept in our clothes, but it was cold and getting colder. I stopped my search to watch Billy grab a couple of his stepfather's unwashed shirts and the heavy overcoat. Billy wasn't satisfied with just the clothing. Now wearing the coat, he knelt beside the snoring bearded head and felt around until he touched the exposed barrel of Mr. Antrim's walnut-handled six-shooter. Slowly and gently, Billy pulled the rest of the gun out from under the bedroll and shoved the Colt into the righthand pocket of what was now his coat. "Let's beat it," he whispered as he scrambled on all fours toward the tent door. I rose to my knees and glanced at Old Bill. He was still breaking ore in his sleep but looked peaceful. I shrugged and followed young Bill out of the tent, going on all fours like him. I hadn't found the jerky or anything else to eat, but I felt like a petty thief anyway.

We silently worked our way down the mountain as the sun rose, somewhat reluctantly, I thought. It was still not full light when we were halfway down and reached the primitive camp of Red Longfellow. He was sleeping in the open, on his back with only his gray beard and long nose showing above his holey blanket. I froze some fifteen feet away, but Billy moved ahead on his toes with one hand clutching the stolen shirts and the other in his gun pocket. I started to feel sorry for Red Longfellow even though I knew little more than his name. That unexpected feeling ended soon enough when I noticed his long rifle lying next to him like a faithful and deadly dog. "Billy, Billy," I said in an urgent whisper. "Look out."

"I see it," Billy replied. 'It ain't about to go off by itself. It appears we're out of luck, though. This old goat is short on supplies worse than that other old goat."

"Why are we here?" I whispered. "Just 'cause he doesn't like your stepfather doesn't mean he's gonna like us."

Mr. Longfellow suddenly opened a lone eye, reached for his long gun, sat up, and flipped over onto his belly. As Billy and I fled, he hollered that we were about to meet our maker, and I didn't have to look back to know he was lining up a shot from a prone position. We zig-zagged in different directions, perhaps each hoping the crazed prospector had taken aim at the other one. We heard the boom but kept going. We must have been a half mile from the camp when we finally converged and stared at each other in disbelief. We had both escaped unscathed but must have looked like wounded soldiers. I dropped to my knees, panting and holding my side. Billy leaned against a juniper tree and with both hands pressed the extra shirts to his chest as if trying to stop the bleeding from an open wound. Neither of us spoke. We kept looking back to see if Red Longfellow had given chase. He hadn't but we still didn't breathe easy.

"Old Bill was right about one thing," Billy finally said. "A fellow would have to be crazy to stay here. And for damn sure he and that Red Longfellow are both crazy."

I was still shaking and not thinking of being hungry yet, but Billy said he wanted food right away and chided me for having failed to grab something to eat from his stepfather's camp. "Look at all I got!" He threw me the two shirts he was holding. "Put 'em both on. You look like you're freezing, Kid." He didn't realize it wasn't the cold that was giving me the shakes, but I did as I was told. "The coat is mine," he added, yanking the Colt out of the pocket. He studied it from butt to muzzle as he weighed it in his right hand, then opened the loading gate to examine the cylinder. "A couple of cartridges," he announced. "That's good for now."

"You gonna try to shoot us a rabbit to eat?" I asked.

"No, not going to waste a bullet. Better save them in this dangerous country."

For the next couple minutes, he debated aloud with himself about whether to make our next stop Lesinsky's store, where plenty of food could be had if we could stomach a little more pilfering, or Dona Juanita's laundry, where we knew tortillas were available if we were willing to work for them. He didn't ask my opinion, but I reminded him that the laundress was not only a good cook but also mighty nice and that I was not averse to doing a little work. I took three or four steps in what I thought was the direction of the laundry as if I were finally taking the lead. He quickly caught up to me, turned me right at a right angle, and kept marching. I followed him, thinking the overcoat looked rather large on him but also thinking what a relief it was that he had put the six-shooter away. And soon enough we reached the welcoming laundry.

20

A MAN NAMED BLOOD

Billy was disinclined to do women's work. For most of the rest of that day, he chopped and stacked wood in back while I helped Dona Juanita with the washing of clothes, including the two shirts that once belonged to Bill Antrim. In return we ate tortillas and beans to our heart's content and to our bellies' content, too. I hadn't eaten so much since the days when Catherine Antrim and Mum had teamed up at the little house on Silver City's main street to concoct grand suppers for Bill Antrim, Fred Schellschmidt, Billy, Joe, and me. There was little chance of either Bill Antrim or Red Longfellow showing up at the laundry as they were the only two white men in Clifton who weren't paying anymore to have their clothes washed.

One of the customers who appeared that afternoon was Bill Blood, a man with no facial hair and a shaved head who seemingly lived up to his name. He showed up with red streaks on his shirt, a red splotch on one trouser leg, a left boot spotted in red, and a rash on his face as if he had the measles. He waved at Dona Juanita a handkerchief once white now a dark red and seeming to turn darker still before our eyes. When I dared take a closer look at the handkerchief, I saw the initials BB stitched on a corner. "Blood feud," he said in reply to my inquisitive eyes. "You're a stranger in these parts. You look too young and well behaved to be a lawman. You aren't by any chance related to the Cahills in the Fort Grant area and formerly of Ireland?"

"No, sir."

"Glad to hear it. And the young stranger with the ax out back?"

"A friend. We're from Silver City, just visiting, not feuding."

"Then we're all friends here. What do they call you?"

"Willie."

"Just Willie?"

"Willie the Kid."

"Good enough. Go out to your friend now, Willie the Kid. You ask him for the loan of his coat and bring it back to me. You got that, friend?"

"His coat, sir?"

"I want to stay decent in the good, clean house of Señora Juanita." He turned his back on me and moved off to the far corner of the room. He removed his boots with some difficulty and shed his shirt, his trousers, and his long underwear. He put them in a neat pile and carefully laid the bloody handkerchief on top. Now stark naked, he clapped his hands. I checked him over quickly but saw no wounds. "Haven't you gone yet, boy," he said, clapping harder. "Go, boy, go. Need that coat."

I ran out back to fetch Billy's coat. Billy came with it. My pal had taken the six-shooter out of the pocket. He saw what state Bill Blood was in and handed him the coat but kept the Colt pointed at the man's chest, which unlike his face and head was thick with hair. Once his body was mostly covered by the coat, Mr. Blood instructed me to take his clothes pile to Dona Juanita at the washing tub. "Thanks, friend," he said. "If anyone can get the blood out, it's her." He had ignored Billy's weapon so far, and I wasn't sure if that made him brave or foolish.

"What happened to you?" Billy asked. "You been shot?"

"No." He lifted his left leg to examine and scratch the calf. "As I made my getaway a jumping cactus pricked me"

"But all that blood on your clothes?"

"It's all Cahill blood. At that range, blood goes every which way. Don't worry, my body's clean, and I won't get any blood on the coat you have kindly provided for me...unless you intend to shoot me, of course. Name's Blood, Bill Blood."

"Mine's Billy McCarty; some know me as Henry Antrim."

"I see. I don't use an alias. Bill Blood is my only name. Glad to make your acquaintance, Billy Henry."

"The loan of the coat is only temporary, you understand."

"Naturally. You can put your pistol away, kid. I'm unarmed. I lost my six-gun after the fight, very careless of me."

Billy lowered the Colt but kept it next to his hip. "You killed that Cahill fellow?"

"No. Put a couple of slugs in him, but Windy Cahill is too mean to die. It happened down Fort Grant way, where I sometimes have call to visit. He's a loudmouth Irishman who operates a blacksmith shop outside the fort. I'm Welsh. We're all Celtic you know, and I generally have nothing against the Irish, especially if you two boys happen to be Irish, but Cahills and Bloods have been feuding one way or another ever since the first haughty Cahills crossed the Irish Sea to Wales during the Reformation."

I remembered Miss Richards mentioning the Reformation one time at school, but all I could recall is that it was something that happened overseas a long time ago. I could tell by Billy's blank look that he must have missed that particular class. But the recent shooting near Fort Grant interested him more than that reformation thing. "Let me get this straight," Billy said. "You're telling me that some ancient feud is the reason you shot this particular Cahill twice."

"I wouldn't say that. He didn't shoe my horse right and damaged its left front hoof. I told him I wasn't going to pay him for his shoddy work. He took exception. We argued, in the course of which he said something to me, the only Welsh phrase he had ever learned, one that his grandfather Cahill had used to insult one of my Blood ancestors. Windy told me I was *dim gwerth rhech dafad*—meaning not worth a sheep's fart, if you'll pardon my English. Now I used to be a cowhand on Henry Hooker's Sierra Bonita Ranch, so naturally I didn't take kindly to that remark. I pulled my pistol, and called him a *bastaird*. That's an Irish word I know. In English and in Welsh it's 'bastard.' I was showing off, didn't want him to think he was the only one who could curse in a second language. Anyway, the bastard didn't scare. Instead of backing off, Windy came at my head with a pair of tongs. He meant to squeeze my brains into a pulp. My first shot went off by accident, the second was well intended. In retrospect, though, I'm glad I didn't shoot with intent to kill. There are worse things in this country than a careless Irish blacksmith with a big mouth."

"I would have shot the blacksmith myself," said Billy, smiling. "But I wasn't going to shoot you." He further lowered his six-shooter and looked around for a place to lay it down. He finally settled on walking up to Mr. Blood and sliding the Colt into the coat pocket. "If you don't mind. I don't want to forget it. It'll still be there when you give me my coat back, right?"

"You can count on that. I might buy your gun, though."

"Not for sale."

"I thought you could use the money."

"I'd hate to part with my pistol."

"Has sentimental value, does it?"

"No, but it once belonged to my stepfather."

"Would you part with it for ten dollars…what the hell, I like you, friend. How about twenty?"

"Twenty bucks, huh?" Billy rubbed his chin with one hand and tugged an ear with the other. "No, better not. My stepfather might come along looking to get his gun back."

Mr. Blood laughed. Billy seemed surprised at first but then joined in, and the next thing I knew they were sitting at the eating table chatting about Ireland, food, feuds, Fort Grant, U.S. Army privates, the San Carlos Apache Indian Reservation, various mining camps, Mexican ladies, and horses, both wild ones and stolen ones. I listened to them while standing by the wash tub watching Dona Juanita scrub Mr. Blood's clothes on the washboard. She was diligently working out the challenging blood stains with soap and salt of lemon.

I answered her call and took the tub outside when it needed to be emptied and refilled so that the clothes could be rinsed in clean water. When I returned, Mr. Blood and Billy were still at it, talking freely with smiles flashing every so often—not the way Billy talked with Bill Antrim or, for that matter, the way I talked with Fred Schellschmidt.

"You need a gun in this country, but you need a horse even more," Mr. Blood was telling his attentive listener. "After shooting Windy I accidentally dropped my six-gun when I ran into the cactus. I rode away fast without it in case the soldier boys or somebody down that way objected to what I'd done to one of their denizens. Not that Windy is universally loved and not that I'm exactly unknown in those parts, but sometimes a man gets labeled something when he only appears to be that and is really something else."

"I know about that," said Billy. "So, you ran away, huh?"

"Running isn't always the answer, Billy Henry. I considered going back, if not to plead self-defense than to at least retrieve my six-gun. That soon became a moot point, though, because my horse, the one with the bad shoe, began to hobble. I pushed on slowly and my horse was game, but my luck was bad, not to mention the horse's luck. It stepped in a prairie dog hole and broke its leg. I wanted to shoot the poor beast to put it out of its misery, but I didn't have my gun, of course. I was at a loss as what to do when I saw Indian ponies making dust in my direction. I took off running and found some rocks to hide behind. I didn't feel too bad because I figured those Apache braves would eat my horse."

"Did they?" asked Billy.

"Not sure. It had gotten dark by then and while they were making camp I slipped away, making a clean escape. Still, my worries weren't over by a long shot. A man on foot with a half empty canteen can't last long in that unforgiving country. My luck changed early next morning, praise the good Lord, when two heavily guarded freight wagons carrying valuable ore to the smelter happened by. I climbed aboard, telling them I had been attacked by Apache horse thieves armed with Winchesters, and just like that I got myself a free, life-saving ride back home to Clifton. Tomorrow, bright and early, I put on my clean clothes to look presentable when I go see Charlie Lesinsky, who owns the store but does some horse trading on the side."

"And what happens after you buy yourself another horse?"

"And a gun, too, since you aren't selling yours."

"Then what?"

"I ride."

"Where to?"

"Whichever way I decide to go, with the wind or against it. I'm no miner, you see, and when you get right down to it Clifton doesn't offer a free man much in the way of opportunity or pleasure. Arizona Territory is big, boy, full of places to see. I'll avoid the Fort Grant area for a time, of course, because self-preservation is important. I may ride over to Sierra Bonito and go back to cowboying for Mr. Hooker. On the other hand, I might round up some horses and get into the horse-trading business myself."

"I sure could use a horse," said Billy. "Clifton has nothing to offer me either."

"Silver City does," I said, which gave both Mr. Blood and Billy a start. They must have forgotten I was still in the room listening to their palaver.

"Hell it does," Billy said. "No more jail time for me."

"Jail?" said Mr. Blood. "What did you do, kid, rob a bank or a piggy bank?"

"It was nothing. The sheriff made a mountain out of a molehill."

"What kind of nothing was it? You can tell me. You see, I haven't always been on the right side of the law myself."

"He stole clothes," I said, but I have no idea why I would pass such a remark about my pal to a near stranger.

"I didn't steal the clothes!" Billy yelled. "I was given them."

His words were somewhat misleading, but I dropped the subject. Dona Juanita did not. "What clothes!" she cried out. "You stole clothes!" Nobody realized she'd also been listening. She temporarily deserted the washboard and put her wet hands on her wide hips. Her face was a dark red, like Bill Blood's handkerchief.

The confusion over what clothes were stolen and by whom took some time to clear up, but at last Dona Juanita was satisfied she was not harboring two devious young thieves and that the Silver City crime would not be repeated in Clifton. Bill Blood seemed amused by it all, but then got the laundress all riled up again by casually asking if the coat he was wearing had been stolen and, if so, whether that theft had occurred in Silver City or Clifton. Billy avoided addressing that issue by getting angry, more at me than Mr. Blood for some reason, and shouting, "It's just a damn coat, not a horse!"

In an agitated voice, Dona Juanita recollected seeing the coat on Bill Antrim several times when he was still paying to have his clothes washed. In response, Billy told her a lie: "He's my stepfather, for God's sake. Stepfathers are supposed to look after the children even if they aren't his, right? Of course, he lent me his overcoat. It gets cold in the mountains, doesn't it?"

"I get the picture," Mr. Blood said, tapping his fingers on his bald head. "I assume you borrowed the six-shooter from your stepfather at the same time you borrowed his coat."

"What of it? You're no lawman. I think you'd better give me my coat back now."

"And your six-gun, too?" asked Mr. Blood as he slid it out of the pocket. With his trigger finger inside the trigger guard, he spun the revolver around several times. For a few seconds the barrel was pointed at a stunned Billy. Then, with a laugh, Mr. Blood repocketed the gun. "Saw John Wesley Hardin do that once in Abilene, Kansas. I've been practicing ever since in my spare time."

"I've seen it done myself," Billy said, although I suspected that was another lie.

"No hard feelings, Billy Henry. I wouldn't shoot you over a gun, a horse, or a coat. Still friends?"

"Sure. Keep *my* coat and *my* gun till your clothes dry."

I was the one who took Mr. Blood's clothes out back to hang on the line behind the wood pile. He and Billy went back to amiable talk at the table. Dona Juanita went back to the washboard and worked like the devil to make Mr. Blood's handkerchief white again.

21

THE SEPARATION

It wasn't until after the sun went down that Bill Blood's clothes dried. I held them out to him and he nodded his approval. "Spotless," he said. "You've done it again Dona Juanita." The laundress merely grunted. She was busy making tamales again. "First things first," he said, motioning me to stay put. He then waved Billy forward so that they stood side by side, their hips and elbows touching. "Let's do this thing right," he said.

What he did was take off the coat and, with great solemnity though naked again, raise the arms of Billy before slipping the coat on my pal. For some reason it made me think of the March 1873 wedding ceremony in Santa Fe when Bill Antrim put a ring on Catherine McCarty's finger. To my great surprise as I was thinking that, Mr. Blood showed off his wit by telling Billy, "Take this well-armed coat as a symbol of my friendship."

While Bill Blood put on his clothes, Billy buttoned the coat and slid his right hand into the pocket as if to make sure the Colt was still there. "Great, Mr. Blood, but all I can give you in return is a jovial handshake," he said flashing his bucktooth smile.

"That'll do for now, kid."

When they shook hands, their bodies shook all over from laughter. I saw nothing even slightly humorous in the exchange. When Dona Juanita called for us to come and get it, I was the first one to the table, but I couldn't enjoy a single bite. It was as if my mouth wanted to taste something good but my nervous stomach was saying *I'm already overloaded with distress and dread.* The problem, as yet unstated by any of us, was that Billy wanted to leave Clifton with his new, older friend to find adventure in the wilds of Arizona Territory while I wanted to leave Clifton with my longtime pal to find security once more at our home in New Mexico Territory.

When Bill Blood went to see Charles Lesinsky about acquiring a horse, Billy told me he was going along and not just for the ride. "He's like me," said Billy, "a man who wants to be free and won't ever settle for bland respectability or sitting inside a jail cell."

"He's twice your age, shot that Windy Cahill fellow, and who knows who else. He very well could be running from the law, maybe from the soldiers at Fort Grant, too."

"I like the cut of his gib."

"Gib? Is that like a handkerchief?"

"Hell no. It's a...well, something on a sailing ship. Miss Richards said it. I mean others have said it before her. She said Sir Walter Scott wrote in a book fifty years ago about liking the cut of somebody's gib. That's good enough for me."

At that moment I wasn't finding Billy's *gib* too likable. He was too easily swayed by the near stranger, too easily influenced by him, too ready to follow. So, what did I do? I followed without thinking any more about it. Hadn't Mum once thought Billy was a bad influence on me? No doubt Fred Schellschmidt still thought it. And Billy's late mom used to think her oldest son was a bad influence on younger brother Joe. I guess everyone is influenced by somebody for better or for worse. I figured Bill Blood was influenced by John Wesley Hardin.

Bill Blood was no miner and no longer a working cowboy but he had accumulated a good deal of greenbacks and gold. Billy and I found that out on the way to the store. He veered off without explanation and Billy followed, then me. In a gulch south of town, our leader paused at a pinyon pine and stepped off twenty paces through the sagebrush to the west.

"This isn't the way," I finally said.

"Shut up," said Billy. "Mr. Blood knows where he's going."

"My friends call me Blood. Mister doesn't work for me. The likes of Windy Cahill called me Mr. Blood. And calling me Bill or Billy might get mighty confusing since we have two Bills in our trio."

"I'm used to the two Bill thing. That's why people started calling me by my middle name—Henry."

"No, Henry won't do for you. My father had a mule named Henry. Let's stick to Billy. And our other friend is Willie."

"I call him Willie the Kid."

"I like it. And you'll be Billy the Kid. After all you are both kids."

"We are sixteen but coming from you, kid doesn't sound so bad, and Willie is used to being a kid."

"That's the spirit. Kids like you keep me young. I'm sure you two have enough sense to follow my lead, to do as I say, and to keep your mouths shut when we aren't alone."

"Sure. Mr...I mean Blood. But why have you led us way out here?"

"We're looking for three flat rocks forming a triangle. They are somewhere in this sage."

It was me who stumbled on the three rocks. Mr. Blood left two rocks in place but tossed the third one aside and told Billy and me to start digging. We both hesitated. "With your hands," he instructed, making clawing motions in the air. "I can't buy a shovel until the diggings done, and once it's done, I won't need a bloody shovel."

Billy and I went to digging, working our paws like a couple of oversized ground squirrels. Mr. Blood gave us verbal support, encouraging us to work faster. What we dug up were two bags, the smaller one full of money, the larger loaded with gold dust. Mr. Blood took a bag in each hand, weighed them as if he were a human balance scale, and laughed. "A bag in each hand is worth two in the bush. Well, fill the hole back up, boys and replace the rock. You never know when we might want to use this hiding place again."

We did as he asked. He didn't thank us, but he merrily clicked his tongue and said, "Now, we can go shopping, kids. Follow me."

And we did. Mr. Blood moved with long, rapid strides and sometimes Billy and I had to run a little to catch up. At one point when we fell behind, I whispered to my pal, "Where do you think he got all that?"

"Worked for it, I suppose," said Billy.

"You think it could have been stolen?"

"No matter to us. We didn't steal anything."

"I know but you didn't steal those clothes from the laundry in Silver City either and you still got put in jail."

"Why don't you shut up, Willie. I'm done thinking about the past."

At the store and the corral in back, Charles Lesinsky treated Mr. Blood like an old friend, not questioning where or how the customer acquired enough money and gold to purchase not one but two plump horses (he said Billy and I would have to ride double for now), two Mexican saddles, a Colt Single Action Army revolver with holster, and enough food to last the three of us up to a week on the trail.

"I see you've taken two willing lads under your wing, Blood," Mr. Lesinsky said after the transactions were completed. "No doubt they can make up for a lack of size and hardiness with youthful enthusiasm and resolve."

"I got me a couple of good kids, Charlie," Mr. Blood said as he adjusted the flapless holster that carried his prized six-shooter.

"I wish you luck. Where you all headed on those two fine mounts I reluctantly parted with?"

"You were well paid as always. We are free to roam, exactly where I cannot say; we may go far or we may stay near. Either way, we can't afford to stay in Clifton at the Lesinsky prices."

The store owner didn't smile but he took no offense. He walked us out the front door chatting about the advantages and disadvantages of living in places like Prescott and Tucson instead of Clifton. "You come back and see me anytime, Blood," Mr. Lesinsky said, "but especially when you're looking to buy anything at all. Always like to oblige."

Mr. Blood mounted the taller of the two horses and sat tall in the saddle with our food secure in his saddlebags. Ready to lead, he watched Billy and I climb aboard the second horse, which I noticed had a sag to its back. Neither of us had much experience riding, but Billy, wearing his overcoat with pride and holding the reins, looked poised and prepared to ride like the wind if our leader so ordered. I squirmed some behind him, thinking about saddle sores and mishaps to come. A hard wind, I figured, was liable to knock one or both of us off that swayback. I wasn't sure exactly why Mr. Blood was taking two inexperienced kids like us along with him. I suspected he wanted us to do his bidding, even if it was his dirty work or involved activities outside the law. I kept thinking of the Cahill shooting and Mr. Blood's bloody clothes. I was convinced, without any other supporting evidence, that he was an armed and dangerous man, if not a killer like John Wesley Hardin then certainly a robber like Jesse James. That made Billy and me his gang.

"Let's move out," Mr. Blood said once he saw us reasonably settled in our saddle. His horse stepped lively but our horse didn't move. "Squeeze him with your legs, boy, and lift the reins up and forward toward his head."

"I know," said Billy. "I was waiting for Willie the Kid to stop shaking."

We lurched forward but then had to move out of the way in a hurry. The stagecoach from Silver City had rolled into town as if it owned the street and pulled up in front of Lesinsky's store. Our horse managed to side step with minimum help from Billy, but then reared on its own. Billy kept his seat through the bucking, but I flew off, hitting the ground hard but thankfully away from the coach and barely missing a water trough. I was stunned and it took me a few minutes to realize I was in one piece and could stand up despite the pain that spread out from the ribs on my right side.

Billy showed no inclination to dismount to help me or for any other reason. Mr. Blood was also still in the saddle, looking back at me with a cross between astonishment and annoyance. It was the driver of the stagecoach who jumped down from his perch to help me to my feet. The second person to reach me was a passenger who alighted from the coach and dusted off his traveling clothes before approaching me. He put a familiar firm hand on my left shoulder, fortunately not on the one that ached the most from my crash to the ground. "Still alive, I see," he said. "That's good. Surely wouldn't want to bring you back to your mother dead."

❖

That Frederick Schellschmidt had been sent on a mission from Mum to bring me home was a mixed blessing. I wanted to go on with Billy to wherever, even on that horse, if necessary, but I did not want to go anywhere with Bill Blood. At the same time, I wanted to go back to Mum in Silver City but preferably not without my best pal and not in the same stagecoach as my stepfather. It didn't matter, though, what I wanted. I had no control over my immediate fate. Mr. Blood showed no desire to keep me with him even before Mr. Schellschmidt showed proof of his stepfather standing—a marriage certificate. I even heard Mr. Blood whisper to Billy that this unexpected development was for the best because my delicate heart wasn't committed to a life of adventure and because the swayback would be hard-pressed to carry two riders for more than a few miles.

The stagecoach driver told Mr. Schellschmidt the next scheduled run to Silver City was two days hence and he couldn't leave sooner even if a passenger wanted to see his dying wife or mother. "And," he added, as if he wasn't worried about losing any customers, "you have said yourself that the boy's mother is suffering from nothing but unbridled maternal instincts and excessive worry. I need a drink."

Fred didn't argue with the driver. He sighed and looked off to the hills. "I suppose if we must be here a couple of days, I should look up Bill Antrim," he said to nobody in particular. "We used to be damn good friends."

"Things change, Mr. Schellschmidt," said Billy. "Bill Antrim used to be my stepfather."

I hoped Mr. Blood and Billy would postpone their horseback departure from Clifton, which would give me time to try to talk Billy into taking the stagecoach in the opposite direction. Convincing him would admittedly be a tall order, one that I figured wouldn't have been so tall had Catherine Antrim been alive in Silver City waiting for her oldest son to come home. At the very least, though, I would have the extra time with Billy and we could pronounce our everlasting friendship and perhaps make plans for a reunion in the near future. Alas there would be no long goodbye.

"I'm making tracks now," Mr. Blood coldly stated. "You come now to see the elephant, Kid, or you remain blind as a bat and green as a grasshopper."

"I got to go," Billy said to me with both hands gripping his saddle horn. "You can see that, can't you?"

"I can see you think you got to go," I said, my eyes already becoming blurry from tears.

"Hey, you aren't crying, are you, Kid?"

"Of course not, Kid. Must be the dust in my eyes from that bad fall I took."

"We'll meet again."

"In Silver City?"

"No, I'm not going back there. It'll have to be somewhere else."

I rubbed my eyes and tried to become mad instead of sad. "Whatever you say, but I'm not coming back to Arizona Territory," I said. "New Mexico is our home."

"We've both had other homes. I can't say where it'll be, but we'll meet again someday."

"In heaven or hell?" The tears were coming back fast. I still couldn't get angry at my best pal.

"We're just separating for a while, not dying."

"That's right, Kid, so separate," said Mr. Blood. "Come on," he added, making a wide sweep of his arm as he rode down the street.

"See you later, Willie the Kid," said Billy. He must have squeezed the horse too hard with his legs and hoisted the reins with too much vigor because the swayback darted recklessly after the man called Blood.

Not until I saw that my pal wouldn't fall out of the saddle was I able to speak. "See you later, Billy the Kid," I called out. I was unsure if he heard me.

EPILOGUE

It would be many years before I saw William Henry McCarty again, and by then most of the world knew him as Billy the Kid and nobody besides him and Mum were calling me Willie the Kid. I have no idea how long Billy stayed at the heels of Bill Blood before breaking away and truly going off on his own. In Clifton I had questioned, at least to myself, the character of that man, and it has remained my opinion that Mr. Blood led Billy down the wrong path in life, glorifying the dangerous practice of brandishing six-shooters and teaching him not only how to ride horses but also how to rope them, corral them, and steal them. I have nothing to back up that accusation because I never heard his name mentioned again and Bill Blood would no more make his mark on history than I did.

I did hear again of Windy Cahill, the man who survived being shot twice by Blood. News reached Silver City in mid-August 1877 that Kid Antrim (the name Billy was going by at that time) had argued for reasons of his own with Mr. Cahill and in the course of the physical confrontation that ensued had fired a fatal .45-caliber bullet into the gut of the horse-shooing bully. Billy, as Bill Blood had done two years earlier, fled the scene of the shooting. Despite extenuating circumstance, Kid Antrim was branded a murderer and considered a fugitive from justice in Arizona Territory. Now using the alias William H. Bonney, he fled on a stolen horse back to New Mexico Territory where he technically was still a fugitive for breaking jail in September 1875. But not even Sheriff Whitehill wanted him for that anymore, and in any case, eighteen-year-old Billy gave a wide berth to Silver City, where no doubt plenty of folks still missed him but where I was the only one having trouble living without him.

I did see Bill Antrim now and then in Silver City because he had at least partially restored his old friendship with Frederick Schellschmidt and, I suppose, wanted to check up on Joe Antrim, who would keep his stepfather's surname the rest of his life (he died penniless and all but forgotten in Denver on November 25, 1930). I'm not sure Billy ever again saw his stepfather, who never forgot that Billy stole his six-shooter and shirts in Clifton and never really got over his two bugs—the wandering one and the mining one. Mr. Antrim rarely mentioned his two stepsons before his death at age eighty in 1922.

In September 1877, according to a rumor Fred heard at his carpentry shop, Billy did run into his brother, who was working on a ranch on the Mimbres River. Fred said that Joe raised an old rifle and was prepared to shoot the suspicious, threadbare stranger leading a spent horse until Billy called out, "Hold on there, Joe, don't you recognize your own brother?" Fred added that the brothers reportedly talked about the good old times and even hugged and kissed before a tearful departure and Billy's resumed flight from justice. I didn't want to believe the rumor. I was jealous. I knew the brothers had gone through some bad old times, too, and didn't always get along, and I couldn't understand why Billy hadn't made more of an effort to see his best pal.

After leaving Joe to his ranch work, Billy pressed on to Georgetown to see our old teacher, now Mrs. Mary Casey instead of Miss Mary Richards, having moved to the new town with her new husband in fall 1875. I heard about the brief Georgetown reunion sometime later from Mum, who had always admired Mary's ability to teach and reach out to the children of Silver City, including the so-called Village Arabs. Mary, Mum reported, had given Billy her best wishes and money for the road, which didn't surprise me since he had been her favorite pupil. I could understand what she saw in Billy (charm, wit, potential, etc.), and I suppose if I'd been in his boots, I would have gone to see her, too. But hearing about it was another sad reminder that Billy hadn't come to see me upon his return to our territory. Of course, I wouldn't have been able to give him any money; still, our friendship should have counted for something!

Don't get me wrong. I wasn't angry at Billy for steering clear of Silver City and me. I was disappointed, of course, but mostly in myself. He was on the run and I knew, as he did, that I wasn't up to being on the run with him. I saw it as a weakness in myself, lacking the courage to go out in the world and experience all kinds of rip-roaring adventures that I could later tell my children about should I ever actually leave Mum, find a wife, and raise a family. Of course, I was only eighteen in 1877 but I would continue to see myself as timid and cowardly for another four years. Some might say I was fortunate not to have been with Billy the Kid during those years considering what he went through—all his horse and cattle stealing, all his fighting and killing as a Regulator during the ferocious Lincoln County War, the bounties that Territorial Governor Lew Wallace put on his head, his capture by Sheriff Pat Garrett at Stinking Springs, his imprisonment in the Santa Fe Jail for three months, his sentencing by a judge in Mesilla to be hanged for murder, his escape from the Lincoln County Courthouse during which he killed two deputies, and his violent end when Garrett shot him down on July 14, 1881, in Fort Sumner. Trying to live such a life alongside my spirited boyhood pal surely would have resulted in an even earlier death for me. Consider that Billy's two best later-day pals were killed in 1880 when ambushed by a Garrett posse—Tom O'Folliard on December 19 at Fort Sumner and Charlie Bowdre four days later at Stinking Springs.

As it was, I continued on without Billy in Silver City, living a quiet, mostly peaceful life devoid of adventure ("a terribly dull life," according to Harry Whitehill, who only saw me from time to time because we had memories of Billy in common). My schooling ended soon enough for three reasons: discontented teachers who made nothing as interesting as Mary Richards had; my dislike for all subjects except reading and writing, and I didn't have to be in the classroom to do those; and my wish to earn my keep so I wouldn't be dependent on iron-fisted Frederick Schellschmidt or a burden to Mum. Fred never stopped reminding me how he had saved my life by rescuing me in Clifton, Arizona Territory, from "the evil clutches of that young outlaw." He didn't want me around, and I didn't want to be around him, yet I went along with Mum and agreed to work for my stepfather as a carpenter's apprentice. I was paid a pittance but, to be truthful about it, probably more than I was worth. Like Bill Antrim before me, I showed no more ability to work with wood than a toothless beaver. Learning the skills of this trade was impossible, especially when my teacher considered himself God's greatest gift to carpentry since Jesus Christ.

After two grueling months of lost labor in Fred's shop I walked out of there for good, which was a relief to both of us. I stayed in the house, though, because Mum didn't want me to leave, and I served as her unpaid kitchen help, something I had been doing more or less my entire life. I never mastered the art of baking pies and such or cooking an eatable meal for her husband, but I was there every day willing to do everything from endlessly loading the cooking stove with wood, straw or cow chips to turning a crank for fifty minutes to churn sweet cream into solid butter. By 1878 I was trying my hand at other occupations, ones that actually paid something, including washing dishes at the old Star Hotel (something Billy had done at a much younger age) and even sweeping the jailhouse and making coffee for Sheriff Harvey Whitehill. The sheriff would gain the distinction of being the first lawman to arrest the infamous Billy the Kid, but I never held it against him or told anyone it wasn't true (there was that false arrest in Denver).

My most satisfying employment was with the *Grant County Herald*. I started at the newspaper in 1878, not actually writing anything but running errands for publisher James Mullen, distributing newspapers, and eventually assisting the printer. It got me out of the house, away from Fred. Even temporarily getting away from Mum was welcome those occasional times I felt I was suffocating in the kitchen or my bedroom. I wasn't making any news in Silver City or even reporting on it, but at least I was helping to spread the news to the citizens. In February 1880 I finally was allowed to put something I wrote into the *Herald*—my coverage of Alfred M. Conner's announcement that he had leased the Bennett building and was converting it into Silver City's premier hotel, the Southern. I quit, though, a year later, just before the *Herald* merged with the short-lived *Daily Southwest* to become the *New Southwest and County Herald*. I had good reason: I had finally received a letter from Billy. I had sent off maybe a dozen letters, addressed to "William H. Bonney, General Delivery" in Lincoln, Fort Sumner, Albuquerque and Santa Fe, but I'm not sure he ever got one of them.

By the end of 1880 Billy the Kid had become a national sensation after his surrender to Pat Garrett at a one-room rock house near the boggy waterhole known as Stinking Springs and his well-publicized transfer in shackles north to a jail in Las Vegas and on to the Santa Fe Jail. In his cell in the capital city, not far from where his mother had married Bill Antrim seven years earlier, he awaited trial for murder but was hoping to receive a promised pardon from Governor Wallace. It is well known that on January 1, 1881, he dashed off a one sentence note to the governor: "I would like to See You for a few moments if You can Spare Time." He signed it "Yours Respect. W.H. Bonney." Lew Wallace was out of town and never replied.

In March, Billy wrote four letters. Three were further desperate appeals to Governor Wallace to see him. In the first, written on March 2 and signed "Yours Respect—Wm. H. Bonney, Billy suggested, "It will be to your interest to come see me." Two days later, after not receiving a reply, Billy wrote, among other things: "You had ought to have come see me as I requested you to. I have done Everything that I promised you I would, and You have done nothing that You promised me." He signed that one: "Patiently waiting/I am Very truly Yours, Respt./Wm H. Bonney" Lew Wallace again did not respond or come down to the Santa Fe Jail. Billy's third letter to the governor was written on March 27, the day before he was to depart Santa Fe for trial in La Mesilla, three hundred miles to the south. "For the last time I ask," Billy penned, "Will you keep your promise. I start below tomorrow. Send Answer by bearer. Yours Respt. WBonney." That same day Billy requested more ink and paper to compose his fourth and most lengthy March letter, in which he made an appeal of a different sort to an old friend—me! His letter writing had greatly improved since he wrote me those letters in the old days before he got his best schooling in Silver City from Mary Richards.

Dear Willie the Kid,

How's it going, Kid? Long time no see. If you could only see me now! If anyone from the old Silver City days could see me now—my mother, your mother, Old Bill, Fred the Hammerhead, Joe, Clara Truesdell, Sheriff Whitehill, the Village Arabs who weren't so bad, the lovely señoritas I danced with, our dear Miss Mary Richards, you name it. For three dreary months I been locked away in this snake pit of a jail, and Satan knows, Kid, it ain't no Goddamn respite (I don't imagine Mary would approve of my language but I've heard language a hell of a lot worse). There's no escape, not by way of a chimney (remember how I pulled that off when I was a skinny kid of sixteen; not that I'm what you'd call plump now at twenty-one) or tunneling out (last month some of the other occupants joined me in trying to dig out with spoons and our bare hands but we were done in by an informer; which reminded me how Joe used to tell on me to Mom).

In truth I'll be out of here tomorrow but in the custody of three cold-blooded lawmen who are escorting yours truly to La Mesilla. The authorities plan to try me down there for two different killings that I admittedly took part in (but so did a bunch of other Regulators): Buckshot Roberts, though it wasn't my bullet that finally silenced that hard-to-kill son of a bitch at Blazer's Mill, and Sheriff William Brady, who deserved to die in Lincoln though I can't say for sure one of my bullets actually struck the bastard. Don't you judge me too harshly, Willie. I killed some men for certain but not nearly as many as the newspapers say. What's more, every one of my so-called gunshot victims was asking for his fate.

I should have written you earlier. Ever since we went our separate ways from Clifton five or six years ago, I've been a mite busy, but I know that's no excuse. I admit I've been BAD about letter writing, at least until this month in the Santa Fe Jail. I am assuming you are still in Silver City and that you will get this letter in time to come over to La Mesilla as early as possible in April to lend me support. I figure I'll need it, even if it's only your moral support. I don't believe you'll be busting in with six-shooters blazing to free me from a hostile judge and an unfriendly courtroom.

Hope your Mum is feeling right peart and still baking the best damn pies in the territory. As for your imperious stepdaddy, I don't wish him to be cold as a wagon tire but I wouldn't mind if he has gotten himself catawamptiously chewed up. Then there's you. I figure you're still being a good kid, but I hope not too Good.

See you later (in La Mesilla I hope)—
Your pal, Billy the Kid

(P.S.: I told you back in Clifton, I'd see you again someday. Better make it some day in La Mesilla in April just in case they decide to hang me)

❖

I did make the 110-mile stagecoach trip from Silver City to La Mesilla, arriving late in the afternoon of April 9. I learned from a bundled-up Mexican woman sitting under one of the shade trees next to the side of the courthouse that the charge against Billy for the murder of Buckshot Roberts had been dropped three days earlier on some technicality over jurisdiction. I expressed my joy, but the woman slumped, squeezed her eyes shut with her fists, screamed, and sobbed. I attempted to console her, but she tightened the shawl around her head and chanted: *Bilito esta perdido, Bilito esta perdido, Bilito esta perdido.* I wasn't sure what she was saying but I knew it wasn't good. Later I got a translation, "Billy is lost," and that is what I chanted in English after I found out the verdict in the Sheriff Brady murder case had come in that very day. My old pal had been found guilty of murder in the first degree and given the death sentence.

That night and for the next three nights after that I slept under the stars in the plaza. I heard more than a few Spanish-speaking residents or visitors call Billy *El Chivato*, which meant "the little goat" or "kid." I wasn't able to actually see Billy until he was called into the courtroom on the afternoon of April 13 and stood shackled, silent, and sullen while Judge Warren Bristol sentenced him to "be hanged by the neck until his body be dead" in Lincoln County in May, Friday the 13th. As Billy was being led out of the courtroom, I shouted out to him, *Te Quiero*, which means "I love you," according to a Mexican gentleman who had also made a sleeping space for himself in the plaza. "Very good," Billy replied, making the guards wait for a moment as he flashed a grin over his shoulder. "Tell it to a señorita someday, why don't you. Glad you made it, Kid. Safe journey home."

So much for my reunion with Billy. I spent one more night in the plaza but I was back in Silver City when heavily armed lawmen handcuffed and chained the shackled Billy to the back seat of a Dougherty wagon at 10 p.m. on Saturday, April 16, and began the long trip to Lincoln. Later, I remembered thinking how Billy should instead have been a free man dancing freely with enchanting La Mesilla girls that Saturday night and for many Saturday nights to come. On April 21, his escort delivered him into the custody of Lincoln County Sheriff Pat Garrett. For many nights at home I had bad dreams about the old Mexican woman wailing for *Bilito* in front of the La Mesilla Courthouse and, worse still, me weeping while watching Billy's body dance at the end of a rope on the gallows in front of the Lincoln County Courthouse. Nevertheless,

I told myself I had not shown enough support for my old pal in La Mesilla and must show further support, no matter how painful it might be to me, by attending his hanging on May 13.

Whether or not I would have gone through and been a witness to an execution is a moot point. As everyone knows, Billy the Kid did not hang. On April 28 he escaped from custody at the Lincoln County Courthouse, fatally shooting Deputies James Bell and Bob Olinger in the process. Some of the folks (both Anglos and Mexicans) who had sympathized with Billy up to that time turned against him for those two killings. But in Silver City, whether he knew it or not, he still had my undying support. More importantly to the Billy the Kid story, the young fugitive still had so much support in Lincoln County from men and women alike that he chose to stay there rather than flee again to Arizona Territory or to Texas or better yet to Mexico. In Fort Sumner at around midnight on July 14, 1881, Sheriff Garrett fatally shot Billy in the bedroom of the Kid's longtime friend Pete Maxwell. Fittingly, my romantic old pal was at the Maxwell home to see the sister of Pete, Paulita Maxwell, who was half French, a quarter Irish, and a quarter Hispanic. I heard tell that at the end, Paulita was the señorita whom Billy the Kid loved the most.

Billy's death, to my surprise, did not leave me miserable and forlorn. I had fond memories of him and felt his loss, of course, but somehow his dying opened up another side of me and set me free. On July 30, 1881, at age twenty-two, I moved out of the house built by Frederick Schellschmidt. No doubt that pleased him, but my stepfather was not the reason I decided to leave (another surprise to me), nor was it because I loved Mum any less. She would go on to teach for twenty years in the territory's oldest public school and continue baking in the Silver City house until dying peacefully in her sleep at age eighty in the spring of 1921, twenty years after a runaway overloaded freight wagon ran over Fred and crushed his skull during one of Silver City's recurring floods.

I left the house in 1881 for a room I rented from the family of Mexican entrepreneur Lorenzo Carrasco, who had smelted the first marketable silver bullions in Silver City. But that was just the beginning. I became a traveler and a full-fledged newspaperman. I demonstrated I could write (thank you Mum and Miss Mary Richards) and find stories to write about. Working for the *Silver City Enterprise* I covered the big stories, such as the November 1883 train robbery at nearby Gage and how Sheriff Whitehill tracked down the robbers, the Santa Fe reaching Silver City in 1886, and the flood of 1895 that turned Silver City's Main Stret into a gorge that became known as the Big Ditch. In the 20th century, I moved frequently, working for newspapers in Lincoln, Fort Sumner, Albuquerque, Santa Fe, Las Cruces, and El Paso, Texas.

On vacations I always came back to Silver City to visit Mum, who didn't miss her late husband as much as she thought she might and was always glad to see me. After she died, I quit reporting to newspaper editors and publishers and moved back to the old house. At age sixty-two, I was home to stay, soon reporting only to my young Mexican wife. It was on July 4, 1921, that I married Sabrina, a very mature twenty-one at the time. She saw something in me that nobody else ever has (but don't ask me what). The Silver City house that Fred Schellschmidt built became livelier than ever; I would not spend my last years alone.

I had met Sabrina the year before while I was in Fort Sumner visiting Billy's final resting place. It was springtime. I saw this pretty black-haired girl in a blue cotton dress placing blue forget-me-nots on his grave, and I knew I must talk to her. She was living at the time with her family south of the town and revealed to me, once I had told her of my strong connection with Billy, that her great aunt had given Billy the Kid refuge after his escape from the Lincoln County Courthouse. "This old aunt said, according to my mother, that she wanted to keep Billy safe from the men hunting him, even if he was the biggest desperado in the land," Sabrina explained, sweetly holding my arthritic hand as we sat on a bench within sight of the grave. "He was small, with long hair, delicate hands, and a nice little smile when he kept his mouth closed. Plus, when he spoke Spanish, he sounded like a true Mexican. So, what my aunt did was have Billy dress up like a girl and stay mostly in the kitchen with her two actual daughters. No one was the wiser."

I am delighted to report that in the twenty-four years we've been married, I have been exceedingly happy with Sabrina and she keeps telling me I've aged exceedingly well. She's great in the kitchen, her specialties being tamales and fruit pies. We both adore our pet sheep, Freya. I am finally learning Spanish and her English is steadily improving; we read books to each other in both languages. Even though I turned eighty-six this year and she is slightly more than half my age, we still dance together four or five times a week in the privacy of our home. For the longest time, she couldn't conceive due to female problems, though I accept some of the blame. On my latest birthday, however, she told me that her gift to me would be arriving in about five months—our first child. I fully intend to live to be one-hundred so Sabrina can have my support and our child can know a father. It brings me great joy to think of this small blessing on the way, and I pray each night that everything will work out. Girl or boy? Doesn't matter. Either way is fine with me.

READERS GUIDE

1. Why does the author include an introduction in which the book's narrator, William Tweed Bonnifield, recalls a 1939 meeting with Billy the Kid pretender Bushy Bill Roberts?

2. What kind of woman is Charlotte Bonnifield? Does she change when she becomes a mother?

3. What influence does Freya O'Neill have on young Willie's life?

4. Why does the author deal only with Willie the Kid's early life in New York and not have Willie meet Billy until they are in a classroom together in Indianapolis at the end of Chapter 3?

5. Why do Willie and Billy become friends? Is it a friendship between two boys who consider themselves equals?

6. What influence does John Caven have on fatherless Willie?

7. How does Willie feel about Billy's relationship to pigtailed Laura Blakney? To other boys?

8. What does Billy think about mother Charlotte's relationship with William Antrim? Does it change after Antrim becomes his stepfather?

9. Why do Charlotte and son Willie follow Catherine and Billy to Wichita?

10. Did Willie want his mother to marry Fred Schellschmidt? If not, why not?

11. How did Willie handle news of Billy's arrest in Denver?

12. How did the move to Santa Fe change the lives of Billy and Willie?

13. How do you rate Mr. Antrim and Mr. Schellschmidt as stepfathers?

14. What role does dancing have in the lives of Billy and Willie?

15. Was Billy really a troublemaker in Silver City or just an average boy in a frontier town?

16. How did Catherine's consumption (tuberculosis) affect the lives of the two families? Her death?

17. Can Billy be blamed for escaping from the Silver City Jail? For running away to Arizona Territory?

18. Did Willie have good reason to leave his mother and go west with Billy?

19. Would Billy and Willie have separated if not for Mr. Blood?

20. How did Willie feel about Billy's later life as an outlaw and Billy's death?

Printed in the USA
CPSIA information can be obtained
at www.ICGtesting.com
LVHW030733220324
775102LV00005B/101